SKIN

THE RENEGADES
BOOK ONE

SYBIL KNIGHT

THE RENEGADES SERIES

SKIN

A DARK FAIRY-TALE RETELLING

SYBIL KNIGHT

SOCIALS:

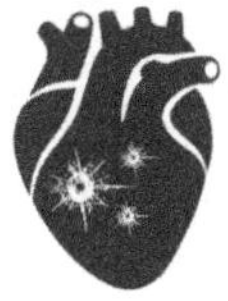

EMAIL: AUTHORSYBILKNIGHT@GMAIL.COM

NEWSLETTER: WWW.SENDFOX.COM/DAHLIAANDSYBIL

FACEBOOK GROUP:
WWW.FACEBOOK.COM/GROUPS/DAHLIAANDSYBILSLITTEDEVILS

INSTAGRAM: WWW.INSTRAGRAM.COM/AUTHOR.SYBIL.KNIGHT

FACEBOOK PAGE: WWW.FACEBOOK.COM/AUTHORSYBILKNIGHT

TIKTOK: WWW.TIKTOK.COM/@QUEENSOFCHAOSBOOKS

AMAZON: HTTPS://WWW.AMAZON.COM/STORES/SYBIL-KNIGHT/AUTHOR/B09QW5R3MB

DEDICATION

It's easy to tell someone you love them.

It's much harder to show them... unless you're not afraid to stalk them for ten years, lock them in a room you converted into a cell in the basement of a former sanitorium, and force them to have your kid so they can never run away from you again.

This book is for those of you who prefer option number two.
At least in book boyfriend form.

TRIGGER WARNING:

Please be advised that the male lead in this book is a complete narcissistic, egotistical prick. And the relationship portrayed between him and the female love interest should in no way reflect how anyone should be treated.

If you come across someone like this in the real world, the author urges that you run as far and as fast as you can.

But between these pages, in the land of fiction, there's no point in trying. Because he'll be right behind you.

That said, the author asks that you heed the following list of potential triggers:

- Overall sexually explicit and violent content
- Forced drugging
- Death and murder
- PTSD and trauma
- Graphic injuries
- Torture

- MENTIONS OF DRUG USE/ABUSE AND DISTRIBUTION
- ALCOHOL USE AND ABUSE
- CAPTIVE/CAPTOR RELATIONSHIP
- MEDICAL GORE
- LOSS OF EYE AND FACIAL DEFORMITY
- NATURAL MISCARRIAGE
- ACTS OF DEGRADATION AND STARVATION
- ASSAULT
- NONCON AND DUBCON
- STALKING
- MENTIONS OF PAST CHILD ABUSE
- BC TAMPERING AND FORCED INSEMINATION
- SPITTING
- SOMNOPHILIA
- SKIN MARKING
- ICE BATHS
- FORCED ORGASMS
- MASKED ASSAILANT
- AND MORE...

BLURB:

Obsession was a five-letter word. Ten years in the making. And her name was Emily.

But the real question was who was I?

When my pretty little pet leaned forward. Offered me a view of her tits and tried to make a deal, I said why the hell not?

Five days. Thirty minutes. She could ask me anything to her heart's content. Anything but my name. She had to figure that one out on her own.

It should have been easy enough. I was the man she stole from. Whose life she ruined and future she destroyed.

I was the man she left behind and she was... **mine.**

SKIN is a dark *Rumpelstiltskin* retelling and book one in <u>The Renegades Series</u>. Each title is a standalone in an

INTERCONNECTED WORLD WHILE EACH STORY IS A RETELLING OF A FAIRY TALE, NURSERY RHYME, FABLE, ETC. THE FOCUS IS DARK ROMANCE, SO PLEASE HEED THE TRIGGER WARNINGS AT THE BEGINNING OF EVERY BOOK.

"MERRILY I'LL DANCE AND SING,
FOR THE NEXT DAY WILL A STRANGER BRING.
LITTLE DOES MY LADY DREAM,
RUMPELSTILTSKIN IS MY NAME!"
—WILHELM AND JACOB GRIMM
GRIMMS FAIRY TALES

PART ONE

THE PRESENT

You ever get the feeling you're being watched?

I think the only thing being watched… is waaaaay too much of that true crime channel.

Yeah, you're probably right.

PROLOGUE
HER

It was the feeling of being watched that first had my eyes moving under my lids, my lashes fluttering just enough to be noticeable as I fought to pry them apart. They were heavy, so fucking heavy. Like two bricks were placed on my face to hold me down and there wasn't shit I could do to swat them away. Because my hands... weren't moving either.

I didn't have time to question the gravity of my situation before the damp air was bristling my skin, causing my muscles to spasm involuntarily as the antiseptic smell—a mix of alcohol and too much bleach—burned the insides of my nostrils. Followed by the buzzing of the harsh fluorescent lighting penetrating my eardrums. My temples throbbing in rhythm with my quickening heartbeat. Which was all I could hear now.

The *thump, thump, thumping* against my rib cage.

I was in a hospital. That had to be it. But why? What happened? Was I in some sort of accident?

I couldn't remember anything since the airport. Since

grabbing my suitcase from baggage claim and following my boss to her town car. Everything after that felt fuzzy. I didn't know what day it was or where I was supposed to be right now. Or if I even had a job anymore.

And I still couldn't move my arms or legs...

My internal panic was rising to the surface as I tried to take a mental inventory of the rest of my anatomy and quickly realized my fingers and toes were twitching. My breathing slowed along with the pounding in my chest until I heard his voice... the one that accompanied the eyes I could still feel boring past the layers of flesh and bone, severing all nerve connections and rendering me immobile.

I didn't need the drugs I was certain were rushing through my system. Not with the weight of those eyes watching me.

"Welcome back, pet." His tone was low, raspy. Like someone who'd spent far too many hours screaming at the top of their lungs and was now forcing air through a set of damaged vocal cords.

I didn't have much more time to think on it as I felt a pair of heavy palms slam down on each side of my head. My lids flung open, forcing me to stare into two black holes where eyes should be. And weren't. But I could still feel them. Staring at me. Through me.

That's when I realized I wasn't in a hospital. Doctors didn't wear black tactical pants or have knives strapped to their hips. And emergency room walls weren't made of concrete. No, I was below ground. Maybe in some sort of basement?

Before I had a chance to piece it all together, or at least try to, the figure was pushing back from the mattress and positioning himself across the dank room, drawing my attention to what I could only assume was the biggest

threat to me getting out of here—wherever here was—
alive.

Him. The man in the cloth mask. His head tipped to the side as he continued to glare at me through the thin fabric that kept his identity as much a mystery as the rest of him.

1
HER

"What do you want?"

"I already told you. And I'm not a fan of repeating myself."

He tossed the small wooden chair across the room, watching it hit the concrete wall and splinter before turning his icy glare on me—I could feel the chill behind his eyes even if I still couldn't see them. Then he stalked forward, pinching my cheeks between his thumb and index finger.

"I want everything you took from me, my pretty little thief." He sank his teeth into my earlobe, piercing flesh through the thin material of his mask. There was an audible pop as he imprinted the likeness of his canines into the malleable cartilage.

I bit into my lip, trying to hold back the tears. I didn't want to give him the satisfaction of seeing me cry. "I've never stolen anything in my life..."

"A thief and a fucking liar, I see... Honestly, I'm disappointed in you, Emily."

I watched him pull away and circle me, his steps

measured, precise, nearly soundless until he forced his boots to squeak when he pivoted to look at me again. Sensation was finally returning to my upper limbs, but only enough so that I recognized the weight of the chains currently riveting me in place. There was no point in fighting against them. I knew it wouldn't get me anywhere.

I needed to be smart. Not impulsive, no matter how hard my fight-or-flight instincts were urging me otherwise.

He knew me, my name, but how? Or did he…? Maybe he'd just found my driver's license… Or overheard my name somewhere… Honestly, his knowing who I was did little to tell me who *he* was… and I needed to know that, to also know what he wanted.

"Who are you?" It was the next obvious question, not that I thought it would be that easy.

"I already told you, pet. I'm the man you stole from." I could hear the grin curling his lips. But it wasn't something pleasant. No, it was the sort of grin that preceded a sudden bout of rage. A violent grin.

"How am I supposed to know what I took from you, if I don't even know who you are?" I tried again.

"Not my problem," he hissed in response.

"It is your problem if you want it back…"

Keep him engaged, Em. Interested in continuing to play whatever game this is.

My subconscious urged me to maintain the façade. Be whatever, whoever it was he needed me to be. Part of me knew my inner voice was right, while another part was wondering how long it would take to chew through the meat of my wrist in order to free myself. The same part that realized I would bleed out long before I was able to make it to the door.

He was growing impatient—who was I kidding? The

psycho was impatient from the moment I first laid eyes on him, likely long before that too. It was evident in the tense posturing of his shoulders. In the way the biceps of his crossed arms flexed and loosened as though he were moments away from closing the distance between us and landing the full force of his knuckles into my face.

He hated me but why?

There was nothing about his voice that was recognizable, nothing about his build that was the slightest bit familiar. The man was a stranger to me. I was sure of it, as sure as he was that I'd taken something from him...

He pushed off the wall and stalked towards me again. I closed my eyes and held my breath, waiting for the blow that never came. Until I chanced a glance through my lashes and watched as he stomped to the only entry point instead. A metal door. Fireproof, I was certain. And not something I could break down.

"Wait!" I couldn't be left alone in here. Alone with my thoughts and rising panic... I just couldn't... "Let me help you—"

His laughter broke through my plea. The sound was humorless and bitter. "Help me? How the fuck do you expect to help me, pet? Do you even realize how fucked you are right now?" It took seconds for him to appear at my side again, less than that for him to bring us nose to nose.

"That's not what I meant—"

"Then tell me what the fuck you meant, my sweet girl..." His tone was suddenly gentle, like something you'd use to soothe a small child, and I didn't know what to make of all the mood swings.

"If you won't tell me who you are, or what it is you *think* I stole..."

He raised a questioning eyebrow, the tight material of

the mask lifting with the movement, but I continued all the same.

"...then at least give me an opportunity to figure it out... please?"

He threw his head back in genuine laughter this time. "*Please?*" He wheezed in a breath, obviously amused. With himself or me? I couldn't tell. "Yes, because proper manners will get you out of this one." He dropped his jaw and glared at me with his neck cocked to one side, as if observing me for a moment. "Go on. What's your proposal? I'm just dying to hear it, pet."

2
HIM

Emily Shaw was...

Well, for as long as I decided to keep her alive, she was mine. The object of my obsession for the past ten years. All the planning, the hours dedicated to this moment, and I was holding on by a thread. Less than that. I was dangling over the precipice of hysteria and insanity. My rage threatening to tip me over one way, then the other.

Neither would do.

I couldn't let her ruin this for me. This was more than a means to an end. This was about taking back everything the little bitch had stolen from me. This was about degradation, control, ruining her. And it was about savoring every second of her beautiful destruction.

Because that's what it would be. I'd paint these walls in her blood. Mark her body with my cum and shatter her will to live along the way. She would beg me to end it, end her, and I'd refuse... until her pleas no longer brought me joy. Until the taste of her tears no longer stirred my cock to life. Until her cunt was nothing more than a gaping hole, her tight muscles loosened beyond repair.

Then my pretty little pet would be free game for all the monsters far worse than I was...

SHE WAS STARING at me now, waiting to see what I thought about her offer. As if she had any bargaining chips left in this little game of ours. She didn't. There was only one way for this to end. But she still had hope, and I liked dangling it in front of her, just long enough to watch the devastation in her eyes when I ripped it away again.

"You want something from me? Fine." I grinned, chewing on the fabric of the breathable mouth covering. I could still taste her blood there. "But I want something from you first."

"I—what?"

I didn't answer her. Instead, I pulled the set of keys from my left pocket and approached the makeshift hospital bed, releasing her wrists. She watched my every movement, likely seeking out some sort of weak spot, leverage, an escape. There were none of those.

But Emily would figure that out soon enough.

Once I'd freed her arms, I stepped around the bottom rail and unburdened one of her ankles, yanking on the chain clasped around her second leg to allow her the illusion of a slightly longer leash. The metal clanked against the bedframe and scraped along the cement flooring before it was left to coil at her feet like a viper ready to strike. Which was fitting really.

"Knees," I barked the order. The half-life of the paralytic agent meant that I knew she could stand on shaky limbs at this point. She was only pretending otherwise. Attempting to hold all her cards close to her chest. When she didn't immediately comply, I added, "And I want to hear the thud of bone hitting concrete, or I'll break them." I pivoted to face her. "Your kneecaps, I mean. Curious as to what that feels like?"

Her eyes widened. My grin did the same.

"It's a trick question really. It depends on if it's a clean break... or more of a shattering of the bone and cartilage. Do you have a preference, Emily?"

She shook her head.

"Then. Why. The. Fuck. Aren't. You moving?" I ground out between clenched teeth.

She scrambled off the bed like the good little cunt she was before sinking to her knees in front of me. I tilted my head and watched her, my fingers gripping the ends of my belt and loosening the straps. I yanked the thin strip of leather free from my waist and dropped to my haunches so that I was at eye level. Slipped it around her pretty little neck and tugged it tight. Her reactionary whimper wasn't just music to my ears. It was a symphony, a series of well-practiced notes only I could hear as I threw my head back and tapped the tips of my fingers to the haunting tempo.

She wasn't broken yet. She was far from it. She was playing along. Calling my bluff. I knew as much. But it was the first step towards my pet's submission, and it wouldn't take long before her resolve was cracking and crumbling as easily as a fly between my fingertips. I'd pluck out her tiny little wings and watch her squirm. Then I'd toss her carcass aside and stomp it with the heel of my boot until what remained no longer resembled something tangible. Something... *human.*

"Please..."

The soft whimper had my neck snapping back in place as I glared down at the pathetic creature pawing at my feet and scuffing my shoes. She had more fight in her than this. I knew it. I just needed to force her to show it.

I tugged on the end of the belt, the makeshift garrote further constricting her airway and causing her wide, panicked eyes to shoot upwards. Then I raised to my full height, the fingers of my free hand nimbly dancing along the zipper of my black tactical pants before I reached inside to release my straining cock. Her pupils dilated as tears began to form on her lash line.

Are you scared, pet? Or turned the fuck on? Maybe a mixture of both? The two weren't mutually exclusive.

"Suck," I hissed, enjoying the way she tried to shuffle back on all fours, only to be halted by the snap of my wrist and the taut leather of her leash. "And if you even think about biting down, I'll knock your teeth out and force you to swallow them."

3
HER

*S*uck.

The four-letter word rang in my ears like a death knell. Worse. Because death was an end. And this was just the beginning of my downfall. My deterioration. The slow atrophy that would leave me rotting in my skin. Decomposing with each forced breath.

This man, whoever he was, didn't want to simply kill me. That much I could accept. Make peace with. Because I wasn't afraid to die. No, he wanted to destroy my humanity. He wanted me crawling on my hands and knees. He wanted me begging for mercy that I was certain would never come.

I just couldn't figure out why. What had I done to deserve... *this?*

He didn't repeat himself. He didn't have to. I didn't have much choice in the matter as he twisted the belt around his arm and yanked me forward. If I wanted to breathe, I had to open my mouth. I wasn't getting enough oxygen through my nose, and he wouldn't loosen the leather constricting my airway until I did as I was told.

I tried to be logical about it. Tell myself it was about

survival. That the discomfort, the debasement, would be fleeting and I could figure a way out of here. But none of this kept my lower lip from trembling as I leaned forward, lowered my jaw, and took him into my mouth. He tugged me closer again without warning and his cock slipped past my tonsils, forcing me to sputter and gag around the thick base while attempting to keep my last meal from coming back up.

My inner voice was screaming at me to do something. To snap my jaw shut and take a part of him with me. But I doubted my ability to tear into flesh, while the thought of his blood pooling in my mouth had me struggling to keep the bile down. Far worse than the feel of his cock between my lips. That and I had no doubt he would follow through with his threat. Something in his tone told me these weren't just threats. They were promises.

So I did my best to block out the smell of his cologne, the taste of the soap on his skin—he'd showered at the very least—and the feel of him thrusting forward and pulling back out, only to repeat the rhythm with more force. I refused to acknowledge the way his fingertips pressed into my cheeks as he held my head steady and gave himself leverage. And I ignored the way my knees burned as they scraped across the concrete flooring, the first layer of skin rubbing away with the friction.

None of it was real. It wasn't happening.

That's what I told myself. Even as my lips cracked and bled, and I struggled between trying to suck in air and attempting to keep the vomit from rising up.

He drove forward so that my nostrils were pressed against his pelvic bone, and I lost balance, my hands reaching out on instinct and clawing at his thighs to brace myself. He stilled, his chin resting against his collarbone and his head cocking to the side as he paused to observe me. I didn't know what he was looking for. I couldn't read his expression through the mask. But I could guess. Something I'd done had halted his movements. And it wasn't my struggle. He obviously didn't care whether or not I could breathe. Whether I lived or died. Just that I suffered.

Truth was I didn't understand why I was trying to figure it out. His motives didn't matter. Why people were the way they were didn't matter. Some individuals were just assholes. There was nothing more to it. No rationale behind their psychotic tendencies. And so I put him into that same category, as my right hand reached behind him to grip the splintered piece of wood that skid across the floor when the chair ricocheted against the wall. The little stake was small enough to fit into my palm and sharp enough to dig into my skin as I tried to conceal it.

He cracked his neck from side to side, breaking his self-imposed trance before he slipped free from my lips and tugged me to my feet, using the belt and his grip on my throat to lift me. When I was finally standing on shaky legs, he shuffled me back until the bones of my spine were digging into the far wall, and then he shoved his fingers into my mouth. I hissed with the impact, allowing him better access as he continued his ruthless assault, his tongue lapping up and tasting the blood along the seam of my split lips through the woven fabric still covering his face.

I couldn't help the moan that escaped when his chest rubbed against my peaked nipples. And I hated myself for not hating it. *I did hate it.* I just couldn't stop my body's natural reaction to the chilled air.

Once again, the sound gave him pause and I used the momentary distraction to lift my arm and jam the jagged piece of wood into his right eye, only to jolt when the makeshift weapon veered to the side and cracked in my grip.

It penetrated the mask. I saw it myself, as the stake seemed to suspend in the air and bounce with the movement of his head. It would be comical if my life didn't hang in the balance. Like something out of a vampire movie gone wrong.

My hands shot up to cover my gasp, while he threw his head back and laughed as I attempted to pull the piece of wood free and jab at him again.

4
HIM

She fucking stabbed me. More like stabbed *at* me. But the sentiment was the same.

My lips curled beneath my face covering into my first real grin since entering this room—the rest had been forced—and my fingers reached out and closed around her delicate throat. Her eyes widened as she struggled to gasp for her next breath of air.

And there it was. That fight I needed in order to get off. The added adrenaline that rushed through my veins as she kicked, clawed, and attempted to shove at my chest.

I gripped the hem of the mask with my free hand and peeled it back before yanking it over my head. "Talk about bad luck. Fifty-fifty shot and you still chose wrong." I waited for her to look at me. Really look at me. The terror coming off her in waves. "Should have aimed for the other goddamn eye, pet."

My smirk widened the longer she stared into the prosthetic I'd popped in just for today, her focus hitched on the gaping socket where my eye had been all those years ago. Long before I lost it. She swallowed down the gasp, the bile, the disgust and I felt the slow up-and-down movement beneath my palm.

I lowered my lips to her ear and licked the lobe as she trembled under the weight of my fingertips. "I agreed to your terms, your little game. But my... *kindness* comes with a price. Each day I allow you to breathe, I will take something of yours. Something you can't get back. I'll take your dignity, your sweat, your blood, and your tears. I'll take your self-respect and I'll decimate them so that there's nothing left of you. Nothing but a shell of someone you thought you were. Till you are a living fucking corpse, Emily. And then I'll leave you to rot."

My hand was already lifting the hem of the hospital gown I'd dressed her in shortly after her arrival, as I punctuated the statement with the upward thrust of my cock into her tight cunt.

She sucked in a sharp breath and whimpered. And fuck, if it didn't send an extra chill down my spine. Straight to my balls. Which drew up with the impending orgasm. But I refused to give into my body's natural instinct to end this so soon.

No, each forward drive of my hips. Each tear that fell from her eyes and each small break in her psyche was a slow, sweet indulgence. I pounded her tiny frame against the cold concrete, over and over again, and felt the way her body caved to me. How her legs trembled, her cunt salivated, her muscles tensed and sucked me deeper. It wanted me no matter how much her cognitive functioning refused to surrender to her desire to submit to me.

I wouldn't allow her to come. Not now. Maybe not ever. I would leave her on that edge, teetering between hating me and needing me. Between begging me for relief and refusing to accept she wanted it. I'd leave that pretty cunt between her legs drenched and fluttering. To the point she would be tempted to touch herself even as I watched. And then I'd tie her arms above her head, her thighs spread wide on the cool sheets, and leave her to squirm like the greedy little bitch she was.

It was that thought, that image, that finally had my cum coating the walls of her womb and claiming her as mine. We both knew it. There was no coming back from this.

I kicked her legs apart, watching as the white semi-translucent substance dropped from between her thighs. Trailed down to her ankles and landed with an audible plop on the uneven flooring. I could feel her eyes on me the entire time, boring into my flesh as if her hatred could somehow penetrate me as easily as I'd penetrated her.

I glanced up from the soiled ground to meet her gaze, and she hocked back the pooling saliva in her mouth and discharged it at my face. It clung to my cheek, the tacky liquid still warm to the touch as I swiped it with my thumb and sucked the digit clean.

If hatred had a tangible form, it would be the flames I saw staring back at me in the reflection of Emily's dilated pupils. And all I wanted to do was fuck her all over again.

5
HER

I wrapped my arms around myself as I watched him open the metal door and slam it shut again before I screamed my frustrations to the empty room. The high-pitched sound seemed to echo off the barren walls and scream back at me. There was no satisfaction in it, but I was able to breathe a little easier as I tugged at the chain on my ankle still tethering me to the hospital bed. Which I just now realized was bolted to the floor.

Fuck...

I took a deep breath. I couldn't give up. Not yet. I'd barely seen what this man was capable of and I was certain far worse was to come. Especially now that he'd revealed himself to me—the fact he was a stranger didn't mean I couldn't pick him out of a lineup. And he was definitely a stranger. I'd remember having met someone whose face was so, um, *fucked up...* and whose eye was, well, missing.

Nearly half of his profile was mutilated, as if the skin had been peeled away and reattached at some point. Which was probably why he grew out his facial hair. That wasn't to say he didn't have some attractive attributes. His jawline defined and his singular eye a piercing blue. Hell, if he weren't so cruel, I might even say that he was hot.

If scars were your thing. I wasn't certain if they were mine.

I also wasn't certain if the fact that he was a stranger should be comforting or not. It sure as hell didn't help me determine what it was that he wanted from me.

I ground my teeth, hoping the sensation would somehow ground me too. Help me focus on the bigger picture and the deal we'd arranged. One I was second-guessing the longer I sat in my solitude—though I'd been so certain it was the right move to make just a few hours ago...

"Go on. What's your proposal? I'm just dying to hear it, pet."

I took a deep breath, reminding myself to treat this like any other negotiation. A regular day at the office. I'd seen my boss do it a million times. I could do it too.

It came down to simple math. This guy wanted something and so did I. It didn't matter how much those two wants conflicted with each other. We just had to meet in the middle or as close to it as we could get without me ending up in a body bag.

I glanced down at my chest before thinking better of it. I wasn't above showing a little cleavage to brokerage terms. That was something else my boss had taught me. But we were beyond that at this point. I was barely dressed and I had no doubt this guy would use me like an old tube sock without breaking a sweat.

I shivered at the thought. I had to hope there was at least one line he wouldn't cross—because not all kidnappers were rapist too. A realization that should have been comforting... and wasn't.

"You claim that you know me..." I began.

"Oh, I more than know you." His eyes were roaming up and down my body. "But I never claimed anything. I told you that you took something from me."

I could feel it whenever his glare seemed to flick across my skin as surely as if he reached out and touched me. I'd never met anyone who had this effect on me, especially when I didn't even know what he looked like. It was a sickening sensation, the curiosity warring with the terror. Like being dropped in a maze at midnight on Halloween, only this time all the monsters were real—at least the one in front of me certainly was.

"Right..." I crossed my arms, trying to keep the chill from rousing my nipples. "So you've said. Look, we both know you have the upper hand here. But humor me. I'm sure a lot of planning has gone into all of... this." I gestured to the room. The creepy-ass medical devices and the rusty hospital bed. And tried not to appear disgusted.

"More than you know." He seemed to grin. He was proud of himself. Cocky. Too sure of his failsafe. And it would be his weakness. He'd already determined how this would go. Which meant even the slightest deviation could tip things in my favor. "You're stalling now, pet. Get on with it before I lose my patience."

"Give me five days. Five days to figure out how you know me, who you are. Thirty minutes a day where I can ask you anything and you'll answer honestly."

He appeared to choke on his laughter, his sputtering ending with a deep vibration in his throat. "And why the fuck would I do that?"

"Because, if there is anything I've learned about you in the *past few minutes, it's that you are the sort of man who likes to play with his food before he eats it..."*

6

HIM

I slammed the door and engaged the industrial-size lock before punching the code into the keypad. Could never be too careful. Emily had gotten smarter over the years. But I was prepared for her games. I expected her to have something up her sleeve. What I hadn't seen coming was how easy it would be to agree to her bullshit terms. She didn't know what she was asking of me.

I had no issue with the truth. I was the most honest man I knew. *She* was the pretty little liar. The thief between the two of us. And I was ten steps ahead of her before she'd even placed her pieces on the board.

Five days? Five days was fucking child's play. A joke. For me anyway. For her? It would be the worst one-hundred and twenty or so hours of her goddamn life.

"Morning, pet," I sang a little too loudly as I shoved the metal door closed behind me, the gears clicking into place and ensuring only one of us was capable of getting out of the room again. "Trust you slept well?" I grinned as I eyed her from a distance.

She was curled up on the cold floor, behind the hospital bed, using its frame to shield herself from my view. She probably thought she was being watched. She was. The entire 20x20 space was wired with hidden cameras, which were monitored 24/7 from a surveillance room located just down the hall. She was lucky it was also climate-controlled, or she could have frozen to death overnight.

That would have been a shame, seeing as we'd only just begun to reacquaint ourselves. And my cock, the pathetic bastard that he was, had yet to have his fill.

I'd foregone the mask today. I didn't see the point. It'd been more for her benefit than mine. So that my... *distinct attributes* didn't immediately send her into a panic when she woke from her drug-induced coma for the first time. I was used to the figure I saw staring back at me in the mirror. Others? Not so much.

When she didn't seem in a hurry to move her ass up off the floor, I placed the tray I was carrying on the desk and crossed the room. "Come on, Emily." I kicked at her arm with the tip of my boot. "Let's not add laziness to the list of all your other sins."

Silence.

"I can see the slight rise and fall of your chest, the fluttering of your eyelashes, even as you try to hold your breath." My eyes dropped to the face of my watch. "And now you're cutting into your thirty—correction, twenty-eight minutes."

With that, she huffed. Reached out an arm and pulled herself to her feet.

"Really? Playing dead?" I shook my head as I walked back over to the desk and plucked the apple I'd brought her from the tray. I sank my teeth into its juicy skin before adding, "I would have thought you more creative."

"Yeah, well, I can only work with what I'm given..." She flicked her eyes from corner to corner. "Which isn't much."

"The accommodations not to your liking, princess?"

She narrowed her glare on me, causing my lips to tip up at one side. "The accommodations could be better but it's the company that's really lacking."

My jaw clenched as I slammed the half-eaten fruit on the desk top, bruising what remained of its flesh. If Emily kept up her bullshit, the apple wouldn't be the only thing to change colors. "Pretty sure my company was requested, Emily. But if you are so set on spending the rest of your days —*hours?*—in solitude, I'm more than happy to oblige." I pushed away from the furniture, as if I were planning to leave.

I wasn't. But she didn't know that. My every action was conflicting, irrational, left her guessing. So that by the end of this all, she would be begging for my attention. My companionship. My condemnation as much as my praise.

"No! Wait!" she called out, and I paused.

Hook. Line. Sinker. Like taking candy from a spoiled fucking baby.

"What the fuck do you want now, Emily? Eat your goddamn breakfast and then we can try this again—when you aren't so hellbent on being such a stuck-up cunt." I tossed the tray on the floor, watching as the bowl of oatmeal toppled over and sprayed most of the contents across the room. "You'll appreciate what I do for you. What

I give you. Or you'll fucking starve. Now, clean up this mess. I won't step another foot through that door till you've lapped up every last drop."

I didn't wait for a response before I pivoted on the heel of my boot, turning my back on her and the remnants of her meal. And stalked out.

7
HER

DAY 1

The only thing worse than the bastard's presence was the sudden lack of it. Being alone with my thoughts was the most torturous form of punishment.

My childhood had been spent in isolation. Not too far off from this, nearly as cruel. If the son of a bitch knew anything about me, he'd realize that this wouldn't be the first time I'd been given the ultimatum of licking my meal off the floor. I was a survivor. I did what it took to get where I was in life. Despite my upbringing. Not because of it. And I would do the same here.

He dished out insults like they meant anything to me. Like I hadn't heard the worst of it long before I even understood the meaning of the colorful vocabulary hurled my way. And he called me princess, as if his wounds were somehow more significant because they were visible.

Fuck that. I'd take damaged flesh over a damaged psyche any day.

There was nothing he could do to my body that hadn't already been done to me before. Nothing I wouldn't endure as I plotted my way out of here.

He wanted a pet? I'd give him one. But something told me he didn't want that at all. No, he was pleased when I fought him. When I talked back and spit in his face. His eyes twinkled and his dick hardened. My submission was never the endgame, whether he realized it or not. What he wanted was a worthy opponent. Because when he did finally break me, *that* would be the ultimate satisfaction.

What that knowledge didn't do was help me determine my next move. How to play this or play him.

My initial offer was only meant to buy me time. And it had done that… I guess. Every crime show I ever watched said the first forty-eight hours were the most important, and I'd requested more than double that. But then again, who really knew how long he planned on keeping me here…?

IT TOOK eight hours for the hunger pangs to set in and my will to finally break. Eight hours plus how ever long I'd spent in that hospital bed after being knocked out. Which didn't seem all that significant in the grand scheme of things. But my pride didn't outweigh my survival instincts. Being weak and half-starved only steeled your spine long enough for death to set in. And I refused to die in this basement. In captivity. Like some forgotten zoo animal.

My dry tongue scraped across the concrete flooring, the granules of dirt, dust, and mummified insects overpowering the flavor of the bland oatmeal. I told myself it was protein. That I'd stomached far less appetizing meals in my lifetime. I'd grown plump and pampered over the years, more so than the bag of bones I'd been in my teens. And a little grime wouldn't kill me.

But I was starting to realize *he* just might...

8

HIM

I watched her lick the ground and imagined each stroke was lapped against my cock. That she was on her hands and knees in front of me instead of alone in her tiny cell. It was the most disturbingly erotic image. More satisfying than any fantasy I'd conjured up of her over the years.

I pushed to my feet and exited the small security room. Descended the stairs two at a time and stalked towards her door before disengaging the locks and barging inside. She peered up at me from the floor, her eyes alight with fury and disgust despite her attempts at schooling them.

And I realized how much I needed it. Fed off her indignation and disdain. My boots echoed with each step into the cavernous room, the sound robotic and methodical, as I marched towards my target. Tugged her to her feet and bent her over the foot of the hospital bed. She twisted her hips, bucking beneath me, and I stood back a moment to watch the action. The vision before me like a worm on a hook tempting me to take a bite.

Emily wasn't just a fixation; she was my ruin. In so

many more ways than one. And she didn't even know the power she held over me.

Apparently, neither did I or I never would have kept this shit going...

I reached out a hand and bunched up the fabric of her hospital gown, my fingers lingering between the apex of her thighs just long enough to test the waters. She was drenched for me. Part of her, deep down, enjoyed the degradation. Got off on it as much as I did. She just didn't want to admit it yet. But she would. Eventually.

The more she fought me, the more we each were turned the fuck on.

Keeping her wrists pinned above her head with one hand, my elbow digging into the arch of her back, I freed my cock with the other. Then I grabbed her ass cheeks as she continued to buck beneath me. And thrusted home. Her tight cunt gripped me in place as I attempted to drive deeper before pulling back and pistoning forward again. With each forceful jerk of my hips, her body gave way to the penetration till it accepted me as readily as my pet would come to accept her fate.

Her whimpered pleas spurred me on while my trimmed nails embedded themselves in the supple skin of her waist to the point of drawing blood. This time, it was the image of red tainting the white of the bedsheets that sent that familiar tingle to the base of my spine as I came inside her. Coating her walls with my cum like I planned to coat her flawless skin with her blood.

And that's when I realized my fatal mistake. I was goddamn addicted.

9
HER

Everyone's reaction was different. Shrinks liked to tell you otherwise—at least mine always did. That same stuck-up bitch in the chair with her glasses sitting on the tip of her nose also liked to look at me like I was cold. Or maybe just a bit crazy. While narrowing down my symptoms and tossing me into one of those boxes from the many books lining the shelves behind her. Beating me down and shoving me inside until I fit. But it was so much more complicated than that.

There was anger, sure. At the asshole who took your choice away. Yourself and society as a whole. Then came the shame. Feeling like something was wrong with you, just as much as there was something wrong with them... the person who did it to you.

It. The word no one wanted to say because it felt nearly as dirty as the act. But alongside all the usual emotions, there was also detachment. The part of you that floated away and could pretend like it didn't happen.

Screw diamonds. Detachment was a girl's best friend.

It meant survival. The ability to compartmentalize. To

pretend you enjoyed it until maybe part of you did. And there was absolutely nothing wrong with that.

There was nothing wrong with protecting yourself how ever you could. *That* was what I told myself when he bent me over the hospital bed and violated me in the worst way possible. When I felt my body accept what was happening to me. When I heard the sounds he made when he was finally done and part of me didn't hate the audible grunts as they rang in my ears.

It was rape. There was no nice way to put it. No more accurate definition. And I hated him for it. Hated the way my body vibrated, because whether I wanted it—him—or not, he'd found a way to stimulate my every nerve ending. To turn me against myself. So I shut down. Switched my brain off like a simple reboot could somehow make it all go away. Help me forget where I was and who put me here. And focused on finding a way out. No matter the cost to my mental state.

10

HIM

She hated me. I could taste it in the air as readily as the piece of chewing gum I popped and gnawed on while lost to my thoughts. A smoke was what I really wanted but my eyes were glued to the screen, watching her watching me from a distance. If there was an antidote for what this woman did to me, I'd take it. But short of castrating myself—which *wasn't* an option—there wasn't much I could do. Outside of killing her. And I wasn't ready for that yet either.

It was like burning a bunch of ants with a magnifying glass. Once they were gone, so was the fun. Thus, Emily and I found ourselves at a stalemate. Neither of us could surrender without the other claiming the win. And I didn't fucking lose. Not since that night. Not again and certainly not to her.

Fool me once and all that bullshit...

I had to kill her. The decision had been made for me. I think I knew it deep down. That this was never meant to be a long-term arrangement. And getting rid of her meant that I finally got to move on. Stop obsessing. Accept my life for what it was and forget about everything it could have been if it weren't for her.

And what she stole from me...

But my cock had a mind of its own. And addiction replaced the obsession. Until I became near animalistic with need. Like a cokehead constantly chasing that high. The truth was, if I didn't kill her, I had no doubt she'd kill me. In some fashion or another. And as much as I didn't fear death, I wouldn't let her take my life from me either. Fuck no, if I was forced to live in this perpetual hell, she sure as fuck would feel the same burn.

That's what really got me going. Her pain, her tears, the sound of her voice when it broke on a sob...

My cock twitched at the thought. And I knew it was too late to do anything but jump on this crazy train and follow its crash course to my demise.

I shot up from my chair. I didn't give a fuck that she was sleeping—or pretending to sleep. Who really knew with this bitch? After all, she was great at pretending. Pushed out of the surveillance room and made a beeline for her door. Emily startled awake the moment it creaked open and slammed shut again.

11

HER

DAY 2

He was positioned in that same fucking spot on a wooden chair in the corner of the room. Sinking his teeth into another goddamn apple and watching me. Always watching. Eyeing me like a subject under a microscope or a creature in the zoo. With curiosity and something more. Sometimes rage. Others lust. All while giving me little to nothing when it came to who the fuck he was.

He reminded me of that Ryuk character from *Death Note* back when I was cutting down on caffeine and anime was my go-to indulgence. It was all I could picture every time he bit into an apple. He liked the red ones, appeared to tolerate green, never chose yellow. It was a fitting comparison, this fucker and the Shinigami, considering he held my life in his hands.

Some sick part of me couldn't help but wonder when my name would be added to that little black book of his...

It was only the second day and I already knew my situation was hopeless. But maybe I could figure out something that could get me out of here. Whether it be by his hands or mine. I wasn't ready to die yet. The will to live still flickered in my chest, forcing my heart to beat and my lungs to expand with each breath I took. It wasn't over. I refused to accept that.

I had thirty minutes to ask him as many questions as I could come up with. But it was like a dance, and he would skirt around the truth in whatever way he could. Not that it mattered. The truth. Just his reaction to it and to me. He wanted something and it was more than seeing me dead.

"How long have you known me?"

He grinned, a minute curl of his lips on the left side. The scar tissue never moved, no matter the expression he made. It was eerie. "It feels like it's been forever." He shrugged, and I huffed.

"That's not a good answer."

"Then ask better questions, pet." The chair scraped across the cement flooring as he scooted back and leaned against the wall, with his arms above his head and his eyes glued to the ceiling like he was soaking up his fill of UV rays on some tropical beach. Instead of sitting in this dank basement beneath the handful of flickering fluorescent bulbs.

"What's the point of agreeing if you weren't planning on participating?"

Another shrug of his shoulders. "Who am I to begrudge someone their need for a ticking clock?"

"A man who rapes women, apparently," I hissed in reply.

"Not women. Woman. One woman in particular." He rocked forward on his seat and planted his feet back on the ground. Then his gaze landed on me like a pair of laser beams that could somehow sear their way through to my soul. "Ticktock, pet. Your time is running out."

"One woman or twenty. Rape is rape, you son of a bitch."

"You can throw that word around as much as you want, darlin'. All you're doing is making my dick harder." He tilted his head as he observed me for a minute, adjusting his cock in his pants before adding, "Look at me." He gestured to his face, along his right arm, down to his scarred hands. "Do you really think I care what kind of monster you see me as? I know who and what I am. Can you say the same? Or do you lie to yourself as much as you lie to me, Emily?"

12

HIM

She seemed to consider my question for a moment, chew on it as if it were a complex math equation with a veritable answer. That was the problem with people like Emily Shaw. They always thought they were smarter than everyone else. Give them enough time and they could unravel you, sniff out your weakness and use it to their advantage.

But I saw her for who she really was. A monster just like me. Perhaps worse. Because she hid it better.

"You sure like to hurl insults, don't you?" She was running out of clever retorts. That much was clear.

"Was that one of your questions, pet? Or more of a rhetorical thing?" I raised my good eyebrow at her growing irritation.

"Fuck you," she seethed, and I grinned and took another bite of my apple.

Maybe I will. After I'm done with my lunch.

I kept that thought to myself. I was much better company after all. Because I always laughed at my own jokes.

13
HER

"Why apples?" It was a waste of a question. But one that honestly piqued my interest.

Was it a weird obsession? Some kind of dietary need? Was I kidnap by Johnny Appleseed's creepy older brother?

I still couldn't remember how I got here. There was just a bunch of blank spaces in time that my brain was trying desperately *and* unsuccessfully to fill. So I decided to focus on what was right in front of me instead. Him and his obnoxious chewing.

He lowered the fruit from his mouth for a moment, flicking his gaze down before lifting his eyes back to me again. "Because they're a lot like people. We choose 'em based on what we see on the outside, but it's not until we peel back the skin that we're forced to bear witness to how truly rotten they are. Take *you*, for example."

His lips twisted into a grin that would be charming if it

weren't so sadistic at the same time. Then he canted his head to the side as if examining me. My arms shot up and crossed over my chest without me realizing it. His scrutiny left me feeling far more vulnerable than the flimsy nightgown.

"You're pretty enough. Decent packaging. Fuckable, of course." His brow twitched as if he found himself amusing. "But slap that ass on an aluminum table and hand me a scalpel? Oh, the stories that body would tell. Every bruise, every tiny pin prick and failing organ—everything you try so desperately to hide under the business casual pantsuit and sensible shoes—would be mine for the viewing. I mean, really, Em, pantsuits? When did you become so basic?" He bit into the apple again, making a show of spraying the juices down his chin and licking it off. He was trying to goad me. He was also trying to distract me from what he was really telling me.

"You're a doctor," I gasped at the realization.

"No, I'm not." His tone was dry, too dry, and it lacked the usual humor and cockiness he wore like a coat of armor.

"But you *were*, weren't you." I didn't need his verbal confirmation. I could feel it in my gut. I was right.

HIM

I waited for it. That glimmer of recognition that told me she understood. That she realized what she'd done to me. It never came. Instead, she seemed proud of herself.

For what? She didn't remember shit.

I chucked the apple against the far wall. Listened to it splatter and watched it slide down the concrete. Imagining it was her brain matter that now brightened the dark-gray paint job. I'd love to say that I was too pissed off to fuck her. But my cock had other plans. So I tossed the chair aside, oblivious to whether or not I'd cracked the wood in the process.

At this rate, I was gonna need a warehouse full of goddamn replacement furniture. Not that it mattered. Regardless of whatever game she was playing, Emily's days were numbered.

I stalked forward, closing the distance between us, as she observed me from where she'd holed herself up in the corner of the room. For all that backtalk, she was no better than an injured bird.

I guess not much had changed after all...

The fire in her eyes was a total contradiction to how she folded into herself the closer I got. And I couldn't help but wonder how much of it was actual fear and how much of it was Emily trying to play games with my head.

Did she honestly think the bullshit act would earn her some sympathy?

Nah, she knew better than that. She also knew I liked the fight. So maybe this was her way of trying to dial it down. To play coy like that would stop me. No matter what she was trying to do, I saw the truth in the way she looked at me. How her pupils dilated. She wasn't afraid. She was fucking pissed.

My steps were slow, measured, as I closed the distance before dropping to my haunches and tipping her chin up so she was forced to meet my gaze. And my lips curled into half a grin, whether I wanted them to or not.

I lowered my face to her ear, watching her hold her breath in my peripheral as I whispered the singular word. "Run."

She sucked in a lungful of air and exhaled on a gasp, her eyes flicking to the door. She hadn't even realized I'd left it open. Barely an inch.

Emily scrambled to her feet, the panic heightening the rush of adrenaline presently coursing through her veins as she shoved the mattress in my path and bolted towards the other side of the room. The moment she yanked the door open and slipped into the hallway, I rolled up my sleeves. Cracked my neck from side to side and sprinted after her. I gave her a good running start, which meant that she'd already tugged on the first few doors. Found them locked and was forced to round the corner and barrel head-first into the unknown.

She wouldn't get far—a fact she'd figure out soon enough.

"Come out, come out, wherever you are," I sang after her, my words bouncing off the walls and encasing her along with the darkness. I could hear her panted breaths. The pitter-pattering of her bare feet on the concrete and her muttered expletives each time she was met by more resistance.

This was what I needed. The hunt. Not the frightened little girl ready to crack into a pool of obedience beneath the heat of my gaze. Maybe there was a time when I was attracted to that side of her. A part that wanted to care for Emily and tend to her every need. But that part of me was buried along with the rest of my face.

Two more long strides and I reached the end of the hall and the last room. She'd just turned the knob. Slipped inside and slammed it shut. My little pet was desperate. I could taste it in the air.

But what my poor, sweet Emily had failed to realize was that she'd just walked into my trap. Like a rodent reaching for that tempting block of cheese, only to find themselves cut off at the tail.

15
HER

I slammed my palms against the ice-cold walls, searching for something. A door. A way out. A goddamn window. Anything. And all I found was more concrete. Leaving me no choice but to spin on my heels, pressing my back to the closest surface, and face the pitch-blackness of the room.

It was sheer stupidity. To think anything the man did was a mistake or an error in judgment. But that was the fucked-up thing about hope. It struck you dumb. Let you believe in childish ideas like chance, luck, fate, and love. And there was no room for any of that shit in the real world.

It took a moment for my eyes to adjust to the sudden lack of light. But I could finally make out different shapes. Four walls. A low ceiling and a cot. Nothing else. If I thought the last spot was a prison, this was a veritable jail cell—a steel door where the bars should be. There wasn't even a light bulb dangling from the ceiling.

I'd run from the comforts of a dungeon straight into my grave. My heavy breaths thickened the air as I awaited whatever would greet me on the other side of that door. I knew it was only a matter of time.

When your senses were hindered by a lack of light and an eerie soundlessness, it was hard to tell how much time had passed. But the creaking of the heavy door was both fear-inducing and a welcomed reprieve from the stifling silence. I could smell him before I could see him. Not to say it was a bad odor. Just one I'd grown accustomed to over the last few days. Something akin to cedar-scented soap, mint from chewing gum, and a hint of cigarette smoke.

I remained glued to the wall, even as his boots squeaked across the floor with each step he took in my direction. It wasn't like there was anywhere to go anyway. I mean, I could try to run past him. But that would only lead me back to where I started...

"Did you enjoy your little bit of freedom, pet?" He grinned. I couldn't see it but I could hear it in his voice as it bounced around the small room before sending a shiver down my spine.

His fingertips brushed against my cheek, and then panic had me ducking under his outstretched arm and sprinting for the door. He gripped my wrist and slammed me into the far wall. My head snapped back with the impact and I felt a sharp chill and a slight dampness that likely meant I was bleeding. The adrenaline kept the pain at bay as I struggled beneath his grip.

This had all been part of his game. Foreplay for a man who got off on breaking me. If my brief time in captivity hadn't told me as much, the way his dick pressed into my stomach certainly did. He restricted my breathing with the webbing between his thumb and forefinger while his free hand shredded my hospital gown down the middle in his urgency to take what he wanted.

The moment he had unrestricted access, he spit into his hand. Slapped the saliva between my thighs and penetrated me. I hadn't even heard him loosen his zipper before the bare skin of his pubic bone was grinding into me like some beast during mating season. The force of his thrusts had my spine scraping against concrete, while layers of flesh peeled away with each back-and-forth motion.

I had no choice but to lean into him, clawing at his shirt with both hands to relieve some of the pressure from my raw skin. His animalistic grunts warmed my ear, and before I knew what I was doing, I was slamming my mouth on his and shoving my tongue down his throat to muffle the sound. He tried to pull away and I sank my teeth into his bottom lip deep enough to taste copper.

"Emily," he hissed in warning. Though I didn't know what about. Whatever it was, he seemed to change his mind, or lose his conviction as he dropped me onto the cot, spreading my thighs as far as they could go as he pressed between them and continued to drive forward.

This was the point where consent and the complete lack of it blurred. I didn't want this or him. To be caged against my will or be treated like an animal. What I wanted was to be human. Feel human. Escape the pain for a moment and make the best of a terrible situation. Which I understood didn't make much sense. But neither did being imprisoned by a stranger who swore he knew me better than I knew myself. If he did, this would be a good time for him to explain a thing or two about why I was so broken.

My back was on fire, but the stiff canvas material was far more forgiving than the wall, and if it weren't for the friction burns and the fact I fucking hated him, the experience would almost be pleasant. His rhythm decreased from frenzied to impassioned, which eased the strain on my tired muscles.

I closed my eyes and imagined I was somewhere else. With someone else. But this man had imprinted himself on my brain. And his beautifully grotesque features were the only thing I could conjure up. So I decided to work with what I was given and deal with how fucked up I was later.

If there was a later...

I skimmed a hand down his face, over the thick scars that marred his skin, and pressed my mouth to his again, offering myself like a sacrificial lamb to this monster, who at his core was just a man. At least that's what I wanted to believe.

He hummed my name, breathing in the scent of my hair as he finally came undone. And put an end to his brutal assault on my body.

I should have felt dirty. Used. Disgusted with myself. But all I felt was relief that it was over and I was still breathing.

16

HER

He'd fallen asleep on top of me. And for a brief moment, I saw him in a different light. In the very real darkness. I guess we all had our demons to fight—some were just more ruthless than others. Not that it excused anything the sick fuck had done to me. Just that it helped explain his motives.

Was this what Stockholm Syndrome felt like?

I was aware enough to realize there wasn't much of a chance of me getting out of here. If nothing else, the man was intelligent. Calculated. And I was no match for that. I could be tender or I could be cruel. I had a much harder time switching between the two.

Meanwhile, my friend here was Dr. Jekyll and Mr. Hyde. Sometimes both at once. It must have been exhausting. To have all that pent-up rage inside you.

Part of me wanted to reach up a hand and stroke his cheek. I was curious about the underlying damage, about what really caused him to become the monster on the outside that matched the one I recognized on the inside. It was obviously a result of trauma. Some sort of accident. And deep down, I knew it had to do with a woman.

Maybe I reminded him of her? Whoever she was...

I was so lost to my thoughts it took me a moment to hear the tapping. My heart thrummed in my chest when I realized it was coming from the other side of the door. There was someone else here. Which could either be my damnation or saving grace. Though one instance was much more likely...

But at this point, what did I have to lose?

"Help..." I hissed the word, simultaneously hoping that whoever it was could hear me and that the man whose full-body weight was presently holding me down *couldn't.*

There were a few beeps of a keypad before the door swung open with a loud screeching sound and the clanking of metal, revealing a blurry silhouette standing at the threshold. Their features obscured by a fuzzy mask and... bunny ears?

"Yo, Frankie," the baritone voice called out at the same time it hit me that this man wasn't my savior any more than the one holding me captive.

17
HIM

I woke with a start. *Fuck.* I'd passed out. I couldn't remember the last time I'd slept for more than a few hours at once. The lingering pain was a son of a bitch, nearly as agonizing as the nightmares that always ended with my face burning off and melting into a puddle in my hands.

PTSD was one sick fuck. It turned your mind against you. And there was no escaping that shit.

"Frank, you fucking listening?" Donnie's prattling was grating on my nerves. For a man of few words, he sure had a lot to say right now. "Or was the cunt just that good?"

I pushed to my feet, tugging my pants up to my waist while shoving my cock into my briefs. My back was to Emily. I really didn't feel like dealing with her moods this early. And I knew she would be less than pleased with me after the game I'd played with her last night.

That said, it was exactly what I needed. Other than a little bit of muscle tightness, I felt like a million bucks.

"Cunt was just fine. Now what the fuck do you want?" I ground out between clenched teeth. The bastard knew better than to come down here. Everyone did. I liked my privacy. We all had our vices. And this basement was mine.

"Casper got fucked up real bad. Needs ya to stitch 'em up."

"And where the fuck's Adrian?" The kid wasn't my problem. Neither was his coke addiction.

Donnie shrugged. The dumb fuck wasn't good for much more than disposing of a body and even that was questionable.

"I'll be there in fifteen. Now get the fuck out." I slammed the door in his face, waiting until I heard the elevator doors ding before grabbing Emily's wrist and dragging her back to her room.

She kicked and screamed and spit along the way but it was all in vain. We both knew there was nothing she could do but surrender. To me and everything I was planning to do to her.

I keyed in the code to the door, disengaging the lock, and shoved Emily inside her little cell.

"Wait! Frank!" she called out as if she'd just uncovered some deep, dark secret of mine.

I turned on my heel and grinned at her. What was left of her hospital gown hung off a shoulder. Her pussy was bare and the one breast bounced with her heaved breaths. Her hair was a rat's nest while her cheeks and lips were flushed with the afterglow of being properly fucked. I grabbed at my cock and readjusted it in my pants, wondering if fifteen minutes was enough time for another round. Then quickly dismissed the idea. I didn't need the rest of those fuckers coming down here looking for me.

"Your name," she tried again. "It's Frank. *Frankie*. I don't know a Frankie." She sounded so sure of herself. So proud that someone else had unraveled the riddle she was supposed to put in the work to solve.

"Wrong answer, pet."

Her eyebrows drew down, her jaw bobbing as she tried to shove together what was left of the puzzle. Only to realize she was missing most of the pieces.

"Don't look so confused, sweetheart. It's a nickname, short for Frankenstein. On account of my face. Idiots think they're clever—except they're too stupid to realize that was the name of the doctor, not the monster."

"And you're the monster..." she whispered, her words trailing off as her posture seemed to deflate along with them.

"You bet your sweet ass I am."

18

HER

DAY 5

Two things happened when I saw the guy in the bunny mask leering at me from the other side of the door moments before I was shoved back inside this death chamber. One, I accepted the fact that no one was coming to my rescue. And two, I was reminded of the time my mother's boyfriend had switched off my cartoons in favor of one of those gory nature shows—*I couldn't for the life of me remember his name.* Which told me he wasn't all that kind or all that abusive. I always remembered the ones who were.

I must have been about six or seven because my feet didn't reach the floor yet so I kicked them back and forth as I ate my breakfast. He had the Discovery Channel playing on the TV, focused on a scene where this pack of wolves cornered and tore a helpless bunny to shreds. I was traumatized for weeks. No matter what I did, I could hear that bunny's screams. See her white fur turn a bright shade of red whenever I closed my eyes.

My mother told me it was natural. The way things were in the world. *"You are either a predator or their prey."* Mind you, she said all this while smoking a pack of Marlboros and using my bowl of stale cereal and spoiled milk as her ashtray. Truth be told, I was just happy she was talking to me. The woman rarely acknowledged my existence. So every word she did say was ingrained in my brain with that sudden surge of serotonin.

The point was, that stuck with me. The fact that some of us were predators while others were prey. Especially now, as this man stared at me like I was his next meal. And for the first time, I felt like that bunny.

I knew he was going to kill me. He'd made up his mind. There was no doubt anymore. And I couldn't help but wonder what that bunny was thinking in her last moments. Had she accepted her fate or was there some part of her that held out hope? Thought if she fought hard enough, there'd be a way out.

A chance...

19
HIM

It was day five when I positioned myself in the corner of the room, crossed an ankle over a knee and watched her. It was also the final day of our little agreement. Fuck if I knew why I indulged her to begin with, other than I found this shit amusing.

Truth was, it was that cunt of hers that kept me from slitting her throat up until now. *That* and the fact I was a man of my word even when she wasn't a woman of hers. But goddamn was she a good fuck. I wasn't too proud to admit I'd miss it.

I adjusted my cock in my pants as she sipped on cold chicken broth. Her glare boring through me while she did everything she could to convey her hatred.

The feeling's mutual, pet.

"So?" I prompted. Not because I couldn't stand the silence but because I was irked with the mundane. With the same thing every day. "Have you figured it out?"

The clanking of her spoon in her bowl told me she hadn't. She was buying herself time, trying to at least. Something in that twisted little brain of hers had her lips curling into a grin. I should have known better than to assume my little fighter would admit defeat so easily. It was time for whatever power play came before acceptance.

"Your name? No, I'm certain I don't know you," she replied, while eyeing her nail beds. Trying her best to appear nonchalant. "That's what bothers you, isn't it? That I mean enough to you to warrant all of this." She gestured to each corner of the room to emphasize her point before landing her glare on me again. "And you mean *nothing* to me. It's all about your wounded ego."

"Is that your final answer?" I hissed between clenched teeth. I shouldn't let her bait me, but the woman knew how to sink her teeth into my skin. Gnaw past flesh and get to the real meat beneath the surface. Like some sort of parasitic creature.

Emily fed off me, and I bled for her.

"You want more?" she fired back. "Fine. Beneath all that toxic masculinity is a little boy with a lot of mommy issues. Did she hurt you? Is that why you are the way you are? Is she the one who did that to your face? So now you have to take it out—"

Before the rest of the shit she wanted to spew had the chance to fully form in her mouth, I'd crossed the room and shoved Emily against the mattress. Drew the knife from my waistband and pressed the serrated blade across her throat. A scalpel would have been more effective but I enjoyed the sensation of sawing across flesh. The push and pull and the sound of snapping tendons. It was like cutting into a taut rubber band.

"Enough about my mother, pet." I grinned, my voice eerily calm as I hummed against her cheek.

"I've struck a chord, huh?" Her throat bobbed, causing

the blade to bite into her skin and bright-red liquid to drip down her throat and onto my hand.

"*My mother* was a saint, Emily. How was yours? Did she pass down those same nurturing instincts to you? Or are you just too goddamn selfish to ever have children of your own?"

Her eyes widened before narrowing in my direction. "FUCK YOU," she hissed, pulling saliva between her cheeks and launching it at my face.

Obviously, she hadn't learned after the first time. A little spilled bodily fluid was nothing to me.

"As much as I've enjoyed that cunt of yours, right now, I'd rather not. But if I'm careful enough, you'll sure make for one pretty corpse." I repositioned my knee. Dug it into the pressure point on her thigh and drew my knife back for a second time. Aimed for her cold dead heart and...

"Cohen! Wait!"

My arm stilled midair as if tethered back by some invisible force while Emily stared up at me with those goddamn doe eyes of hers. She was sobbing but she wasn't afraid. I could tell by the way she was looking at me.

"I... I lost the baby..."

PART TWO
TEN YEARS PRIOR

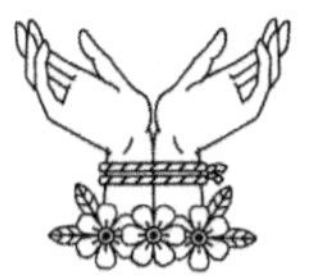

He's looking at you again!

Who?!

You know who!

EMILY

The first things to catch my attention were his eyes. Not the color. They weren't different when it came to that. Though I had to admit they were a pretty shade of sky blue. Sometimes a darker navy when he seemed really focused on whatever it was he was looking at.

But like I said, it wasn't the color. It was the way they watched me, trailed my movements across campus like they were locked on their target. Like I couldn't hide from them—*him*—if I wanted to.

I didn't. Want to.

I liked the way he looked at me as if I was all he saw without even knowing me. It was flattering. To feel like the center of someone's universe. Even if that someone was a stranger. And especially if that stranger was hotter than fucking sin.

Funny, wasn't it? How being attractive gave you a free pass to do something that would seem otherwise threatening.

A handsome football player follows you home and it's

romantic. The start of a love story or some Hallmark shit. The nerdy loner does the same thing and you're being featured on Dateline or starring in your very own Lifetime movie.

Truth was sometimes it could be both. I just didn't realize it at the time, struck dumb by the feel of those eyes on me. Otherwise I might not have smiled as wide when he decided to approach me halfway into the fall semester. Or held my breath when it sank in that he was actually talking to *me*. A nobody. That I hadn't imagined it. I didn't even bother to question the fact he didn't belong on campus anymore.

"Tonight." He told me. Because Cohen Michaels didn't ask. He didn't have to.

I nodded and then he was gone.

The first red flag should have been the fact he never asked me where I lived. Where he should pick me up or even attempted to get my phone number. None of that came to mind as I watched him walk away though.

Instead, I felt lucky. *Seen.* And girls like me didn't feel that way often. That was the psychology behind it. Behind growing up the way I did with the parents I had. Mommy and daddy issues made for a deadly combination. Throw us in a room with a true predator and we were easy pickings. Like the slowest gazelle trying to outrun a pack of lions.

I didn't have a chance.

21

COHEN

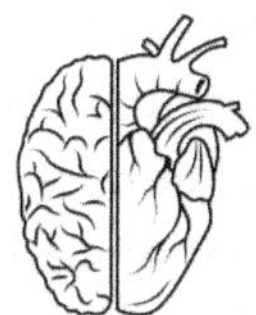

Obsession was nothing new to me. Something caught my eye. I became infatuated with it. Needed to know everything about it. Every detail. How it worked and what made it tick. Naturally, medicine became my calling, because there was no more curious an animal than mankind.

Some people would throw a label on that. Something like narcissistic personality disorder with compulsive tendencies. Those people were wrong. I didn't love myself. I just knew that I was better. It was fact, not opinion.

But nothing had ever captivated me as much as Emily. At first, scrolling through her socials had been enough. Knowing her class schedule and learning her usual coffee order. Then I began following her home. Back and forth between lecture halls. I studied her like I studied the human body. Waiting for the moment boredom would hit and I'd move on to bigger and better shit. Girls never kept me interested long. A few weeks at most. But it had been months and I just wanted... needed more.

So I decided fucking her would put an end to the infatuation. It usually did the trick. Then I'd find someone or something else that would drive my curiosity in another direction. Which was what had me walking up to her and telling her we were going out. Had me pulling up to her dorm and leading her back to my car.

Watching her close up was odd at first. I had to remind myself to do more than stare. To blend in. Converse. Pretend I didn't know everything about her already.

It took me a good portion of that first night to figure out what it was about her that piqued my interests. But then I realized it was the fact that Emily Shaw was so beautifully broken. And I enjoyed piecing things back together. Repurposing them and making them whole. And she carried so much delicious damage beneath that brittle shell. One quick tap and she'd shatter.

"Eat your food, Emily." I gestured to the nearly full plate in front of her. The restaurant lighting was ambient but not so dark that I couldn't make out every detail of her face each time the faux candlelight flickered in her direction.

I noticed how she moved the food around with her fork more than she ate it. She was hungry. I could tell by the way her pupils dilated each time she eyed her meal. But something in her psyche told her she didn't deserve it. Didn't deserve to eat. To *enjoy* her food. That same broken something.

She smiled before taking another tentative bite. The girl also smiled a lot. Almost like she was afraid if she didn't, she'd cry. And I was addicted to watching her teeter between the two emotions. Pushing her towards the ledge before yanking her back again.

"Thank you," she whispered, and I quirked a curious brow.

"For what?"

"For tonight. For taking me out to dinner. For... making an effort, I guess." Her cheeks turned that rosy shade of pink I'd yet to see up close. A color that made her eyes so much grayer in comparison.

I reached across the table and closed my fingers around her hand. I could feel her pulse beating at the base of her wrist, the bpms increasing with the slightest touch. "Spending time with you doesn't take effort, Emily. It's one of the easiest things I've ever done."

"You say my name a lot..."

"Do you not like your name, *Emily*?" I grinned when that pink deepened.

"Never really thought about it, to be honest. But I do like the way you say it."

"And what way is that?"

She shrugged as she attempted to pull her hand back. I held on tighter. I was making her nervous. I liked making her nervous. "I don't know. Almost like you're tasting it."

Now I was the one grinning. Or maybe smirking. I couldn't tell the difference when the action wasn't forced. "I'd much rather taste something else... Emily."

She sputtered on her water, choking down a few more sips as I gestured for the waiter to bring us the check.

By the time we made it back to my car, I had Emily squirming in her seat. She was doing her best to hide it. To pretend she didn't want me. And maybe she would have been successful if I hadn't studied her mannerisms. If I didn't know everything there was to know about Emily Shaw.

"You missed the turn..."

"I'm taking you back to my place." I kept my eyes straight ahead while catching Emily's glare in my peripheral.

"No, you're not."

The fire was new. I hadn't noticed it before. It was the wounded girl I'd analyzed, not the brat.

"I don't argue facts." It wasn't the right thing to say. But my mask was slipping the more my blood rushed to my cock. Her mouthiness shouldn't have been such a turn-on. It usually wasn't. Like I said, I enjoyed all the broken parts of her. I was attracted to them. At the same time, the thought of her fighting me had me nearly feral.

"Neither do I. And the *fact* is, while I appreciated dinner, that doesn't give you an open invitation to get into my pants."

"Are you a virgin, Emily?" I knew she wasn't. I'd done my homework.

"What? No!"

"Okay, then what's the problem?" My eyes flicked from the road to her dropped jaw and back again.

"Your entitlement, apparently."

I shrugged. She wasn't wrong. I was entitled. To a certain life. To enjoy myself. To everything that body of hers had to offer me. I kept that bit to myself though. Slammed on the brakes and made a U-turn in the middle of the road.

"Where are you going?" Her voice was much more timid all of a sudden.

"I thought you wanted me to take you home? Or have you changed your mind again, Emily?"

"No..."

"No, you haven't changed your mind? Or, no, you don't want to go home?"

"I... don't know."

"Well, you better figure it out before morning, babe. Wouldn't want you to miss class..."

"How do you know I have class in the morning?"

Oops, I was slipping again.

"Good guess. You look like a morning person."

She wasn't. Emily despised mornings. She could barely function before her second cup of instant coffee. A splash of milk and a packet of sugar—whenever she had it on hand. Otherwise she'd drink it straight black while scrunching up her nose in that way she did.

She was watching me. Studying my profile while I remained impassive. She didn't need to know how much I wanted her right now. That would give her the upper hand. And truth was, I would have her either way... eventually.

"I'm not, you know."

"Not what, Emily?"

"A morning person."

"Hm, guess I was wrong." I was never wrong.

Five minutes later, we were pulling up to her dorm. I slid out of my seat. Walked around the hood of my car and opened her door. She took my hand tentatively, almost as if she were afraid to touch me. She should be. Because her body betrayed her. Her breaths quickening and her chest heaving. It was sheer stubbornness that kept her legs closed. That and the slight friction it offered her with each step she took towards the door that was meant to separate us.

I punched in the code to her dorm, without giving her the chance to question me as I lowered my head and tugged her forward. Her lips parted on an almost silent moan before I slipped my tongue inside her mouth and finally kissed her. For the first time. And realized it would never be enough.

22
EMILY

Cohen Michaels was... well, the guy was fucking arrogant. Full of himself. Cocky with a capital COCK swinging between his legs. He was also good looking enough to get away with it. The cherry on top... was the way he kissed me. Both hard and soft. Pulling me in while simultaneously pushing me away. At ease. Like he didn't have a care in the world. But so tightly wound I was afraid he might snap.

That was the intoxicating thing about him. How many different versions of this man were tied up in one. And I admit I was too naïve to see the danger right in front of me. In a navy-blue button up, loose around the collar and tight around the chest, and a perfectly pressed pair of khaki dress pants.

I wanted to hate him. I should have hated him. Hell, I *would* later come to hate him. But by the time he stepped back, his lips kicked up at one side, I was breathless. A little dazed and a lot turned on. I knew it wouldn't take much more than me asking him to come inside with me. That at the very least I'd get a *good night* outta this one night. But something about his thinking I was easy didn't sit right with me. Even if it meant I'd never see him again.

Thing was, I knew that was impossible. I *saw* him every time he walked into a room. He just wasn't likely to see much of me. And I wanted it that way. More like I'd come to accept there was no other choice.

"Good night, Cohen." I glanced up at him through my lashes while doing my best not to actually look at him.

He reached out a hand and brushed my hair behind my ear, the brief contact enough to send a shiver down my spine and curl the toes in my shoes. "Good night, Emily." Then he dropped his arm and turned on his heel before calling out over one shoulder, "See you tomorrow, babe."

Tomorrow? Tomorrow when? That was what I'd wanted to ask; instead, I slipped through the door and watched him walk away until his car was nothing more than a dot on the road.

THE REPEATED BEEPING of my alarm clock startled me awake, the sunlight streaming in through the curtains of my dorm room window. I didn't remember leaving it open. But the truth was I didn't remember much after being dropped off last night. Almost like that kiss had rendered me stupid.

In a way, it had. I was a little dazed, cock-drunk, attracted to a man whose ego barely fit in the room with the rest of him. Then again, wasn't that what college was for? Being young, dumb... making mistakes and doing your best to forget them?

That's what I was telling myself anyway. When I threw

on a pleated black skirt, an oversized off-the-shoulder sweater, and my usual worn-out white sneakers. Before glancing at my reflection in the mirror. I wouldn't call the girl staring back at me... *hot*. But she wasn't ugly either. Cute was a more accurate description. Wavy brown hair that fell almost to my waist when I left it down, pale gray eyes that never even hinted at blue. A pert nose and pink cheeks.

Like I said, cute but never anyone who really turned heads or made any sort of entrance into a room. So it wasn't hard to figure out what guys like Cohen Michaels wanted. I was another notch on his bedpost. A girl he assumed was a sure thing, only for him to realize I was far more stubborn than I looked.

It was probably the cheeks, which gave me a heart-shaped face and made my twenty appear more like sixteen. And young meant easy. To fool. Manipulate. Coax into bed and never see again.

I'd been staring at myself so long in the mirror I'd lost track of time. Until my emergency second alarm started going off and sent me rushing out the door.

Ten minutes later, I was settling into the seat of my first lecture hall with a notepad and pen in front of me. I flipped my textbook open and watched a shadow darken the page. I didn't have to look up to know who that shadow belonged to. I could sense his presence the moment he walked through the door, though I told myself I was crazy at the time. And I could smell the distinct scent of his cologne and feel the way his glare seared through the side of my face before he ever spoke a word.

"Good Morning, Emily."

"Morning, Cohen."

He dropped his bag at his feet, then lowered himself down in the seat next to me. "You didn't eat breakfast."

It was another one of those questions that was really a statement and not a question at all.

"I didn't have time." I glanced in his direction without meaning to. I couldn't help myself. The guy was nice to look at.

He slid a paper bag in front of me before nudging a coffee cup over along with it. "One cream, one sugar."

My eyes bounced from the cup, which smelled as good as I'm sure it tasted, to Cohen. Then back again.

"How did you know...?" I asked, taking a small sip before peering into the bag. A chocolate muffin. My favorite. Even if I didn't get to have them often. And not because I was watching my figure. Fresh pastries just weren't a necessary expense when every penny went towards my housing and textbooks.

"Lucky guess." Cohen shrugged. But I could sense his focus on me again. I was pretty sure he was getting off on... watching me eat? Maybe the guy had a food fetish?

Not that it mattered. I'd eat a dozen chocolate muffins if it meant someone else was fronting the bill. It sure as hell beat selling used underwear on eBay...

I was kidding, of course. It hadn't come to that just yet. Though I had to admit that I'd thought about it more than once.

23
COHEN

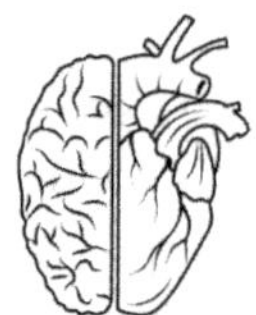

I knew I was staring, my attention hyperfocused on the way her throat moved when she swallowed. Almost as if I could see past the layers of dermis and subcutaneous tissue to the muscles of her larynx. The epiglottis closing over her windpipe to keep those little morsels of chocolate from making their way into her lungs and embedding in the alveoli.

I was the first to admit that my fascination with the woman was odd. At the same time, it made perfect sense when you really thought about it. What I was doing here wasn't all that different from feeding and watering a collection of lab rats. Studying what made them tick, how they reacted to their internal and external environments. Assessing if they could be conditioned and encouraged to seek out the reward at the end of the maze.

In this case, that reward just happened to be allowing her to drop to her knees in front of me... and the privilege of sucking my cock.

Not forcing Emily to come home with me that first

night had nothing to do with morality and everything to do with ego. I wanted her begging me, frothing at the mouth and clawing at my back. I wanted her screaming my name when I gave into her and cursing it when I refused. It was about more than sex. It was about complete submission and total domination. About the chase. The game. About outsmarting my opponent because I *could* and not because I needed to.

Her eyes were locked on the whiteboard in front of us and the professor droning on about some topic that wasn't worth the energy I would have had to expel to even pretend to pay attention. While my glare stayed glued to the tautness of her jaw and the little beads of sweat that trickled down her forehead before getting lost in a loose curl. She chewed on her bottom lip, absentmindedly, realizing it every now and then. Attempting to stop herself, only to gnaw at the plump flesh all over again a second or two later.

Her central nervous system was in overdrive beneath the weight of my scrutiny, trying to compensate for the panic rising in her chest—her body's way of preparing itself for a threat.

And that's exactly what I was. What I would be. A threat to her physical and mental fortitude.

By the end of the sixty-minute lecture, I could count every strand of hair that made up the right side of her head. Could tell you how many respirations she averaged per minute, depending on her stress level. Recognized which of her little sighs meant she was interested rather than annoyed. Frustrated instead of confused.

Maybe there was more to my obsession than science, but even I knew you shouldn't turn a lab rat into a pet.

She was pushing to her feet and slinging one strap of her bag onto her shoulder before it occurred to me that I'd stopped staring and started daydreaming.

"Have somewhere to be in a hurry, Emily?" I grabbed her wrist as soon as she tried to brush past me.

"I'm surprised you don't already know. Or would you like to have another go at a *lucky guess*?"

My lips curled into a smirk without me meaning to do it. I liked my girl timid but I thoroughly enjoyed it when she wasn't. "If you're not running to my bedroom, babe, you shouldn't be in such a rush. Sit and finish your coffee."

Her eyes flicked to where my hand was still wrapped around her tiny breakable wrist, over to the cup of coffee on her tray, then back to me again. "I don't have—"

"Time?" I finished for her. "You have precisely forty-five minutes before you have to meet up with Professor Daniels to review your application for his TA position." I watched her pupils dilate, her jaw drop slightly before setting tight again. She was surprised, just as much as she wasn't. "I wouldn't recommend it by the way."

"Recommend what, Cohen?"

"Accepting his offer." I shrugged.

"How do you even know he's going to offer it to me? There are plenty of more qualified applicants."

"Maybe..." I craned my neck to one side, making a show of eyeing her body from tit to toe. "But none of them look as good in that skirt as you do right now."

Emily tugged her arm free—*I let her, of course*—before quickly folding it over her chest. "I'm not sure what you're suggesting—"

"I'm not suggesting anything, Emily. I'm telling you. Show up to his office looking like my favorite little slut and the job is yours."

She pursed her lips, stunned silent. Or maybe she was too turned on to form intelligible words. Either way, I used the opening to nudge her closer to that ledge.

"Tell me, Emily." I quirked a questioning brow. "Did you dress up like that for him... or for *me*?"

24
EMILY

"*M*e. The answer is me. The only person I consider when choosing what I want to wear is me, myself, and I." Even as I hissed the words in his face, I knew they were a lie. I may not have done it consciously, but some part of me hoped I'd see him today. Hoped Cohen meant it when he said he'd see me *tomorrow*.

And now I was pissed off. At him. At Professor Daniels *and* at myself. For tossing my feminism out the window because some guy happened to have piercing blue eyes and a nice set of dimples.

Even knowing this, I didn't pull away when Cohen reached out a hand and tapped a finger on my lower lip. "You know, you're pretty when you lie, Emily." He grinned. "But you're absolutely breathtaking when you tell the truth."

I didn't know how to respond to that. Hell, I didn't know how to respond to half the shit this man said. Considering there wasn't much distinction between his compliments *or* his insults. It seemed the two were fairly interchangeable.

Before I knew what I was doing, Cohen was leading me out of the classroom. Down the hall and into some supply closet that I was certain should have been locked. I wouldn't have questioned it if he hadn't slammed me up against the back of the door, shoving his tongue so deep into my mouth I was surprised I didn't choke. Then his hands were up my skirt, gliding back and forth across the thin fabric of my underwear. I had several classes left to attend before I went home for the day and the last thing I needed was to smell like sex.

That didn't stop me from grinding against his hand, though. Or moaning against his lips before he glided them to that spot just beneath my ear and sucked.

"Why'd you wear the skirt, Emily?" he mumbled into my skin.

"I... I don't know."

"Wrong answer," he grunted between clenched teeth, running quick circles over my clit, his cock grinding against my belly at the same rhythm until he quickly dropped his hand and pulled away.

My chest was rising and falling with my rapid breaths, my every nerve ending buzzing and my blood pumping loud in my ears.

Why'd you stop? That's what I wanted to say. But my mouth couldn't seem to find words. My brain lust-drunk and my hormones in overdrive.

I glanced up at Cohen, who didn't appear much better as he paced back and forth in the small space while combing a hand through his tousled hair. My eyes flicked to the bulge tenting his pants and I held back a smirk.

I wasn't the only one hanging on by a loose thread.

"Tell me." He pivoted on his heel and rushed forward, slamming one hand on the door. Above my head. The other dropping to my waist and tugging me forward so that I had no choice but to feel him grind himself against me. "Tell me why you wore that to class today, of all days, Emily."

"For you," I whispered, but apparently it was enough to have him grinning back at me. Then he slipped his palm down the door and onto the handle. He twisted and I stumbled back a step, before he pushed through and walked out without bothering to say another word. Or even spare me a second look.

25
COHEN

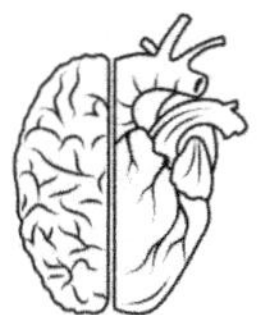

I could feel her watching me. Still smell her scent on my fingertips. More than that, I could hear the little sounds she made on repeat in the back of my head. Which was why I jumped in the shower the moment I got home. Poured a hefty portion of soap on my palm and jerked off to the image of Emily pressed up against that closet door.

I could have had her. Right then and there and been done with it. With her. But like I said, it was about more than sex. I could walk out onto that street right now and find a tight pussy to grip my cock or a pair of plump lips to suck me down. Wouldn't take more than a few minutes. Or a couple of hundreds if I happened to be too lazy to play nice.

This. Her. It was about more than that. I was sure if I looked close enough, went deep enough with the research, I'd find this reaction I was having could be explained away as a chemical impulse, a mix of pheromones emitted from the body that sent my central nervous system into overdrive.

At the end of the day, Homo sapiens were animals, which included the most basic instinct to procreate. Or at the very least, trick our bodies into thinking that's what we were doing. When really it was just a quick fuck.

None of that mattered right now though. As I pumped a slick palm up and down my cock with the image of a certain woman in a too-short skirt playing like a film reel behind my lids. I could still smell her, long after the hot water had rinsed what was left of her away. I could only fantasize about what she tasted like. I'd resisted licking my fingers clean. Fearing that if I hadn't, I'd be breaking into her dorm room to find out... instead of slipping in through that window to snoop.

I didn't like how out of control she made me feel. At the same time, I craved it. Tugged at the leash holding me back. Hoping if I yanked a little harder it would finally snap.

One, two, three more strokes had my left palm pressing against the wall, my right hand and most of the drain covered in the evidence of what this woman did to me. It would look better on her lips. Her chest or fucked deep into her cunt while she cried for me to go harder. Or stop. Didn't matter as long as it was her voice I heard screaming one way or the other.

I woke up the next morning to the feel of a warm hand slipping under the waistband of my boxers. Reaching lower and grabbing my cock around tho base. Before offering it a few long strokes. I could even feel the weight of her straddling my thighs.

My eyes sprung open only to see she was another figment of my overactive imagination, my own hand down my shorts and spread across my cock while my brain told me it was hers.

It didn't seem to matter how many times I jerked off to Emily's image. I wasn't satisfied. My body knew it wasn't the real thing.

I stretched my arms out before tucking them behind my head, my glare hyperfocused on the matte white of the colorless ceiling. Didn't remember even grabbing for it and couldn't tell you when I'd pulled up her number in my contacts but suddenly I was shooting off a message I had no recollection of typing out.

ME:

Wear a sundress today. That one with the white and blue flowers.

ME:

And don't forget a sweater. Daniels always has the air on full blast. Wouldn't want anyone else getting a peek at those pretty pink nipples.

EMILY:

Who is this?

ME:

Don't pretend like you don't know, Emily.

The little bubbles popped up on the screen, telling me she was about to reply—likely typing something snarky before thinking better of it—then disappeared again.

So we're playing games, huh?

My lips curled into a grin. "You can run but you can't hide, pet."

I WATCHED her from three rows down. The cap of her pen clasped between her teeth. Her hair pulled back in a high knot and that blue-and-white sundress hidden beneath a white sweater, sheer enough that I (and everyone else) could see through to her bra straps.

My girl was being bratty. Intentionally trying to get under my skin with that subtle hint of noncompliance. She knew what I wanted, what my instructions were, and yet I had no doubt she would play dumb. Attempt to make a case for herself. Of course it wouldn't work, which was probably what she really hoped for.

Emily liked being punished. Craved it without even realizing that was what she wanted.

I shouldn't give it to her. The best way to knock down her defenses was to completely ignore her little outburst. Make her thirst for the attention until she was on her knees begging me to look at her.

Problem was, I couldn't not *look* at her. If it were that easy, I wouldn't have bothered to spare her a glance from the get-go.

I waited until the lecture was over to push up from my seat and follow her out the door. If Emily knew I was behind her, she made no move to acknowledge me. Her hair brushing the back of her neck with the natural sway of her hips and her ass cheeks hugged by the fabric of her dress each time she pushed off her heel to propel herself forward.

Then she turned the corner, pivoting on her department

store off-white sneakers and pinning me with a glare. "Don't you have somewhere to be?"

I shoved my hands into my pockets with a slight shrug of my shoulders. "Nope."

"What about class, Cohen? You don't even go here anymore."

"Why would I go to class? What could they possibly teach me that I don't already know?"

"Maybe something about personal space..." she muttered under her breath, gasping when I grabbed her wrist. Yanked her forward and pressed her against the wall.

"It doesn't get more personal than this, babe," I whispered against the shell of her ear, smirking when my words had the desired effect. Emily clenched her thighs together, squeezing her eyes shut like she could somehow will me out of existence. So I tipped her chin up with my free hand. "It's okay to admit you want me, ya know."

"What I want... is to get as far away from you as humanly possible," she hissed.

"The only thing worse than lying to me is lying to yourself." I lifted a single eyebrow in challenge before dropping my grip on her wrist and stepping aside. "Nice dress, by the way..."

26

EMILY

Cherry cola, red licorice, and Cohen Michaels. My three vices. None of them good for me. But all of them made my mouth water.

I knew what he was doing. I'd turned him down that first night. Bruised his frail ego and now he needed me to beg for it. To chase him and make him feel wanted again, so he could return the favor and throw me out on my rear.

He was a grown-ass man throwing a toddler-sized tantrum. And I shouldn't feed into it. After all, what kind of lesson would that be?

At the same time, resisting him didn't seem to be an option either. Not when my body was so ready and willing. There was no hiding my attraction. No tamping it down or denying it either. Which left me between a rock and a literal *hard* place.

That place being the hefty bulge that hung between his legs.

Maybe it was better to just fuck him and get it over with. Enjoy myself for as long as it lasted. Then watch him get bored and move on. Because that was what guys like

Cohen Michaels did. They got in your pants and then *got* out of there. There were no flowers, no calls the next day. Hell, if they ran into you out in the wild, they didn't even remember your name.

And if they didn't remember your name, they sure as shit would forget your class schedule.

So, as I watched him walk away for the third time in as many days, I decided I would do my sanity a service and fuck Cohen Michaels out of both our systems. Prove to myself that I wasn't special and neither was he.

FIFTEEN MINUTES into my Fundamentals of International Business lecture, and I felt... nothing. No rise of the hair on the back of my neck. No prickling sensation when I could feel a pair of eyes searing their way into my skin. No sixth sense that told me someone was watching me.

Nothing. But a chill that traveled up my spine at the realization that I was alone. Completely alone in a room full of people.

I should have been used to it; instead, I was becoming used to him. In only a handful of days.

My eyes flicked around the lecture hall, seeking him out without even realizing I was doing it. Until my phone buzzed and vibrated across my desk tray. I glanced down at the screen and the words *unknown number*.

UNKNOWN:

Looking for someone?

I snatched up the device, checking to make sure

Professor Walsh was thoroughly distracted by the sound of his own voice before trying to come up with a suitable response. The stubborn part of me wanted to tell him to fuck off. But being bratty hadn't gotten me anywhere. In fact, he seemed to like it. The challenge. The chase. Playing cat and mouse with my libido.

I stared at the text box, willing a reply to formulate while my thumbs hovered over the little keyboard.

UNKNOWN:

Ignoring me or thinking too hard, babe?

UNKNOWN:

No need to answer that. I can see the stress lines on your forehead. The little beads of sweat pooling at your temples and the way your nose scrunches up whenever you're hyperfocused.

I couldn't help myself and immediately glanced up and around again. Only to come up short. He wasn't here. In this room. I was sure of it. But he could see me. I was sure of that too.

That or he was bluffing. Something told me he wasn't though.

UNKNOWN:

Are you wet just thinking about me watching you, Emily? Your thighs clenching tight and your pussy tensing at the thought of me filling you up?

ME:

No.

Yeah, it wasn't a strong argument but it was the best I could do at the moment.

UNKNOWN:

> Then tell me what has you squirming in
> your seat? You really should be taking
> notes. That's what good girls do in class.

ME:

> And what gave you the impression I was a
> good girl, Cohen? Or is that just another
> assumption you got wrong?

The little check mark popped up, telling me my message was read, followed by the bubbles that indicated he was typing out a reply. But nothing came through. Not five minutes later or ten or twenty. Or even by the end of class.

Couldn't say I was shocked by Cohen's sudden radio silence. I'd taken the fun out of our little back and forth by being so agreeable. The slight flirtation had given him what he wanted and like every spoiled child, once he got it, he didn't want it anymore.

At least that was my own misplaced assumption, which was proven wrong the moment I stepped foot into my dorm room, only to find a pair of stark blue eyes glaring back at me from my bed.

I had no idea how long he'd been waiting for me. In that spot. On my mattress. Appearing so out of place in his designer clothes on my bargain bedsheets.

"What are you doing here, Cohen?" I huffed as I tossed my bag on its usual spot by the door before slipping out of my sneakers and tucking them against the wall. I didn't bother asking him how he got in or even feigning surprise. Because it had been a long day and I just didn't have it in me.

His body didn't move. There was barely a rise and fall of his chest. A flare of his nostrils or a flutter of his lashes as his eyes tracked me across the room. I would think he was dead if it weren't for the sudden dilation of his pupils when I shrugged out of my cardigan and tossed it on the chair.

My roommate was gone for the weekend, not that she was really ever here. Something I planned to finally use to my advantage.

I took three steps forward, prying his legs open and pressing myself between them before bracing my arms on his neck and straddling his lap. "You didn't answer my question."

"Was it a question, Emily?" He hissed when I took his earlobe between my teeth and sank down. "Thought it was rhetorical. Since you know exactly why I'm here," he grunted as he flipped me down onto my bed and quickly climbed his way up my body.

27
COHEN

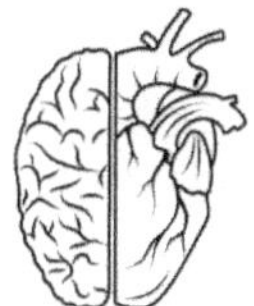

There was something about the feel of Emily squirming beneath me. Her arms pinned high above her head. Her eyes wide and her brain stunted. That fascinated me. Even more than the first time I cut into a fresh cadaver and got an eyeful of intestines. Even more than the feel of cardiac muscle still pumping in the palm of my hand.

Unlike my Jane Doe, I could see the panic on Emily's face, the fear creasing her brow. The desire and the obstinance. She wanted this. She'd used that text to bait me into doing it. But she was also afraid... of liking it. What I did to her and how I made her feel. More than that, she was terrified of not knowing how to survive without it.

In all honesty, we both were. I just hadn't realized it yet.

I kept her wrists locked in one palm, while my free hand slowly slinked down the length of her torso before creeping up her skirt and sliding between the apex of her thighs. I grinned as my fingertips traced over the moist fabric of her underwear.

"Is all that for me, Emily?" I knew it was. But I needed

to hear her say it. Needed her to submit to me fully as much as I needed her to fight me. Though, if we didn't speed things up a bit, the way my cock was straining against my zipper meant either would do.

Consent was a nicety, not a requirement.

When she didn't immediately answer, I shoved the lacy material aside and dipped a finger into her wet cunt, enjoying the way her muscles clenched when she tried to suck me deeper. I gave her three quick thrusts while angling my wrist downward so that my palm pounded against her clit, and she threw her head back, biting on her bottom lip in a failed attempt to stifle a moan.

"Why is it so hard for you to admit you want me?"

"I... I don't know..." Her voice was soft, vulnerable, barely above a whisper.

I watched her face, my gaze flicking from one eye to the other. Searching for any sign of deception. She wasn't telling the truth but she wasn't lying either.

Emily was good at balancing herself between the two.

I dropped my head and pressed my mouth to that spot just under her ear, sucking on the sensitive skin there while grinding my cock against her lower stomach. An inch or so above where she really needed me.

"Tell me..."

"Tell you what, Cohen?" she huffed. She was frustrated. We both were. And the solution was easy enough.

"That you want this as much as I do. That you can't stop thinking about me. That you search me out in every room you walk into. That I haunt your nightmares and star in your fantasies. Tell me you want me to fuck you as much as you want your next breath, Emily. I need to hear you say it."

"Why? Why do I have to say the words? Why is it so important to you?"

"Because we'll both feel a lot better when you do."

"We? Or do you mean your ego?"

"Both." I could see her resolve waning, her eyes fluttering closed when I flicked my tongue across her earlobe before tugging it between my teeth. She tasted sweet and slightly salty from the sweat still clinging to her skin.

"Fuck me, Cohen. I want you to fuck me, okay?"

I captured her mouth in a kiss, grinning against her lips as I tugged my waistband down and flipped her skirt up. I didn't bother to free my other leg from my pants before forcing her thighs apart and thrusting forward. I pulled back. Drove in one more time and quickly bottomed out as Emily clawed at my back. I couldn't tell if she was trying to shove me off or pull me deeper. I didn't care to find out either. She was too warm. Too fucking wet. Her cunt tightening around me and holding me hostage. Even as her palms slapped at my chest.

"Condom!" she yelled out. But it was too late. I'd felt her raw. There was no way I could turn to latex now.

"Don't need it," I ground the words between clenched teeth. "Clean as a whistle, babe."

"You'll have to pull out," she mumbled, but I could tell the logical side of her brain was losing its grip as the endorphins took over.

"Uh-huh."

One, two, three deep thrusts and neither of us was able to form words anymore. I could hear the blood rushing to my ears, the sounds of my own grunts echoing off the bare walls of her dorm room, the slapping of skin against skin, and the banging of the headboard against the thin sheetrock. Until it was all drowned out by her soft whimpers.

I slowed my pace, drawing all the way out before gliding back in again. Emily's spine arched, her gluteal muscles contracting beneath the imprints of my fingertips and her nails raking through my hair.

She was lost to the moment. And suddenly I realized I was lost to her. Not just fucking her. Figuring her out and obsessing over her. It was more than that.

I... liked her. And I wanted her to like me too. That was why I needed to hear her say it. Why I couldn't just fuck her and walk away. Why I couldn't get her out of my head. Why that first kiss outside the dorms had inhibited my ability to think...

When she began chanting my name under her breath like a near-silent prayer, I found my hand reaching up to sweep her hair off her cheek. I needed to see her face. A small smile tipped up her lips just slightly and I couldn't stop myself from bending forward to kiss her again. The gesture tender, almost gentle, my tongue dancing with hers instead of dueling. The fucking affectionate instead of primal.

And I pulled back at the same time my cum marked Emily as mine. For as long as both of us were breathing, this woman was mine. She just didn't know it yet.

28
EMILY

I didn't remember closing my eyes, but suddenly I was fluttering them open as the early morning light poured in from my window. I waited a second, watching the dust particles dance through the air, and took a deep breath, knowing what I'd find without having to look. Cold sheets and an empty bed. Almost like last night was nothing more than some hyper-realistic fantasy made up by the mind of a girl who hadn't gotten laid in a while.

The very real throbbing between my legs told me it wasn't though.

I didn't bother to check for a note or a text as I forced myself to roll off the mattress and changed into a clean t-shirt and a pair of sweats. What I really needed was a shower, to wash the scent of his cologne off my skin and the taste of his mouth from my lips.

But a quick glance at the old-school analog clock on my nightstand told me that was the *real* fantasy. I'd forgotten to charge my phone and had just enough time to sprint across the lawn and slide into my seat for my first class of the day.

I tied my hair up into a high ponytail before setting my notebook and pen in front of me. Most of my classmates used their laptops, but I enjoyed the weight of a pen in my hands and the feel of ink gliding across the page. And right now, I needed the distraction. To get out of my head and ground myself. Because forgetting Cohen wasn't so easy when my senses couldn't escape him.

You'd think getting fucked out of my mind would ease the tension in my muscles, help my body relax. It didn't. I felt hungover, like I'd taken too many shots of vodka instead of too much dick in one sitting, while my stomach growled from yet another missed breakfast. I should have been embarrassed by the way I looked, but the truth was I just blended in with the rest of the masses, who all smelled like sex and last night's bad decisions.

Because that's what Cohen Michaels was. A bad decision. A mistake. Something I was more than a little aware of as I sat with my eyes glued to the door, like thinking about him enough would make him appear. Ten minutes into Professor Hughes's lecture, I'd accepted the fact *that* wasn't going to happen either.

So when I heard the door squeak open, followed by heavy footfalls towards the front of the class, I didn't bother to look up from my notebook. Until my doodles were distorted by the ring of a coffee cup.

"Hey! What the hell—" The words caught in my throat and nearly choked me to the point that all I could do was comply when a hand reached down. Grabbed my wrist and tugged me to my feet.

"You forgot your phone," Cohen said as he set the device in my hand and curled my fingers around it before he deposited a brown paper bag next to the coffee cup. "And breakfast."

Then he lowered his head. Palmed my cheek and kissed me. I found myself unable to speak, standing here and wondering when I'd fallen asleep while asking myself why I was still dreaming about some guy who dined and dashed on me last night. Because I couldn't imagine any other way this could be real.

"All right, Mr. Michaels." Professor Hughes cleared his throat, and I suddenly realized that all eyes were on us. Cohen and me. In the middle of class. When I looked like I'd been thoroughly fucked and he smelled freshly showered. "I've given you enough leeway. If it's not too much of an inconvenience, I'd like to continue with my lecture."

I heard a few chuckles in the back of the room, before Cohen's glare had them stifling their laughter with a fake cough. He didn't say anything else. Just pinned me with that same glare, his eyes blazing a bright blue as he took a step back. Pivoted on his heel and walked out the door like I'd once again imagined the whole thing.

Professor Hughes's voice broke through the buzzing in my ears as he went on to babble about mathematical equations I didn't have the brain capacity to grasp at the moment. I shook my head, trying to reboot my senses while ignoring the hushed whispers and frequent stares, as I reached into the paper bag and pulled out a chocolate muffin.

I wanted to grin, to believe the gesture meant something. I could feel my facial muscles pulling taut without me telling them to, but I'd never been one of those girls. The type to think a muffin and a coffee were anything more than a *muffin* and a *coffee*. A small gesture that didn't signify something it wasn't.

If anything, this was a cheap *thank you*. Like a quick tap

on the ass on your way to the door. A *don't call me, I'll call you* kind of thing in the form of my favorite breakfast order.

It could have been worse though. And my stomach was grateful to not have to eat itself for the next few hours.

The sound of my phone vibrating caught my attention as I plopped a piece of pastry into my mouth and savored the way the chocolate melted on my tongue. I should have been focusing on class. But I couldn't help the way my eyes hitched to the message pinned to the top of my screen.

UNKNOWN:

Stop staring at the bag and actually eat your breakfast, Emily. And don't leave your phone behind again. If I text you, I want to know you're able to respond. And not just being stubborn.

I rolled my eyes. I shouldn't expect anything less than arrogance from the man, even if he was doing something nice.

UNKNOWN:

You still smell like me, by the way.

He was right. I did smell like him. And I was sure everyone in this lecture hall now knew why.

29
COHEN

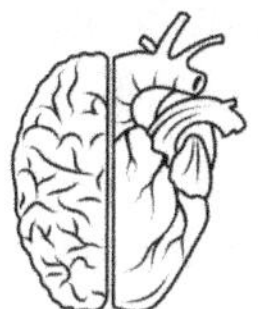

I knew Emily's class schedule well enough to know exactly where she had to be and when. Which meant I also knew that she *wouldn't* be in her dorm room when I returned from the campus coffee shop with her breakfast order in one hand, swiped her phone from the charger where she left it with the other, and slowly made my way over to Roberts Hall. Where Professor Calvin Hughes was sure to be fifteen or so minutes into his lecture on *differential calculus in an applied setting* or something to that effect.

The thing was... I'd studied my girl. Her habits, her routines. Long enough to predict what she would do when presented with any given challenge.

Emily wasn't attached to her technology. She didn't scroll her socials all day or spend much time staring at her phone screen. She took all her notes by hand. And she liked to scribble little pictures when she was trying to stay awake. All of which told me she didn't have any qualms about leaving the device behind if she were to find the battery "surreptitiously" dead in the morning.

Unfortunately for her, not me, a dead battery also meant no alarm. Or secondary alarm, in Emily's case. And a poor circadian rhythm—paired with a lack of fluids and an increase of vasopressin, melatonin, and oxytocin thanks to multiple orgasms I'd been sure to give her—meant the likelihood of her waking up on time was slim to none.

Odds that were certainly in my favor, considering the sort of display I had in mind after deciding that I wasn't done with my pet. That it was more than an infatuation and that I wanted to keep her. Lab rat or not.

I'd spent the better part of an hour this morning watching Emily sleep. Enjoying the way her scent mingled with mine. And I wasn't willing to give any of that up just yet. Maybe not ever. Which gave me more of a reason to ensure she kept part of me with her in class today. Even if that part was mostly an assortment of plasma and dead cells by this point.

Like I said, I knew my girl. Break it down how ever you wanted, it was simple human behavior and probability. When forced to choose between taking care of herself and being late to class, she'd forgo the former and rush out the door. No matter how many meals she skipped the day prior, and even if that meant she was forced to sit in a lecture hall full of people with my dried cum still clinging to her skin.

I smirked at the thought, whistling as I turned the corner, then shoved my way inside room 202, precisely thirty minutes into one of Hughes's drawn-out rants.

I had a reputation on this campus, long after graduation—one I used to my advantage whenever I found the need. I was a rising star in the medical world after all, a credit to the school. And the administration knew that my success meant more money in their pockets. A shiny new name they could add to all their plaques as soon as my fieldwork hit the medical journals. Until then, I was granted certain privileges. Like sitting in on Emily's classes. Or, on days like today, interrupting them entirely. Making sure that everyone in this room got an eyeful of me and my pet together.

This was me staking my claim. In front of enough witnesses to ensure the gossip spread hot and fast to the rest of the school with the least amount of effort. Sure, I could have just told a few acquaintances, posted a handful of photos of her half-naked in my bed wearing my old football jersey, but nothing traveled quicker than a little PDA and a whole lot of speculation.

It was also a good lesson for Emily. A reminder to check her battery and not leave her goddamn phone behind. If she was gonna be mine, I expected her to be available. To answer my texts and not leave me on read. It wasn't too much to ask for everything I planned to give her in return.

My attention, my affection, *myself*.

30
COHEN

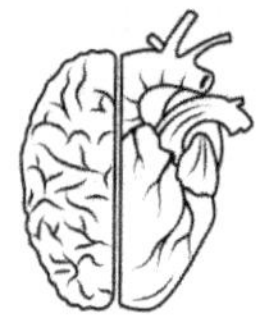

I shoved my phone back into my pocket, not bothering to wait for a reply. I was in a good mood and didn't want Emily's attitude to dampen it.

Sure, I appreciated a little brattiness here and there. Shit got my dick hard. But it also got under my skin for as long as it took to finally get her alone and fuck some good sense into that cunt of hers.

And I didn't have time for any of that today. I'd been

missing too many hours during my clinical rotations and people were starting to take notice. Talk. Suggest my head wasn't in the game.

Of course, they were wrong. Emily might have been a distraction but she also kept me hyperfocused on the end goal. My surgical residency working alongside Dr. Rath. Guy was a sick fuck with a well-deserved ego. Someone who was known to bend the rules. Or so it'd been rumored. I was promised free rein in his operating room—seeing as another thing that was rumored was his affinity for watching.

The first cut into live flesh, the peeling back of muscle tissue, and the last breath. He watched it all. Got off on it. Which was hard to do when you were the one holding the scalpel.

My phone buzzed in my pocket, just as I tossed my helmet on and was about to throw a leg over my bright-yellow bike—because fuck if I didn't like being seen. I flipped open the face shield and glanced at the screen.

J:

Ten minutes early. Blue dress with yellow flowers. White sweater. No breakfast.

I replied with a thumbs-up emoji, my lips tipped up to one side without meaning to as I navigated to Emily's name in my contacts and opened our chat thread.

ME:

Your breakfast will be there in ten. Keep playing games, babe, and I'll be forced to crash another lecture and kiss you stupid in front of everyone again.

I wouldn't be the one delivering her coffee today. I had

people for that. It was amazing what a few forged scripts for Adderall could get you when you were surrounded by a shit-ton of stressed-out college students all itching for a quick fix. Pills really were the best form of currency. Which was entirely too convenient for someone with access to overworked doctors—as long as you weren't going crazy with the opiates, no one seemed to notice. Or care.

A few minutes later, Jason sent through a picture of Emily sipping on a white paper cup from the campus cafe. And I promised to drop off a month's supply of ten mills to his dorm room tonight. Gave me an excuse to see Emily while I was there.

Really was a win-win when you thought about it.

I honestly couldn't decide what was better. The feel of someone's guts in my hands or Emily's around my cock. Though right now, there was definitely one I preferred.

I pushed through her dorm room door, not bothering to knock, and made it to her bed before she had time enough to sit up and gasp. I closed a palm over her mouth and pressed my lips to the shell of her ear, shushing her as she choked back a scream. Then I dropped my hand and slowly pushed her back down on the mattress.

"Cohen, what are you—"

Her words were severed as I shoved my tongue into her mouth while trailing my fingers along her abdomen before slipping them beneath the waistband of her sleep shorts. Emily groaned, low in her throat, and I grinned at the little whimpers that followed.

No matter how much her brain wanted to fight me and my many demands, her body never could. And the truth was, mine was just as inhibited. I craved her, the thought of sliding my cock into her cunt enough to send me into a frenzy.

I thought I'd get over it after the first time. Assured myself I would by the third. Now, I accepted the fact I needed her. That I might always need her. And she needed me too. There was no other explanation for the way she clawed at my back at night and wanted to claw at my face by the light of day.

It was toxic and I fucking loved it. I loved her compulsion to hate me *and* her inability to do so. There was just something so intoxicating about knowing something was bad for you and wanting it anyway.

I tugged her shorts down her soft thighs and she kicked them off her ankles with her feet, scrambling to wrap her leg around my waist through my jeans. I could feel how wet she was each time she ground her cunt against me, her juices seeping into my clothes and keeping her scent locked in the tiny fibers. I would be able to smell her for days if I wanted.

She fumbled with my t-shirt, trying to tug it over my head without breaking the kiss. I pulled back just long enough to tear it off and then my mouth was on hers again. Biting, licking, and sucking. Far more animalistic than human. Then we were both yanking on my jeans, shoving them down my legs before I kicked off my shoes and socks. Emily's tank top was the last article of clothing to hit the floor, and then I was flipping her onto her back. Spreading her thighs and thrusting forward.

It was always a challenge at first, to push through the slight resistance before her cunt was hugging me like I fucking belonged. Holding me in place before sucking me deeper. I knew it was a mix of endorphins and serotonin, this feeling, this need. I knew and I didn't care because it felt fucking fantastic.

Emily's body moved in tandem with mine, her hips lifting up each time I drove forward. She'd stopped bothering to ask for a condom and I never bothered to bring one. Nothing could compare to the slapping of skin to skin, to the friction of her walls closing around my cock. We both knew it even if neither of us said it.

She was close. I could tell by the change in her pattern of breathing. The way her head tipped back and her movements grew languid. The fast and hard brought her to the precipice, but the slow and steady was what sent her flying over. I arched my back and lowered my mouth to one of her pert nipples, enjoying the way her entire body shuddered with the contact. It didn't take but three more rigid thrusts before Emily's muscles were spasming and turning gelatinous beneath my grip.

I continued to fuck her through her orgasm, my attention hyperfocused on her face and the tension leaving her features. Her expression softening and her lips curling into the smirk of a woman properly fucked.

I gave her a few seconds of reprieve before rising up on my knees. Grabbing on to the headboard and setting the tip of my cock against her slightly parted mouth. Emily's eyes snapped open and peered up at me.

"My turn, babe." I grinned.

31
EMILY

I had barely sucked in a lungful of air before Cohen was prying my mouth open and shoving himself down to the back of my throat. I gagged and sputtered, clawing at his thighs as my brain screamed at me to breathe while my nostrils flared with each inhale. Panic was taking over, insisting I was suffocating even though I knew I wasn't. My fight-or-flight instinct in overdrive as he used my mouth like his own personal fuck toy.

The thing was... Cohen needed it rough. He always needed it rough. He'd hold himself back, fuck me slow and soft, wait until I got mine. And then it was like something inside him snapped, and he'd use my body, whatever hole caught his eye how ever he saw fit. As he fed those darker impulses of his, the ones he seemed to hide from the rest of the world. Almost like I wasn't human. I didn't exist. Like my throat was nothing more than a means to an end. That end being a hefty dose of cum chipmunking my cheeks and dripping down my chin while I heaved in a breath and tried to swallow.

I knew how fucked-up it was. How toxic. I also knew it

wasn't good for me. But neither were those chocolate muffins and the knowing did little to help tamp down the craving.

I couldn't deny the familiarity of it either. The comfort I found in the way he treated me. Cared for my well-being, only to completely disregard it on a whim. Some part of me thought this was what I deserved, because growing up, that's what I was told. I was unwanted, unworthy of even the slightest dignity. And I had yet to break the cycle.

But that was tomorrow's problem. Right now, I needed to focus on breathing through my nose. On sucking in air the moment Cohen pulled back while hoping it would sustain me when he drove back in again. I couldn't even say the entire experience was unpleasant. It wasn't. Especially when he would tug on my hair and angle my head back, my spine arching off in the bed in a painful yet pleasure-inducing way. My thighs drenched with my own release and my nipples peaked with the chill of the air.

My clit was throbbing, begging to be touched as his balls slapped against my jaw in rhythm with his frantic thrusts. He was close. I could tell by his pacing, the frequency and depth of his grunts. And just when I thought he was going to come, his cock pulsing against my cracked lips, he pulled back and released himself on my face.

I blinked my lashes, my eyes burning and my skin tacky as Cohen traced his fingers across my cheek before bringing the pads to my lips. He seemed mesmerized by the sight of my face smeared with his cum. Like I was both the most beautiful and grotesque thing he'd ever seen.

He shoved his hand inside my mouth, as far as it would go, and threw his head back on a groan when I gagged and nearly tossed up my dinner. He pulled away again, dropping his palm to my throat before he leaned forward and captured my lips in a searing kiss. Slowly guiding me back down to the bed and straddling my hips.

This was different. I didn't know what it was. Just that it was more tender somehow. Almost as if he were worshiping my body, caressing every part of me and committing it to memory. I couldn't tell you what changed. What shifted between us in this moment. But something did.

Because this was for him as much as it was for me this time.

He flicked his tongue against mine, tasting himself on me as he edged his half-hard cock against my entrance. Rubbing back and forth until my arousal was coating his tip and he was almost fully erect. Then he nudged forward, never breaking the kiss as he slowly rocked us both over that ledge again.

He didn't stop, not when I felt his cum dripping down my thighs before seeping into the bedsheets. Not when my nerve endings were so overstimulated I had to cover my nipples. Not even when my body gave out and my consciousness was waning.

Truth was I couldn't tell you when he finally dropped onto my chest and fell asleep on top of me. Only that, that was how I found him when my eyes fluttered open again the next morning. And the damp spot on the mattress reminded me of how epically we'd fucked up.

32
COHEN

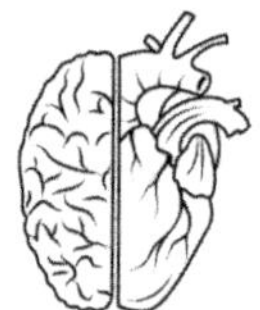

Emily was pacing back and forth across her dorm room, her hair still tangled from where my hands had combed through it, her lips swollen and her voice hoarse. Every part of her was marked by some part of me. And she never looked more perfect. Or agitated.

I could hear the panic underlying her tone while her words filtered through my ears like white noise. I wasn't listening. I was observing. Reading her reactions and seeing how much it matched or conflicted with her tone.

She thought it was a mistake. That much was obvious. She assumed we had both gotten carried away, and right now I had no plans of correcting her. I knew what I was doing. Her schedule wasn't the only thing I had down to a science. I also kept track of Emily's menstrual cycle. When she bled and when she ovulated. Nothing I did was ever *unintentional*. Even if my decision hadn't been finalized until seconds before I was driving into her cunt again.

Sure, it would likely take more than this once and she'd be more wary of me fucking her bare. That just meant I had to play this smart. Keep her guessing and so sated she didn't have time to question what I was doing.

No, kids had never been on my radar before. Something I wanted, let alone was trying to actively produce. But right now, it seemed like the best idea in the world. I wanted to see Emily's abdomen stretching with my child, her breasts plump and weighted down with sweet milk. I wanted a piece of me inside her for how ever long I could keep it there. Then I wanted to repeat the process. Over and over again if I could manage.

I'd thought it through at length. Emily would make the perfect doctor's wife, *my wife*. She was intelligent in the general sense, more than pretty enough, and pliable in a way that meant I could mold her into the sort of woman I wanted at my side indefinitely. I just needed her to see it too.

"Cohen, you're not saying anything..." She stopped moving and the sudden shift caught my attention.

"I'll... I'll take care of it." It wasn't a lie. I would take care of everything. She only needed to sit back and let me.

"What does that mean?"

"What do you want it to mean, Emily?" I allowed her to maintain the position of power, keeping my ass firmly planted on the bed so that I had to peer up at her.

"I... I can't have a baby. I can't get pregnant."

"Okay, so you want a pill? Plan B? I can grab you something from the hospital's pharmacy. If you're sure. Get you a script for birth control while I'm at it?"

"Yes, please. Let's do that. Can you do that?"

I could tell she was still spiraling, her thoughts flying through her brain so quickly she couldn't focus on me and how I was watching her.

"Of course, babe. Whatever you need to feel better." I

pulled her head down, her arms crossed over her chest in a defensive posturing as I pressed a kiss to her forehead. Then I pushed up from the bed, shoving my feet into my shoes before shrugging on my jacket. "I'll be back in about an hour. Stay here." I paused with my palm wrapped around the handle. "And, Emily?"

She glanced up to meet my glare. "Yeah?"

"Don't forget to eat your breakfast." I jutted my chin towards the orange juice and pastries I left on her night-stand, then pushed through the door and clicked it closed behind me.

I watched Emily swallow down the "levonorgestrel" tab I'd switched out for folic acid. And kept my grin to myself.

Her eyes were watery and her hands shook as she twisted the hem of her shirt between her fingers. "So that's it? That's all I have to do and it'll be okay?"

I reached out an arm and pulled her onto my lap, brushing her hair back from her neck and kissing her pulse point. Her heartbeat was erratic. She really didn't want this. Which was fine. I wanted it enough for both of us. I felt her breathing normalize and her body relax as she melted into my touch.

"That's it, babe. One tiny pill."

"Are you sure?"

"The instructions are on the back of the box if you don't trust me."

"Okay." She nodded, her movements almost robotic. It didn't go unnoticed, the fact that she didn't comment on the whole *trusting me* thing. Then again, I suppose she shouldn't. Not with everything I had in mind for her, with or without her knowledge.

"You know, some guys might take it as a blow to their ego that a chick's so obviously repulsed by the idea of getting knocked up with their kid," I grunted against her ear, tugging her ass back and gliding it over my straining cock.

I didn't have to see Emily's face to know her eyes were rolling back in her head.

"I can't imagine anything affecting your ego, Cohen, least of all me." She sighed but I could hear the tension leaving her voice as my fingers traveled along the waistband of her shorts. "I have to get to class soon..."

"I know."

"Which means I have to get in the shower and get dressed."

"I know."

"Cohen..."

I pulled my mouth back from where I was sucking on the soft skin of her neck, slowly pushing to my full height while sliding Emily off my lap and back onto her feet. "Wear the blue one today." I gestured to her closet, where I'd set out her clothes when she was busy panicking. "White cardigan with whatever shoes are most comfortable. Your schedule is all over campus today."

I pressed a kiss to the top of her head and slipped out the door again, as Emily continued to stare at me in stunned silence.

33
EMILY

I'd been taking the three-month supply of birth control pills Cohen had given me. *Religiously.* Every day. At the same time. To the minute. And all it seemed to do was make me sick.

I could deal with the nausea though. The exhaustion. The random lightheadedness whenever I skipped a meal. What I couldn't deal with was the very real possibility that the side effects had nothing to do with the medication and everything to do with the box I snagged from the corner store between classes. The same box I'd avoided all day, pretending it didn't exist before finally deciding at almost midnight that sleep wasn't happening and I'd better just bite the bullet now. Even if the label on the back said it was best to test first thing in the morning.

I couldn't wait that long, not when my heart was beating out of my chest. My palms sweating and my thoughts jumping down that rabbit hole without looking back.

Five minutes later, I was glaring at the two little pink lines staring back at me from where the white plastic stick was perched on my bathroom counter. Eyeing the results as if I could somehow will them to disappear.

This was it. My life was over. I'd carry on the legacy of becoming an unfit single mother to a child I never wanted. My hand drifted to my abdomen with the thought. I didn't mean it the way it sounded, I told myself and the unborn baby who was nothing more than a blip beneath my fingers. It wasn't about me not wanting them. It was about them being better off without me. I didn't know how to do this. I was never *shown how*, and I was almost certain that the genetic trait of being a shitty parent was passed down from generation to generation in my family.

But it wasn't just about me. Cohen needed to know. He *deserved* to know. It was the right thing to do. Then he could decide for himself if I—*we* were worth sticking around for. If this infatuation of his was just that. An infatuation. A few months of getting off on our toxicity.

My hands trembled over his name in my contacts. We barely knew each other, our relationship consisting of a few fucks more than a one-night stand. And he was about to start his surgical residency. At the top of his class. With a life and a future ahead of him. The last thing he needed was a kid holding him back.

I typed out a message. Deleted it and typed again while chewing on my nail beds till they bled. The copper tang grounded me enough to hit *send*.

ME:

Hey, it's Emily. Can you come over?

That was stupid. He would know it was me. But my nerves were all over the place. How do you tell someone you're about to ruin three lives? What if it was my fault? If maybe I rushed out the door one morning and skipped a pill? Or misread the instructions? Worse yet, what if he thought I'd done it on purpose? A girl like me looking to trap a guy like him?

It wasn't unheard of...

My eyes flicked to the clock on the wall. Fuck, my text sounded like a late-night booty call more than an invitation to talk. I swiped my phone off the counter and tried again.

ME:

> If not, that's fine. I just have something to tell you.

Send. Yup, that sounded worse. Like I was about to inform him a series of antibiotics was in his near future. Lucky for us, a baby was only slightly less permanent than herpes. You could walk away from the former, not the latter. My mother taught me that much when she tried to leave me in the grocery store parking lot that one time.

Funny enough, child abandonment came with legal ramifications that STDs didn't.

I watched those familiar bubbles pop up on my screen and disappear. Then pop up and disappear again twice more.

COHEN:

> I can't tonight, babe. I want to. Promise. But I have to be in the OR in the morning with Rath. It's part of the application process. Have to be bright-eyed and bushy-tailed.

ME:

> Okay. I understand.

I dropped my phone onto the counter with an audible clank and a sigh, my eyes glued to the chipped paint on the ceiling until the device pinged with another incoming message.

COHEN:

What are you wearing to class tomorrow?

I glared at the screen as if it had personally offended me rather than the man on the other end of the line. The thing about Leos was that we acted on emotion and impulse. I was a prime example of "fuck around and find out," which got me into trouble on more than one occasion. Especially with Cohen. I liked to grate on his nerves, more so when he was grating on mine.

ME:

This.

I proceeded to snap a photo of the pregnancy test and send it on through without bothering to consider the consequences. Something that got me here in the first place.

34
COHEN

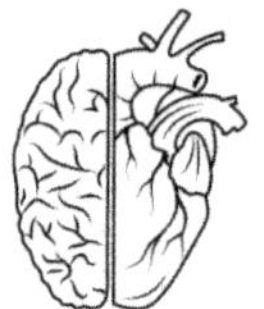

It worked. Much quicker than I thought it would. Emily was pregnant. With my kid growing inside her. Cells multiplying and dividing at a rate that was mesmerizing under a microscope. My DNA mixing with hers, combining brilliance and beauty. I was a combination of both and my girl was the prettiest thing I'd ever seen outside the bathroom mirror. The perfect incubator for our child.

And right now, I was on cloud fucking nine.

I thought I'd feel a certain type of way. Maybe less enthused? One of those getting what you want isn't always what it's cracked up to be situations. I should have known better. That wasn't me. I always knew what I wanted. Did whatever had to be done to get it and thoroughly enjoyed myself in the process. And that's what fucking my kid into Emily had been. Weeks of pure fucking enjoyment.

I considered typing out a reply. But I wanted to do more than tell her. I needed to show her how good this was for us. How good we were together if she just gave in and stopped fighting me at every fucking turn.

Emily was it for me. I knew it even if she didn't. This kid gave me more of a reason to rush things. To force her hand to take mine. She couldn't do it alone. And we both knew that. She needed me, and I needed to see her. Tell her she had to marry me now before I missed my chance. Or she did something stupid. Like take a quick trip to the clinic.

Fuck if I'd let her kill my kid.

So I jumped out of bed, slid on a pair of gray sweats. A white beater and my leather jacket. Grabbed my helmet and rushed out to my bike. Flinging a leg over the black-and-yellow seat and hopping on. Barely checking that the road was clear before I pulled onto the street and merged with the light traffic.

I considered calling her at a stop sign, telling her I was on my way. But I needed to choose my words carefully. Keep my cards close to my chest without her suspecting this was exactly what I wanted. Emily was defiant and easily startled. Like a bird with an injured wing. Except with a much stronger bite.

I was on autopilot, weaving between cars quicker than I knew was good for me, with only one thing on my mind. Her.

Thirty minutes into the hour commute between my apartment and her dorms, I was pulling up to a stoplight. Propping my bike up with one leg on the ground and the other supported by my foot peg. I reached into my pocket and quickly withdrew my phone to check the time.

Ten past two. I had to be scrubbed up and in the OR with Rath in less than four hours but that didn't matter right now...

Or ever really. Seeing as the next thing I knew, my helmet was flying off my head. My bike was propelled forward and my face was scraping against hot asphalt.

Apparently the asshole behind me hadn't seen my bike or, if he had, was just too drunk to care.

Lucky for me, adrenaline kicked in quick and I was able to roll across the highway. Curl up into a ball and hold my face on until paramedics arrived. The pain was indescribable, agonizing, and yet the only thing running through my mind was the fear I wouldn't get to Emily in time. That she'd run off with my kid. Or shack up with the first fucker to pay her the slightest attention.

I lost more than my right eye that night. I lost my career, the man I could have been, and not long after all that, my ability to trust. And it was all because of *her*.

That was the night Emily Shaw stole *everything* from me.

PART THREE
A FEW WEEKS LATER

People are saying he took some elite residency in Europe.

Of course he did.

What are you gonna do?

What can I do?

35
COHEN

The numbness was supposed to take the pain away, right? That's what we were told. As medical students, interns, doctors. That the opposite of pain was numbness. Hypoesthesia. The absence of feeling. Except it wasn't.

I was cold. I felt everything and nothing all at once. My nerve endings hyperalert. My left eye shifting under my lid, seeking out the source of the light that penetrated through the thin layer of skin. Saccadic eye movements my textbooks would tell me. A sign of growing awareness for a patient and his surroundings. Though I'd yet to figure out why the extraocular muscles on my right side were so eerily still...

There was a natural shift in the air, a breeze created by rushing bodies in a temperature controlled room. But it was the hint of iodine that clung to my nostrils, both comforting and not, that offered the first real hint that this wasn't my bedroom.

I recognized the buzz of the magnetostriction in the cheap light fixtures, would hum along to the off-key tune each time I shifted the curtain over and got an eyeful of whatever atrocity was waiting for me on the other side. But I wasn't used to hearing them above me. Nonstop. Like a fly in my ear I couldn't reach, let alone try to swat with deadened limbs.

Because I couldn't move. I tried. My arms, my legs, nothing. The receptors that should light up my brain and tell the rest of my body to comply appeared to be severed, or maybe just dulled. Either way, no part of me was acting as it should. As it was meant to do.

And I was too fucking broken to fix myself. The irony wasn't lost on me. But the magnitude sure as fuck was...

Another forty-eight hours would pass before I learned what the asphalt had done to my hands. The fingers on my right side mangled and pieced back together by someone who clearly never learned how to remove a funny bone with a pair of tweezers—let alone how to properly work a scalpel.

What was a surgical student without his hands? He was dead. Or at least he wished he was. It was a helluva lot better than this...

Several more weeks would pass before I saw myself in the mirror for the first time. By then, the only thing that was numb was my ability to empathize. The rest of me was in agony. Nonstop agony. All the time.

WHAT MATTERS most is not what others see but how you see yourself.

My guess is the fucker who said that didn't see the same shit I saw in the mirror every day.

I ran a finger across the fogged over glass, clearing the condensation while the squeaking sound of rough flesh on a smooth surface echoed off the bathroom tiles like nails on a chalkboard. It didn't matter how much the noise grated on my eardrums. I couldn't stop myself. Too engrossed by the monster reflected back at me in the mirror. I was half a man really. Half a chiseled jawline, half a prominent nose, one blue eye... attractive enough until I turned a cheek and you realized I was half something else entirely. Because I was also half freak in a sideshow.

That was the cruelest part, I suppose. The duality of seeing who I was now compared to who I used to be. Unable to escape either. All I had to do was turn to the side and I was reminded of everything I lost. The perfect half of an imperfect whole.

The shattering of glass broke the silence of my bathroom, my fist embedded in the mirror in front of me and blood trickling down to my wrist. I didn't even remember lifting my arm, barely registered the sting of my broken knuckles. Pain was another constant. I didn't know what it was like to live without it anymore. At the same time, nothing compared to the agony of living without her.

A few more days, I'd tell myself. Until those days turned to weeks, those weeks months. And nothing about me had gotten better. The nightmares were the worst part, imagining the look of horror on her face when she saw what was left of mine.

Truth was, I didn't care. I wasn't about to give her up either way. Because no matter what I looked like, Emily belonged to me.

36
COHEN

At first, watching her was more of a necessity than anything else. Needing to see her without being seen. I understood it would take time for her to accept me the way I was, the things I'd done to survive and maintain the sort of freedom I was used to. I couldn't exactly practice traditional medicine without a license. But that's not to say I didn't have a certain set of skills that other... *less-than-savory* individuals found useful. Especially those who weren't aboveboard themselves. And those skills proved more lucrative than a couple of letters following my name.

That necessity quickly morphed into obsession as the days passed, and nothing about her seemed to change. I was waiting for her lower abdomen to stretch the fabric of her blouse, her breasts to press tighter against her bra. Her cheeks to round out and her skin to glow. Instead, my Emily remained rail thin, gaunt even. She barely ate, and whenever she did, it was nothing more than a few bites before she tossed whatever it was into the closest trash bin.

Hyperemesis gravidarum was my initial assessment.

Severe morning sickness. It was the most likely cause of her weight loss and waning appetite. I gave the woman the benefit of the doubt. Until I saw her walk into this bar and order herself a double. That was when my prefrontal cortex went into overdrive. Distrust bubbled to the surface and congealed.

I lifted two fingers, flagging the bartender over, and repeated Emily's order, the same drink she was currently pressing to her lips. It was the closest I could get to tasting her right now.

Two hours passed before she left the bar, alone. And just as I was about to follow her, a heavy hand slammed onto my shoulder and shoved me back down onto the stool. I could have shrugged him off had I been expecting it, but the several rounds of liquor had dulled my senses while self-loathing had me wanting to dull them further.

Before I could look up, the bartender had placed two more drinks in front of us without having to be told and walked back down to the other side of the counter.

"Dr. Cohen Michaels," the stranger hummed. "It's a pleasure to make your acquaintance."

"Not a doctor," I grunted as I eyed the fucker from head to polished toe. Not a hair was out of place, his shirt perfectly ironed and tucked into his designer dress pants. His belt and shoes real leather from the looks of them. When my glare landed on his square jaw, perfect teeth on display with the catlike smirk curling his lips and dark deadened eyes, I added, "Do I know you?"

I knew I didn't.

He shrugged a shoulder before snapping his fingers. His coat was collected by some kid I didn't even see standing behind him, and then the fucker lowered himself down on the vacant stool between us. The guy looked out of place in this hole-in-the-wall bar. But then again, so did I. For a totally different reason.

"I know *you*, Dr. Michaels. And that's all that matters."

"Already told ya not a doctor." I returned my attention to the amber liquid coating the bottom of my glass before chugging the rest of the contents and pushing to my feet. "Thanks for the drink." I slammed it down again and moved to shove back from the bar.

His hand clamped onto my shoulder for a second time. "I wouldn't if I were you..."

This had one side of my mouth lifting into a grin. The other side was long since dead. "And why's that...?"

"It wouldn't be good for your health."

I barked out a loud laugh that had half the room looking in my direction. Good thing I was used to them looking. "And what makes you think I give a shit about my health?"

"Emily Shaw: female, age nineteen, seen at Mercy General on the 28th of October for a scheduled D&C. Four-hundred micrograms of misoprostol administered orally three hours prior to scheduled procedure. Evacuation completed by attending without incident. Patient alert and oriented times three before discharged to care of emergency contact with aftercare instructions."

I swiped my glass off the bar top, slamming it down until it shattered, then grabbed the largest shard and pressed it to the fucker's jugular vein. I didn't know what kind of nonsense he was spewing while the ethanol flooding my neurological pathways had me swaying on my feet, my cognitive functioning too dulled to piece together everything he was telling me *without telling me.*

What I did know was he said her fucking name. And that shit had my blood boiling beneath the surface.

He laughed and dipped his head forward until the glass bit into his throat, and a small trickle of blood streamed down his Adam's apple before it was soaked up by the white collar of his dress shirt.

"Thought that might get your attention." He grinned while waving a dismissive hand at the kid still hovering at his back.

"Who the fuck are you and what the fuck do you want?" I tossed the shard across the counter and signaled for a top off. There wasn't enough liquor in this bar for me tonight.

"The man whose business you've been stealing, it seems." He tugged off a leather glove and offered me a steady hand. "Dr. Adrian Lambert. But everyone 'round here calls me The Surgeon."

37
COHEN

The towering iron gates flanked each side of the town car, the name Briarwood Sanitorium dangling from a broken chain as we pulled up the long driveway that curled around the front of the abandoned mental hospital. I would say it was the thing of nightmares but that'd be a lie.

I saw far worse shit than this every time I closed my... eye. Every time one of the wounds on my face oozed and my poorly sutured fingers bled. Every time I poked around the empty socket in my head with a pair of sterilized tweezers and tried to locate what was left of my optic nerve. So if Mr. Fancy-Ass Surgeon was looking to intimidate me, it would take a lot more than some rundown looney-bin in the middle of nowhere.

I stepped out of the military-looking SUV and onto the gravel walkway, not believing for one second this was a government-sanctioned facility. The large metal double doors appeared to open the moment we approached. Which told me they were automated or we were being watched. Maybe a little of both. I glanced up, noting row after row of barred windows before following the suit and his silent henchman inside.

The place smelled of death. But not like formaldehyde and cadaver bone. Not old death. No, it smelled like blood. Fresh blood and newer flesh. Like an operating room more than a former sanitorium. It was clean too. Sterile. A blinding white from floor to ceiling. Much more modern than the exterior would suggest. There were doors stretching out in every direction in front of me, cameras staring down at us from every angle.

This was some serious surveillance system for a simple mental hospital. Though something told me these fuckers weren't looking for a quick consultation. If they were bringing me here to pick my brain, it would definitely be in the more literal sense. Full-on lobotomy style.

"Who we got here?"

I looked up, towards the sound of the disembodied voice that seemed to come from nowhere and everywhere all at once. My boots squeaking on the tile floor as I pivoted in time to watch a shadow jump down from one of the rafters in the ceiling. Spring off his fingertips into a cart-wheel and push to his feet in front of me. Silent. Not a sound echoing off the walls. No footsteps, no audible inhalation of breath. Nothing that would indicate the guy was more than a visual hallucination if it weren't for the fact I was certain everyone else saw him too.

He stepped around me, his movements still soundless and half his face done up like someone forgot to tell the guy Halloween was over a few weeks ago. "Those are some gnarly scars, Frankie." He grinned.

"That ain't my name," I grunted as the fucker continued to watch me with a slight cant of his head.

"It is now."

"Casper, enough." Adrian cleared his throat, his glare flicking from The Skeleton King back over to me. "Dr. Michaels, why don't I give you a tour. Show you a bit of what my facility has to offer…"

I nodded, following his lead as he stepped through the first door and made two quick rights down a long hallway. I guess you could say my curiosity got the better of me. And truth was I didn't have fuck all to lose.

38
COHEN

"As I'm sure you're aware, Dr. Michaels..."

I stopped bothering to correct him. It was clear the guy had a bug up his ass when it came to addressing me. And the more I argued facts, the more Adrian made a point of talking over them. Fucker liked the sound of his own voice. Reminded me of a few of the surgeons I met when I was applying for my clinical rotations. So maybe the nickname wasn't so far off.

"...Briarwood Sanitorium has a long, tumultuous history... often misunderstood by those with a lower intellectual capacity. My predecessors were at the forefront of clinical research, developing creative solutions to resolve the challenges many of the residents and their families experienced on a daily basis..."

Blah, blah, blah...

I couldn't hold back my yawn as we turned another corner and landed ourselves in front of the hospital's epicenter. My eyes flicked along the sterile surfaces. The mortuary cabinets lining the far wall. The large metal door that led to an industrial size meat freezer perpendicular to the table in the center of the space.

It was part operating room. Part morgue and part human chop shop.

My heart beat out of my chest, sweat trickling down my forehead and my skin humming after months of desensitized detachment. I ran a finger over each of the instruments lined up on the surgical tray, the cold tungsten—not cheaper stainless steel—calling out my name. Begging me to hold it. To approach the table and perform a simple Kocher or a quick midline long the vertical linea alba.

All I needed was a body.

Couldn't remember the last time I'd sank my gloves into flesh, seen the white elastic turn that bright shade of arterial red. Felt the live cardiac muscles beat in my hands or heard the buzz of the LED lights and the slight hum of the capnography. Except it also seemed like yesterday. This was where I was always meant to be. At the table with a scalpel in my hand. Problem was I didn't have much use of that hand anymore and my Rehapiano reading was a fraction of what it used to be. I clenched my fist in an effort to staunch the involuntary trembling. And cursed under my breath.

"So what do you think?"

"Of?" It took me a moment to register I wasn't alone. Even though I was well aware that I wasn't. There was just something about trying to understand the human anatomy that enlivened me.

Adrian waved a hand in the air, as if the answer should be obvious. It wasn't. I had no fucking idea what he was asking me. Didn't have the faintest clue as to what these guys were really doing here. Just that it was in no way board certified.

"Of my entire operation. My facility." He grinned the

way a cat grins after it's dropped a dead rodent on your doorstep. Fucker wanted me to choke down whatever bullshit he was feeding me. "I would love to hear your thoughts on Briarwood."

"I don't see any patients." I tipped my head from one side to the other, like a horde of mouth-droolers was gonna appear around the corner any minute now, even as my gut told me that wasn't likely.

"You wouldn't." He lifted a single shoulder in a half shrug. "We don't treat. Not anymore. You see, what we do here is much more..." He hummed as if considering his choice of word. "...*specialized.*"

"Yeah, well, not sure how much you've been paying attention. But I ain't specializing in much of anything these days." I held out my mangled hand and did my best to flex the taut muscles. My pinky twitched, offering the slightest movement, while the rest of my fingers were as animated as a few slabs of meat tossed up on a butcher's counter.

"That is a pity. What they did to you on that operating table. Then again, their loss is my gain. Now isn't it?"

The way the fucker's lips curled into a satisfied smirk left me with an uneasy feeling in the pit of my stomach. I was half-tempted to ask him if he had anything to do with my botched surgeries. Wouldn't be the first time some butcher with a PhD behind his name put self-interests ahead of patient care. Had a lot to do with the god complex each of us suffered from on some level or another. Couldn't do the job without it. Not really.

"Tell me why I should trust a word that comes outta your mouth?"

"You shouldn't. I certainly wouldn't." He shrugged. "And...?"

"And nothing. Facts are facts, Dr. Michaels. And the

facts are you have a choice. Accept my offer to come work for me or don't. What happens after we leave this room is entirely up to you."

"And why does that sound like a threat, Doc?" I lowered myself onto the metal chair. Kicked my boots up onto the desk in the corner while leaning back in my seat.

"Because it is. If you decide it is. Or maybe it's not. Maybe it's exactly what you need to get it all back. Use of that hand, an operating room of your own, the girl... it could all be yours again. It really is that simple."

"Ever heard the phrase *if it sounds too good to be true, it probably is?*"

"I assure you nothing we do here is good."

"What does any of this have to do with Emily?"

"The girl? I couldn't care less about your extracurricular activities." He pulled a brown hospital chart from a drawer and chucked it across the desk, waiting for the audible slap when it landed in front of me. "Merely a means to an end. A motivator. Everyone has one and I watched you long enough to find yours."

"Stalk the stalker? Ain't that a little on the nose?"

His only reply was the subtle rise and fall of one shoulder.

My eyes dropped to the chart before flicking back up to meet his smirk. I could sense the tremor in my hand, hear the tapping of my foot against the chair leg, which meant I knew he could hear it too. I was no better than a junkie while that chart was the closest thing to my next fix as I was gonna get right now.

"What's in it?"

"The answers to all your questions, of course."

I couldn't tell you where the bottle had come from... just that it was empty. I watched it roll across the room, the black and white label hypnotizing as it completed its rotations before hitting the wall with an audible clinking of borosilicate glass. My back was propped up against something hard, maybe a chair or perhaps the floor. I didn't remember sliding down but knew I was now staring at a blurry ceiling.

Never had a problem holding my liquor. Sure as fuck didn't have an issue drinking it either. But tonight was different. Tonight I could feel the walls closing in on me, my rage only slightly dulled—lucky for everyone else my central nervous system was too suppressed to do fuck all about it.

Couldn't sleep. Because I knew if I did, I would dream about her. And the last thing I wanted right now was to see her face. It was also the only thing I wanted.

To see her, watch her, taste the air between us as she took her last fucking breath. Thing was, as much as I hated her, I didn't know how to live in a world without Emily in it. Couldn't imagine what it'd feel like to focus on anything other than my obsession.

But I couldn't forgive her either. Not for this. Not after what she'd taken from me. *Stolen* from me.

My future, my career, my unborn fucking child.

I'd kill her for it. Of that much, I'd decided. It was the how, the when, and the where that left me fantasizing. Picturing her face when she realized the type of man I'd become. Because of her.

I reached out an arm, the concrete flooring chilled against my heated skin, while hoping another bottle of something would magically appear. Didn't really matter what it was at this point. I'd drink rubbing alcohol if I happened to find any.

I closed my eye, opening it again when I felt the subtle *drip, drip, drip* of something wet on my face. I took a deep breath, sucking the distinct odor of vodka deep into my lungs.

"Ya looked thirsty." The fucker in a kid's Halloween mask was standing over me, a clear bottle in his hand as he tipped the contents onto my face. I reached up to tug the liquor out of his grip and he pulled it back. "Tut-tut-tut, ya want more, you're gonna have to lick it off the ground."

"You first," I grunted before kicking his feet out from under him.

He landed on his back with a thud and a low chuckle. "Oh, yeah, this is gonna be fun."

Didn't know what the ass clown was going on about. Just that my head was throbbing. My mouth dry and my mind plagued by images of *her*.

The fucker swiped the file outta my hand. I'd forgotten it was even there. His leg crossed over on a knee as he sprawled out on the concrete floor like a bored housewife at a day spa.

"Emily?" He hummed her name. Tasted it the same way I used to taste her. "So all this self-loathing is about some chick?" He threw his head back on a cackle as I pried the file from his bony fingers before he could flip to the first page. "Didn't take ya for being pussy-whipped."

"Say it again," I ground out, swallowing the copper tang of blood in my mouth as I cracked my neck from side to side. "Give me a reason. Just one. To bash your skull into the ground."

"Couldn't see it before. But now it's obvious."

"Yeah? And what's that?" I didn't know what was wrong with this guy. Casper, Adrian called him—though it was apparent the fucker had a few screws loose.

"Word on the ward was you were some sort of quack. With the fucked-up hand and all, didn't make sense. But now it's clear as a silver spoon. It's the arrogance. You got that shit in spades."

"Fuck you."

"Now is that anyway to treat your new bunkmate?"

"What makes you think I want anything to do with a bunch of sociopaths in *Scream* masks?"

The fucker grinned, tugging his shirt over his head before tossing the rest of his Devil's Reject's costume onto the floor. "Ya know he can fix that shit, right?" When I raised a single eyebrow in question, he clarified, "Your hand. That face of yours is fucked. But he can give ya use of your hand. I've seen the crazy son of a bitch work wonders with nothing more than a pot of boiling water and a soldering iron."

I forced out an incredulous laugh. "Yeah, and I'm

Mother fucking Teresa. Go sell your snake oil to someone who doesn't know first year anatomy."

"Suit yourself." He shrugged, twisting his body into a figure eight that looked physically impossible before jumping to his feet in one swift ripple of gelatinous bone.

Then he cracked his neck, the movement soundless as he stepped towards the door, one silent boot in front of the other. He paused with his palm clenched around the knob, the silhouette of his profile prominent in the dim lighting of the room.

"I thought the same thing... Had the rope strung up on the rafters. Shit ready to go. 'Cept a severed spinal cord kept me from being able to lift my ass high enough off the wheelchair to do any real damage."

I craned my head to one side, my narrowed gaze focusing on the medial facetectomy incision on the crazy fucker's L-4.

40

COHEN

Most people saw a stiff on a cold slab and were reminded of their mortality. How insignificant they were. How short life was. Me? I saw another dead ant under a magnifying glass. Bits and pieces of unpurposed meat. Mine for the taking. I felt like a god. Immortal. An artist with unsculpted clay, the amorphous blob just begging me to transform it into something useful. To learn and apply that knowledge to the next lump of fleshy pulp to land themselves in my office. On my operating table. Beneath my knife.

I guess you could say I'd always been this way. Different. While masking myself to be the same. The star football player who examined his teammates' injuries on the field a little too closely. Who didn't gag at the sight of blood. Torn flesh and protruding bone. Because, of course, sports medicine was my interest. When, in reality, the need to dissect—*pick something apart*—ran as deep as a bone saw. As fluidly as an intravenous drip.

I felt empty without a scalpel in my hand. Filled that emptiness with my obsession. And now even that wasn't enough. Instead of need, I was driven by rage. Unsatisfied rage lacking proper output. And disjointed fingers that could barely clutch a butter knife, let alone a fifteen blade.

Truth was, accepting employment at Briarwood wasn't much of a choice. And Dr. Jekyll knew it. Mr. Hyde had yet to be seen. While both versions of the man had me by the balls. With or without throwing Emily's name in the mix.

It was this... or rotting in some gutter until the madness consumed me and everything around me. Until I plunged over that abyss into insanity and took everyone in a five-mile radius with me into that six-foot pit.

As much as I didn't give a fuck about society as a whole, I loved what I could do. The skills I'd fine-tuned over the years. It was that rose-tinted narcissism that wouldn't let me dip my toes into the idea of suicide. The belief I was better, smarter, more capable than those in my midst.

That and the need to make *her* pay. Because how the fuck dare she kill a part of me. The brilliance that could have been and wasn't.

But those were thoughts for another day. After I'd planned out every detail of her downfall. After I jerked off to images of her blood on my mangled hands. Her tears on my stained bedsheets and her juices coating my cock before she took her last fucking breath.

That was what drove me now. Her suffering and this fucker's promise to end mine.

I flipped through the various books on anatomy lining the walls of Dr. Adrian Lambert's office. Some modern, some archaic. It still wasn't clear what went on behind the tall iron gates of the outdated sanitorium. Couldn't even tell you what part I was meant to play. Just that it revolved around my medical acumen.

He wanted my skill set and he needed to make me

whole in order to do that. It was the most basic example of a little tit for tat. A few experimental surgeries, unsanctioned medical devices, and I would be forever in his debt. I wasn't so naïve to believe there was a way out once I was in. It was a lifetime commitment—one I was willing to make if it improved the dexterity of my hands.

I heard him enter the room, his steps not nearly as inconspicuous as his counterpart's. Not that I thought he intended for me to be taken by surprise. It was more of an observation than anything else. I was keen on reading people when I wasn't drinking myself into oblivion.

"You're still here," he hummed.

I pivoted on my boot to face him. "We both know my leaving was never really a choice."

"Wasn't it?"

"No, it wasn't." I paced in front of his desk while Adrian lowered himself onto his chair. "No surgeon from here to the coasts will touch me with a knife. Insisting there is nothing they can do for me. Regulations are far more strict overseas and I can't very well operate on myself without my good hand. Believe me, I've tried. I'm not too arrogant to admit I've done more harm than good. So here we are. Here *I* am. Without any other options."

"You can stay as you are. That's a very real option, Dr. Michaels." He shrugged, the movement subtle, before pinning me with a glare. "I wouldn't recommend it, given the... alternative." His eyes flicked to my hand resting on the back of the armchair before landing on my face again.

He meant more than my present deformities. He meant what he would do to me if I refused. We both knew it. And while I loved a good game of cat and mouse as much as the next guy, I hated being the rodent in this analogy. If I was walking into a trap, shit would be done willingly and not because I was backed into a corner. There was no winning when the loss was self-imposed. Not for men like us. The challenge was the best part.

"Here's the thing, Doc. Bedside manner was never my forte so let's rip the bandage off and get straight to the point. What do you want?"

"How about I show you what I can do first, then we can decide how grateful you feel?"

"You mean *indebted*."

"I mean what I say, Dr. Michaels. Stop thinking you're the most clever man in the room. That's not true in my company." He pushed to his feet, his demeanor calm despite the slight curl of his upper lip. "Learn your place or you'll be re*placed*. You aren't the only asset in need of my services."

"No, I'm probably not." I paused, waiting for his snarl to drop into the hint of a smirk. "But something tells me I have far looser morals."

41

COHEN

The first time the fucker cut into my hand, it was conveniently without anesthetic. I watched Adrian's pupils dilate, his mouth curl behind his surgical mask, his nostrils flare. The crazy bastard was getting off on it. He was enjoying my pain. And I couldn't even blame 'em. Because I knew the feeling.

I felt it too. Or at least I used to. It'd been a while.

By the tenth incision, I was numb to the bite of the blade in more ways than one. The buzz of the antiquated machinery helped lull me into a state of hypnosis, most of my nerve endings severed and pieced back together like some home-sown rag doll.

I didn't mind the aesthetic. The lackluster suturing and lazy tie-offs. I wasn't much to look at anymore anyway. I refused a fucking glass eye just to make everyone else in the room more comfortable. I wouldn't mind if the cocksuckers choked on their tongues when they stared into my open socket.

In fact, I hoped they did.

The fluid trickling down my fingertips was lukewarm at best. I barely registered the dampness pooling at my fifth metacarpal. Lost count of all the *lost* liters. My right arm was hooked up to an infusion, a new bag pumping fresh blood into my system as quickly as it dripped into the steel surgical tray. Didn't know where it came from. Didn't care to ask either.

I was supposed to gain mobility after this. Be able to curl the fourth digit and extend the second. So that at the very least I could hold a scalpel in my hand again. My grip would never be what it was. My fine motor skills impaired beyond reconstruction.

But, as much as I hated to admit it, Ghost Boy's spine ignited a little spark of hope in my chest. I could almost feel my little black heart beating again.

The classical music skipped on the track, repeating the same fucked-up chorus over and over again in tune with Doctor Jekyll's disjointed humming as he snipped the final thread and grinned at his handiwork. "Now isn't she pretty..."

"Not really," I grunted while lifting my hand to glare at the line of unevenly spaced interruptions. I could have done a better stitch with my teeth and a pair of rusty tweezers. I moved to flex my fingers and realized the paresthesia wasn't all in my head. I craned my neck, eyeing Adrian's back as he bent over the large industrial sink mounted against the far wall.

"I can't feel anything." It was an observation and a question rolled up in one.

"Much better than the pain, hm?"

"Why?"

"Why's it better?" He shifted his body to one side, directing his glare at me while rinsing a few pints of my blood down the drain—then again, was it even *mine* anymore? Possession being nine-tenths of the law and all that.

Yeah, shit was definitely getting to my head. I wanted a drink. What I needed was a hefty dose of iron shoved down my throat. Maybe another few bags of fluids.

"No, why'd you use an analgesic?"

"I didn't."

"What do you mean?" My head was throbbing, the temporary hypovolemia causing my lower limbs to wobble when I tried to stand. "I can't feel anything."

"So you've said."

"*Why?*"

Adrian huffed out a breath. Fucker was losing his patience with me. Good, seeing as mine flew out the goddamn barred windows about a week ago.

"Because that's what happens when you cauterize the ulnar and median nerves. Once it's done, it can't be reversed. The sensation's gone. Given your credentials, I didn't think I'd have to explain myself like I'm talking to a first year med student."

I knew better. Lack of sensation did not mean lack of internal damage. My quick temper didn't seem to care.

My swollen fist snapped forward and connected with the cocky fucker's sharp jaw. I heard the cracking of bone. Didn't know if it was mine or his or a combination of both before I felt a sharp pinch in my carotid.

In a perfect world, I would have been able to narrow down the paralytic agent by factoring in my height and weight and calculating my body's overall response time. Today I didn't have that luxury. The blood loss expedited the onset and the compound had taken full effect by the time my knees hit the floor.

I blinked twice, the only thing in focus a set of teeth outlined by a pair of curling lips before I was left to stare at the fleshy underside of my eyelid—awake but incapable of moving.

The son of a bitch had drugged me...

42
COHEN

Thump-thump, thump-thump, thump-thump.

The sound was rhythmic, like the beating of my own heart pounding in my ears. Pulsatile tinnitus and possibly a traumatic head injury. The dull ache at the back of my skull told me I'd cracked it against the cement floor when the drugs took effect. When my knees gave out and gravity took over.

Couldn't say I regretted it though. Felt good before it felt fucking terrible. As did most bad ideas.

I didn't know what damage I'd done to my hand, and blocked nerves meant it would be difficult to figure out without doing a full assessment. Which wasn't happening anytime soon.

The forehead restraint pinched at my left temple where the buckle had been ratcheted down and I could feel the burn of the IV seeping into my bloodstream. Fluids. With a hint of some sort of analgesic.

The thumping was replaced with the repetitive dripping, amplified by the soundlessness of the room. And I realized the sick son of a bitch was trying to slowly drive me insane.

By the time the metal wheels of the med cart clanked to my bedside, much louder than necessary, I was ready to puncture my own eardrums and claw out my remaining eye.

"An apple a day keeps the doctor away," Adrian hummed, before dropping a plastic lunch tray on the small table to my right. With a dramatic *thud*.

"Didn't realize the EBM included old wives' tales," I grunted.

"Apples are actually quite high in natural quercetin. Helps with the inflammation by lowering the C-reactive protein in blood."

"You gonna add it to my bag? Or just hold the shit in front of my face long enough for me to take a bite?"

"Not very fond of the restraints." It was a statement. Not a question. Fucker knew given the chance, I would be aiming for his jaw again. Then he *tsked* his tongue, without bothering to drop his smirk or even turning to look at me, his focus glued to my bandaged hand still pinned to my side. "You nearly destroyed all our hard work. Didn't leave me much of a choice, now did you, Dr. Michaels?"

"And I'm the one with the ego..." I grunted under my breath but I knew he could hear me. Not that I cared if he did.

I continued to watch Adrian move around the small hospital room, as much as I could without moving my head. Straining to track his steps with a limited field of vision while my brain tried to fill in all the gaps. He closed a few drawers and prepped a couple of syringes from cloudy vials, tapping his foot to a song only he seemed to hear before spinning on the heel of his designer shoes and landing me with a glare.

"Glad you finally admit it. Explains why you're having so much trouble expressing your gratitude."

I barked out a laugh, the sound harsh and disconcerting against my strained vocal cords. "Grateful for what? All you did was ensure I'd never pick up a scalpel again."

"How's that? You have almost full mobility of all five metacarpals, ninety percent flexion of the phalanges, and your baseline HGS score nearly doubled from what it was before *I ensured you'd never pick up a scalpel again.*"

"And I still can't feel shit." I wasn't sure what was so difficult for Dr. Dipshit to understand.

"Ah, I see."

"About damn time."

"You're afraid of the challenge. And here I thought being the top of your graduating class, rumored to be the next big thing in medicine actually meant something. Guess I was mistaken. Sorry for wasting your time, Dr. Michaels." Adrian shifted to my bedside, releasing each restraint one at a time with a quick flick of his wrist. "The door's right there. Please don't let me keep you from all the job offers filling up your inbox."

I swung my shaky legs over the edge of the mattress, flexing my wrist and relieving some of the tension in my tight muscles. I hated to admit it but the fucker was right. I had decent mobility in my palm, each of the digits moved independently, and most noticeable was the lack of pain. Which brought me right back to the problem literally at hand.

"How?" I ground out the question between a clenched jaw and scraping teeth.

"What's that?"

I could hear the satisfaction in Adrian's voice, see it in the indent of a slight dimple on his right side. "How am I supposed to cut into a live patient without being able to feel the depth of my incision, without being able to control the force and pressure of the blade?"

He shrugged a single shoulder, his grin wider than the cat that ate the goddamn canary. "Very carefully, Dr. Michaels. Very, very carefully."

"Fuck you."

"No, *fuck you*, Cohen." Adrian shoved a hand against my chest and had me sprawled out on the hospital bed before I had a chance to react. It was the first time I'd seen him break that cool-as-a-fucking-cucumber demeanor. The first time I'd seen the rage rise to the surface and darken those emotionless eyes of his. Like his long-held tight leash had finally snapped.

And now I was the one grinning. "Look at that. Adrian Lambert does have a breaking point."

He lowered his head and leveled his glare so that there was barely a breath between us. "Don't say my name like you know me. You don't know a goddamn thing about me. But I know everything there is to know about you, Cohen Michaels. Every secret, every skeleton you thought you buried. Don't you ever forget that." Then he pushed himself upright, adjusting his lab coat before canting his head to the side. The grin plastered on his face again like it had never left. "Now, I suggest you get to work and show me you're worth the second chance I so graciously offered you. Before I change my mind."

Adrian stalked to the door without waiting for a response. Pausing at the threshold to pull an apple from his coat pocket and toss it in my direction. I reached up on instinct, catching it with my dominant hand before I realized what I was doing. My fingers closed around the firm flesh a second too late and the apple toppled to the floor.

I cursed under my breath but I could tell Adrian was still grinning. Didn't matter that his back was turned. I could see it in the tautness of his neck and shoulders.

"Looks like you have some work to do," he called out as the click of his heavy footfalls echoed down the hall in time with his self-inflated steps.

Yup, even the way the fucker walked somehow screamed *I'm better than you.*

43
COHEN

I took a long drag of my cigarette, holding the smoke deep in my lungs before forcing it back out again. I didn't get that buzz of nicotine that shot through my bloodstream and left me feeling momentarily light. Almost drunk. My central nervous system had built up a tolerance, which meant my body craved a fix more frequently with little to no benefit of that high it used to offer me. It did help me stay awake though. And I needed to be awake so I could watch her.

"That shit'll kill ya, ya know?" Casper hummed from where he was perched on the branch above me, his legs kicking back and forth like a kid on a swing set instead of a grown-ass man too old to be climbing fucking trees.

"Yup," I grunted, as I dropped the butt into Emily's flower bed and stomped it out with the toe of my boot. It was reckless to leave it behind... and I wouldn't have. If it were anyone else. But I wanted her to know I was here. That I was watching. Her blissful ignorance was getting under my skin after all these months.

Nothing seemed to faze her, not even her complete lack of a social life. Thanks to yours truly. She'd tried. Tried to fuck someone who wasn't me. Tried and failed. The first guy was easy enough to scare off. A few photos snapped of his bedroom, more specifically his bed with him sleeping in it, had him blocking Emily's number before the shit was hot in his phone.

The next fucker took a little more effort. Not much but some. Had to leave a couple knives stabbed into his front door. But the look on his face was totally worth the loss of a good blade. A few more asshats would come and go but none of them stayed when I was done with them. She seemed to resort to self-care after that. Alone in her bed under the cover of night when she thought no one was watching.

But of course, someone was. Someone was always fucking watching. Waiting.

It would be so easy to snatch her right now. Drag her out of that house and hole her up in a basement somewhere. But I wasn't ready for her yet. I was still working on getting everything in order. Setting up my bunker and acquiring the appropriate equipment.

Emily was the long game. And I refused to be rushed, even by my own subconscious. I could almost taste her as she flitted in front of her bedroom window. Tugged her dress shirt over her head and began to unhook her bra.

"Time for you to go," I hissed in Casper's direction, knowing his eyes were on Emily as much as mine were. You couldn't not look at the woman. It was how she lured you into her trap. "I don't need a fucking babysitter."

I could hear the rustling of more branches as Casper jumped down, his landing silent despite the full force of his weight hitting the ground. That was how the fucker got his nickname. He was a goddamn ghost when he wanted to be.

"Yeah, I ain't leaving now that the show's just getting good." He grinned, the whites of his teeth glowing in the darkness of the shadows as he slung an arm over my shoulder. "What do ya think she tastes like? Bet it's something sweet..." he whispered against my ear while fixing his glare back on that window. "I could go in there and fuck her for ya. Bend her over and press her up against the glass since watching seems to be your thing."

I drove two fingers into his brachial plexus, forcing his arm to drop before I pressed on his chest and shoved him back a step. The fucker didn't feel pain, not like any normal person should, but that didn't mean I couldn't immobilize him for a few minutes.

"You can do whatever you want with what's left of her body... as soon as I'm done with it," I ground out between clenched teeth. "And not a moment before that... or I'll carve you up and use ya for spare parts."

Casper threw his head back and barked out a laugh, much louder than was good for either of us. "Yeah, and which parts you gunning for, Doc? My eye or my cock?" He ran a hand down his chest before tugging on the bulge in his pants. "Shit's prime real estate. Can't go wrong with either."

I grabbed onto the front of his shirt, curling my fingers around the material and dragging him back towards our blacked-out SUV. Fucker could stop me if he wanted, but he enjoyed the games. It was his favorite form of entertainment. And sometimes it was safer to indulge him, for both our sakes.

I slid into the driver's seat, waiting for the blonde

Johnny Knoxville to fling himself over the hood on his hands and pivot back onto his feet on the other side. Rumor was the fucker was some sort of Russian gymnast whose visa expired after a career-ending injury. My guess? He was just a coked up asshat who didn't get enough attention as a kid.

He jumped through the window into the passenger seat, pulling his legs up under his ass in a way that should be inhuman or at the very least uncomfortable before stretching them out over the dash. His arms raised and his hands clasped behind his head.

I peeled off down the street, breezing past the red light when Casper tipped his chin in my direction. "So, she the one who did that shit to your face?"

"Something like that," I grunted between clenched teeth.

"Ouch. That's brutal."

"Yup."

"I like ' em brutal."

I could hear his smirk without having to look in the fucker's direction. "Don't go there. I'm not gonna tell you again."

"And if I do? If I break in to that nice little condo of hers, slide right into one of those windows we both know she doesn't lock... whatcha gonna do about it, Doc?" He leaned back in his seat and tapped a foot against the dash. "We both know you can't kill me."

"Oh, I don't need to kill you. Killing you is too easy... too quick. Instead, I'll slowly cut away at your body. Starting with your eyelids... Do you know what happens when someone removes your eyelids...? What it feels like? It's a slow burn that becomes more excruciating with each hour that passes. You can't sleep. Not really. And as time goes on and insanity seeps in, so does the blindness. And that's just step one."

Casper was quiet for a long minute until the crazy son of a bitch slapped a hand on a thigh and broke out in a fit of dark laughter. "Now that's the spirit. I knew I liked you."

44

COHEN

It didn't take long before I graduated from watching Emily through her bedroom window to helping myself to her condo. I'd memorized the code to her door after the first night, and bypassing her limited security measures was child's play after that. She didn't know how close I was, still blissfully unaware of the danger within arm's reach.

I traced my fingertips over her skin and watched it pebble beneath my touch as she slept. Curled the ends of her hair around my hand and fought the urge to tug before tucking it back behind her ear, while the simple gold studs she wore at night glowed under the moonlight that streamed in from her window. She really was the ideal specimen of a woman.

If she weren't such a manipulative little cunt...

I stalked around her bed. Lingered by the footboard and continued to observe the gentle rise and fall of her chest. Listened to the soft sounds she made in her sleep. Her dark hair sprawled around her like a halo she hadn't earned. Begging me to reach out and touch her. To see the fear in her eyes the moment she realized she wasn't alone. That she hadn't been alone for a very long time.

My little pet stirred, rolling onto her side and showing me her bare back. The curve of her spine and the soft globes of her ass. So pale without the darkness of a solid hand-print. My handprint.

I slipped onto the bed, positioning my body behind hers. Unable to stop myself. My movements slow, predatory. I'd been watching Casper. How he moved so seamlessly. Soundlessly. Learning how he could navigate a room without being heard or seen. And right now, I was using that skill set to my advantage.

Emily sank against my hold, like it was the most natural thing in the world for her to do. Her respirations moving in time with mine as I lowered a hand from her flat abdomen and dipped my fingers beneath her waistband. Circling her clit in soft, slow, barely there motions. The pressure not nearly enough to get her off but fuck if she wasn't drenched. Grinding her hips against my tactical pants and whimpering low in her throat.

"What are you dreaming about, Emily?" It was barely a whisper against her ear. So quiet it would have been carried off in the wind.

She moaned in reply. Still lost to the deepest stage of REM sleep while her body was thrumming. Electrified and in desperate need of relief. Relief I wouldn't give her. Because this was about me. A little indulgence after all the effort I'd been putting in. All the time I'd been dedicating to my surveillance. All the hours I'd spent watching her. All those instances where I'd been forced to see her laugh and flirt at a distance. Slutting her ass around the city like she hadn't made a deliberate decision to kill our child. Then pretended as if neither of us ever existed.

I could feel my rage boiling beneath the surface. My hand fighting the urge to sweep up against her throat and squeeze. And squeeze and squeeze. Until her eyes were bulging out of her head, her lips turning that pretty shade of violet blue, the capillaries bursting and changing color.

I forced myself off the bed, tamping down the aggression beating against my chest and screaming at me to give into my instincts to destroy her. Because that's what it would be. Destruction. Not death. I would destroy everything that made her, *her*. Until her body was unrecognizable, each part of her as pulverized as the connection between us. So there wasn't even the slightest urge for me to fix her.

My steps were slow, deliberate as I backed out of the room. Still watching her motionless form on the bed until all I could see was the hourglass silhouette against the darkness of the mattress. Then I slipped out the front door, locking it behind me and turning around to find Casper staring at me with that usual stupid-ass smirk on his face.

"You smell like pussy," he hummed, like he could taste her on my fingertips.

"And you don't. Maybe you should go get some," I grunted in reply. Walking past him and making a beeline for the van.

Fucker was worse than a coked-up toddler. Followed me around like he was looking to suck my dick or some shit. Though it very well could be Adrian's way of keeping my ass on a short leash. Making sure I didn't go rogue again. I didn't care enough to put too much thought into it as long as I continued to get paid. So I could feed my habit. My addiction to one particular cunt.

Casper jumped into the passenger seat, waiting for me to slide behind the wheel before landing me with a glare.

"So what is it about this chick? I mean, sure, she's hot. I guess. In the girl-next-door kinda way. But I've seen better." He shrugged.

"You won't be seeing shit after I remove your eyes from their sockets."

"Always so violent, Franks." He *tsked* his tongue. "Is that what happened to you? Were you looking at some fucker's girl a little too long for his liking?"

I threw the van into drive and screeched the tires down Emily's street. Hoping the shit was loud enough to wake her. Have her sitting up in that bed all hot and horny. Without a fuckable cock in sight. I patted my pocket, where I'd tucked her vibrator away for safekeeping, and one side of my lips tipped up into a grin.

"No, because I'm not stupid. I know when to keep my mouth shut."

"I'm gonna find out eventually, you know. What she did to you and what it has to do with your face." Casper tossed his hands behind his head and leaned back in his seat. "Hit a drive-through, would ya? I'm dying to dig my teeth into something pink."

45
COHEN

I'd dusted away most of the cobwebs and cleared some space in Briarwood's old corpse-grinder, a series of rooms and tunnels located at the lowest level of the building used for body disposal. Amongst other things the quacks didn't want the other residents to know about. Which also meant no one could hear ya scream once the giant metal door to the basement clicked into place.

It was no happy accident.

I sprawled out across the metal bedframe I'd found tucked away in some corner, equipped with a brand-new mattress because some shit was not meant to be handed down, and stared up at the rafters. The wood creaked and cracked every time the wind blew outside and I didn't have much confidence in the foundation. But my options kinda flew off the bike and skid across the road along with all my potential job offers—something Adrian liked to remind me over and over again.

So here I was. Home sweet fucking home. In the basement beneath a former crazy house.

Shit was no Four Seasons but it sure beat bunking it

with Ghostface for another day. Besides, I liked my privacy. It would come in handy when I figured out what I was doing with Emily long-term. That didn't seem to stop the fucker from following me down here whenever he got the chance though.

Like right now.

I glanced over to Casper, who was tossing one of those little rubber balls you get outta of a gumball machine against the far wall, watching it bounce before repeating the process over and over again. Until the sound was slowly driving me mad. Which I was pretty sure was his intention all along. The stupid son of a bitch was the annoying little brother I never wanted and would have drowned in the bathtub given the chance.

Only children didn't know how good they had it.

Bounce. Bounce. "How long before it catches on?" *Bounce. Bounce.* "Oh, and what about business cards? With invisible ink. Shit only comes through when you dip it in blood." *Bounce. Bounce.* "Yeah, The Renegades. Just you wait. It's gonna be a thing, Franks." *Bounce. Bounce.*

"It's a stupid name. So's the whole mask thing by the way." I reached up an arm when the ball finally hit a crack in the concrete and veered off in my direction. Swiping up the damn thing before throwing it down a darkened hallway. Never to see the light of day again. Or so I could only hope.

Casper appeared unfazed as he plopped down next to me, kicking his feet back and forth like one of those kids bobbing up and down on rusty playground equipment. Too fucking dumb to realize how close to danger they were teetering.

"Really? And here I thought you'd jump at the chance to cover that ugly mug." He smirked.

"Yeah? And why are you so quick to wanna cover yours, pretty boy?" I grunted in reply. Guy was acting like playing dress-up was something to get your nuts off about. Truth was I couldn't care less what the fuck we called ourselves as long as it came with a payday. "What's the cash flow situation like? I'm guessing this ain't no biweekly kinda deal."

Casper was a talker, which meant he was the easiest one to pry information out of. At the same time, he was ADD as fuck, which meant it was also hard to keep him on topic.

He lifted his shoulder in a half shrug before flipping onto his back. Kid didn't know what it was to stay still. "It comes and it goes."

I pushed off the mattress and onto my feet. This whole conversation was fucking pointless. I wasn't gonna get much of anything except maybe the occasional riddle.

"Why? Having money problems?" he asked, stepping up next to me as soon as I left the room. I turned down the first passageway before quickly realizing I was lost. And turned right back around.

I didn't bother answering him. But that didn't stop the barrage of questions that continued to be slung my way.

"What about your parents? Can't they help?"

"They died."

"From embarrassment? 'Cause you look like that?"

"No. I killed 'em. 'Cause they wouldn't stop asking dumb questions." It wasn't all that far from the truth. My mother kicked it not all that long after my accident. Pretty sure the stress did it to her. While my father might as well be dead to me. The fucker was off on some tropical island, pretending his less-than-perfect son didn't exist.

I was two steps down the next hallway when an eerie sound had me frozen to the spot.

Bounce. Bounce. Bounce. Bounce.

I cursed under my breath before pivoting on my boot. Either that crazy fucker had a pocket full of bouncy balls or his luck was far better than mine. And right now, I didn't know which was more irritating.

46
COHEN

Casper clamped a hand down on my shoulder, grinning like the idiot he was as he maneuvered around me. Crouching low enough in the shrubs that his six-foot-something frame collapsed in on itself, while I could barely bend at the waist without the skin on my right side pulling tight against my muscles.

The elasticity was gone, the new layers of epidermis transplanted from my thigh combined with subcutaneous cadaver tissue taut and inflexible. But I refused to let Dr. Lecter anywhere near me with a scalpel again. The pain reminded me of the rage. Fueled it. Kept me focused on the task at hand. Which had nothing to do with a certain woman curled up in her bed. As much as I wish it did.

I hadn't seen my pet in two days. Not close up at least. And my skin was beginning to itch. Like insects were clawing beneath the surface and eating away at the layers one by one. I knew the shit wasn't healthy. *My dick didn't give a fuck.*

I waited for the signal before following Casper's lead, Donnie at my tail with Bugs on the comms. The brothers didn't talk much. Though it was clear one was the brains and the other was the brawns. The lobotomy scar next to Donnie's nasal cavity gave me a good idea as to why that was. Not that it mattered. The fucker in front of us talked enough for everyone. Except whenever he was hyperfocused on a target. Then, the ass clown turned assassin. Like some sort of switch had been flipped.

There were five of us in total back at Briarwood. Adrian at the reins, the rest of us the muscle. The whole operation was a bit of a mystery—the sort that involved both sides of the equally corrupt law. Though I had to admit the pay was decent, if not inconsistent. I didn't care enough to question it. Not yet anyway. I had more important shit on my mind. Shit that involved me keeping my mouth shut and my eye open.

I was an observer after all. And human behavior was my favorite curiosity.

Two more taps on my shoulder had my attention focused in front of us as Casper compressed his body, like a rodent collapsing its ribs, and slipped through a tiny hinged window with ease. I listened for a thud, some sort of indicator that he made it on the other side but there was only silence. Guy was definitely some sort of circus freak, if nothing else.

Seconds later, the large front door to Prescott Estates was squeaking open and Donnie and I were rushing through. I glanced up, a crystal chandelier swaying above us and a tapestry on the far wall bristling with our movement. My eyes flicked to the portrait of some rich white guy hanging front and center along the grand staircase before swooping corner to corner. Other than the pendulum swinging from the old grandfather clock to our immediate right, there were no signs of life.

Didn't know why we were here. Didn't much care either. Shit was just another paycheck to me. If my hands got dirty in the process, even better.

"Up the stairs, third door on the left. Alarm's down and cameras blacked out for the next ten minutes. In and out and don't fucking touch anything," Bugs hissed over the mics in each of our ears.

None of us bothered to reply. He knew we heard him.

I glanced behind me. Casper was nowhere to be found. Fucker could be on the roof for all I knew. He was quick; even more than that, he was efficient.

Ten minutes wasn't much time. But it was enough to have us grabbing Tate Prescott from his Egyptian cotton sheets and pillow top mattress, a bag over his head as we dropped him kicking and screaming into the back of the van. A quick dose of ketamine had the fucker sedated within minutes, Donnie pinning our target at the waist and securing his limbs while Casper jumped into the driver's seat.

My job was to make sure Prescott didn't cause a problem before we made it back to Briarwood. I had every cocktail imaginable on hand. Including a few bottles of Narcan. I had to ensure he made it there alive too. At least in this instance. Every job was different.

Had to admit I didn't mind the thrill either. It was a different kind of high from the operating room. Mix up one of the vials and the guy would be sent right into a seizure, foaming at the mouth, his eyes rolling to the back of his skull right in front of us.

The temptation was there. To send him over the edge just to bring him back again. But right now, the cash was more enticing. Bugs had an in with some tech guys and I needed better surveillance equipment to keep an eye on

Emily. Wouldn't be long before I had an entire setup dedicated to her and everything I wanted to do to her.

The sound of the gates creaking open and welcoming us home to Briarwood had me looking up and packing away my kit. Before Donnie and I were hefting Prescott onto a shoulder each and dragging him through a different set of doors.

"WHAT'D HE DO?" I grunted in Casper's direction.

We had Tate Prescott strapped to the metal slab in Adrian's personal operating room. An IV strung up on a pole. A cardiac monitor hooked up to his chest and a respirator at his side. I'd done my part. Now I was just curious.

"Do you care?" Casper jumped down from the counter, taking two steps forward to lean over the table. He pried open one of Prescott's eyelids, dropping it only to repeat the process on the other side.

Before I could respond, Adrian was pushing into the room. Dressed head to toe in a sterile gown and med boots. He eyed Casper, then quickly landed his glare on me. "Scrub up or get out."

47
COHEN

The air was tinged with the distinctive scent of copper, my gaze honed in on the rib cage cracked open in front of me. Like some fucked-up Sunday roast. Slightly pinker in the middle against the aging not-quite-white bones while the buzz of the suction tube drowned out the rest of the machinery. I could almost hear the contracting of the cardiomyocytes whenever the suction stopped as Prescott's heart throbbed in time with the blipping of the machine to my right.

There was that sound again. The rhythmic pulsing in my eardrums.

Thump-thump, thump-thump, thump-thump.

My nerves were still misfiring, sending faulty signals to my brain, which made it difficult to determine which sensations were real and which were phantasmal. I cracked my neck from side to side, trying to release some of the built up fluid in the joints, and watched in stunned silence as Adrian used a makeshift tattoo gun to scrawl a name across the thin tissue of Prescott's pericardium.

Marisela.

I canted my head to one side, unable to stop myself from taking some visual measurements. Shit was more than a habit. It was second nature. By the time my eyes swept back along the chest cavity, I was certain if we didn't kill Tate Prescott, heart disease would do the job for us.

Adrian eyed his handiwork for a moment before lifting his gaze to meet mine, a smirk curling one side of his mouth.

"Who's Marisela?"

The good doctor dropped the gun onto the medical tray, ink mixing with blood as it splattered across the blue surgical pad. "Our client." He shrugged, then gestured a red-tinged glove to the slab. "Also his wife."

"His wife paid you to do this." It wasn't surprise that had my brows pulled tight across my forehead. I didn't give a shit about the Hippocratic Oath or follow any sort of moral code outside my own. Again, I was just curious. Enjoyed figuring out what made someone tick. What drove them. Their motives. Who hired us and why.

"No, she paid *us* to take him from the house and hold him for a few days. Scare 'em straight. Keep him out of his mistress's bed. I did *this*..." Adrian threw a hand out towards Prescott again. "...on the house. Want our clients to know how much we really care about their overall... customer satisfaction." He grinned, and if fear were something I was prone to feeling, a shiver would have traveled down my spine.

Good thing for both of us I didn't scare easy.

I stared at the man sprawled out on the stainless-steel mortuary table. His weathered skin and the tiny pinpricks that suggested he received regular Botox treatments. His manicured nails, which told me he didn't do much with his hands outside of signing checks and playing the occasional game of golf. The wide pores dotting his scalp that screamed hair transplant. Throw a bottle of those magic blue pills inside a shiny red sports car and Tate Prescott screamed midlife crisis.

"So what do we do with him now?" I grunted past my disgust. Only one thing pissed me off more than cheaters. Big fat fucking liars. And this fucker was both.

"We aren't doing anything." Adrian pivoted on his heel, his leather shoes squeaking on the cement flooring. I'd been so focused on the body on the slab I hadn't noticed him strip off his gown and boots and toss them in the trash can by the heavy metal door. "You're keeping 'em alive or we aren't getting paid."

He waited and watched the confusion flick over my face. Then the panic. Before I settled on irritation. Twisted together with a shit-ton of defiance. "And how the fuck do you expect me to do that?"

I knew the grin was coming. Expected it. And I should have known better than to react. But untethered rage was volatile, especially when mine had been simmering for months. And I rushed the door just as it clicked closed, Adrian staring at me through the little panel of bulletproof glass on the other side as the padlock dropped into place.

"You son of a—"

Adrian *tsked* his tongue. The lines of his eyes, the only part of him I could still see, crinkled by that same stupid grin. "Go tend to your patient, Dr. Michaels. Open-heart surgery is no small procedure."

THE INCREASED BEEPING of the O2 machine told me that Prescott's oxygen levels were dropping, his heart rate following a similar rapid decline. It'd taken me too long to wire the fucker's sternum back together. Plating would have been the more medically sound choice, given my patient's age and lowered bone density. But that shit was much more complex. Time-consuming and not a fucking option.

My right hand was fatigued, the slight tremor an obvious sign of muscle weakness as I tightened my grip around the metal clamps and alternated between an intra-cutaneous stitch and surgical staples. While hoping it would be enough to stave off infection. At least until the exchange. I didn't give a fuck if the guy's chest exploded and his heart fell onto his lap, as long as it happened *after* I was done with him. I didn't like having my fucking time wasted.

Time was money after all. And money was the only fucking reason I was here.

I was fighting the urge to pull up the app on my phone that would give me a direct view into Emily's bedroom as I deposited my gloves into the red sharps bin and washed my hands in the industrial sink. I could feel my foot tapping again, my eyes seeking out the clock, my knee bouncing and my skin on fire. I needed to get out of this fucking room. I needed to see her. Touch her. Taste her. Make her bleed. Taste that too.

I glanced at my palms and envisioned them turning my favorite shade of red before the cardiac monitor started screeching in the background, and I realized my patient was crashing.

Jesus-fucking-Christ.

48
COHEN

I spent six fucking hours watching Tate Prescott die and come back to life. Over and over again on that metal slab. The irony not fucking lost on me and the stupid nickname. Tonight I really was Dr. Frankenstein, my current monster a serial cheater who'd obviously scorned the wrong woman.

The thing was, it didn't matter why the fucker was here. In front of me. Stitched together like some practice cadaver and being pumped with the same kind of adrenaline that ran naturally through my veins with the rush of holding his feeble life in my hands. Because my skin was buzzing, sweat clinging to my overgrown beard as I watched the steady rise and fall of Prescott's chest. His respirations and oxygen level decent enough for me to move 'em from critical to stabilized.

I tossed my seventh pair of gloves into the red bin and approached the metal door, knowing someone was out there watching me. I had no doubt every frantic moment was caught on live video feed and streamed into Dr. Dick's office, his feet kicked up on his desk and a permanent smirk on his face. Though that might have been a bit of an exaggeration. Adrian wasn't the *kick up his feet* type. But that smirk? That shit was dead-on.

And glaring at me from the other side of the glass again as the door creaked open. The prick didn't say a word. Just pivoted on his heel and strolled down the hallway, veering left before stepping into his office. Carefully lowering himself down on his chair and waiting until I took the seat in front of him.

Then he reached a hand inside his top drawer. Pulled out a stack of cash and plopped it down on the desk between us.

I eyed the—going by a quick perusal—ten grand. Then peered up at him again. "What the fuck is that?"

"Your cut." He lifted a challenging brow. "Unless you prefer to work for free?"

I swiped out the stack before the fucker could pull some BS and try to snatch it back. "Thought you said we didn't get paid until the live drop?"

"Oh, my mistake. I was using the universal *we*. Really leaning into that whole working as a unit thing. What I meant was *you* weren't getting paid. We..." He gestured to the air around him. "...get paid upfront of course. With a signed risk-agreement listing fatality as one of the possible outcomes. I'm a businessman after all."

"You son of—" I jumped across the desk, my knees knocking over his carefully laid-out piles of paperwork and my arm outstretched and ready to strangle the fucker with my bare hands the moment I made contact. Only to pause when he waved a disciplinary finger in my direction. I was more curious than I was intimidated. That's what kept me from following through on my very real threat.

"I wouldn't if I were you."

"Yeah? And why the fuck not?" I threw myself back in my chair, my posture open and my legs wide spread. Fucker didn't scare me. I had a good fifty pounds on him. And all he had was quick access to a needle. That would only get him so far now that I was aware of his tricks.

He shrugged a single shoulder. "Because you're so focused on the resources that got you here you're missing the objective."

"Is that your bullshit way of telling me the ends justify the means?"

He arched that eyebrow again, which only seemed to enhance the smugness of his expression. "It seems withholding your funds is a decent enough motivator. Good thing too. At least it is for that pretty little college girl you're so fond of. Inch upon inch of flawless skin. Would hate to have to give her a scar to remember me by."

I leveled Adrian with my glare. He wanted me to react. And I refused to give him what he wanted. "Emily is off the table."

"Then don't make me put her on mine."

I grunted in response. Saying more would have been dangerous. The fucker liked to play mind games and I wasn't about to let him probe around in my brain anymore.

I pushed up from the chair and stalked back towards the door before slamming it behind me. Which, I suppose, told him exactly what he wanted to hear anyway. He'd gotten under my skin.

By the time I made it back down the hall towards the bunks—the basement was too far from our liquor stash—I could sense Casper trailing my steps. Couldn't hear him but I knew the creepy fucker was there. Almost as if the temperature had dropped a few degrees. There was just this odd chill to the air whenever he was lurking in the background.

Like every time he sucked it in through his lungs it came out colder.

Maybe the guy really was a ghost?

"Do you know anything about the job we just did? Specifically the client? Prescott's wife from what I hear?" My gut told me that something was off. That this target was personal somehow. To Adrian. I was certain tonight had to do with more than just teaching me some fucked-up lesson.

I needed to find out what that *more* was. Gain some leverage and tip the scales so the sick son of a bitch didn't have me by the balls anymore.

I stopped short when instead of replying, Casper started humming a familiar nursery rhyme, the haunting tune bouncing around the corridor and echoing back on all sides of the stone walls.

"Mary had a little lamb whose coat was white as snow. And everywhere that Mary went that lamb was sure to go." He alternated between singing and mumbling, the lyrics slightly different from the way I remembered them. But fuck if I cared enough to ask him why.

Guy was seven sorts of crazy on a good day. Definitely swinging towards the manic side of bipolar from what I could tell.

I didn't have the time or energy to figure out the other six.

49
EMILY

I stifled a yawn with the backside of my hand as my date prattled on about his day. My eyelids heavy while the sound of his voice lulled me into a sleeplike trance.

I know! It was rude. I needed to be more attentive. Which was why I ordered the steak, hoping the persistent chewing would be enough to keep my mouth active and my brain stimulated. Unfortunately, my second glass of wine had the opposite effect. A third would knock me on my ass for sure. Though I had to admit the idea was tempting.

I glanced across the table. Grant Nielson was a decent-looking guy. A strong jaw and chocolate-brown eyes that sparkled an amber color under the flickering of the candle-light. His face clean-shaven. His hair brushed back and neat and his mannerisms open and engaging. I also had to admit his cologne smelled nice whenever it wafted between us.

I continued my visual perusal as my gaze drifted along his bobbing throat to his wide chest. His dress shirt was freshly ironed, an off-white color tucked into perfectly creased suit pants. It was clear he made an effort to impress me tonight. Which was more than I could say about my dating life over the last couple of years.

I was a living, breathing man repellent. Someone who couldn't even pay a guy to take her home. Not that I'd stooped to that level. Yet. I wasn't far off though. A battery-operated boyfriend could only get you so far. I mean, it got me *there*. Obviously. Shit was an investment well-made. Until the damn thing found a way to leave me too.

I mean, who loses their vibrator?

It also wasn't the same as being fucked into unconsciousness. Hurting so good you couldn't move the next day.

My glare flicked across the table again. And I couldn't help but wonder if Grant was the type of guy who'd be willing to throw me up against a wall. It was always the quiet ones. The ones you least expected who were the freakiest in the bedroom. At least that's what all the articles said. I was out of practice, remember?

"You wanna go back to my place?" I arched a brow and watched my date nearly choke on a mouthful of mashed potatoes before washing it down with his glass of sparkling water.

"Um, yeah, let me get the check." Grant fumbled with his cloth napkin while waving a waitress over with more vigor than I'd seen him display all night. I could only hope that was a good sign.

A short cab ride and a lot of heavy petting later, Mr. Nielson and I were stumbling through my front door, tearing each other's clothes off on our way to my bedroom. He was a little clumsy but that could have had a lot to do with the two whiskeys he'd downed at dinner without me giving him the chance to finish his meal. Poor guy was probably starving.

Speaking of...

The underside of my knees hit the edge of my mattress and I tumbled backwards. Grant dropped his slacks and attempted to crawl over me.

Nice try, pal.

I shoved at his shoulders, until his head was exactly where I wanted it. I was gonna get mine first. It'd been too long and I couldn't risk the chance that Grant here was a two-pump chump, prone to passing out before his balls even finished unloading.

Clearly catching my drift, Grant tugged my underwear down my legs and lifted my skirt around my waist. His face hovering and his hot breath sending tingles up my spine. I spread my arms out, clinging to the sheets as I prepared my body for the first lap of his tongue. Which would be everything or nothing, depending on his skill set and my possible disappointment. When the front door slammed shut with the force of the wind and I realized I'd completely forgotten to lock it.

"Want me to...?" Grant hitched a thumb over his shoulder, and I groaned my annoyance.

"Yes, please. Lock the deadbolt too, if you don't mind?"

He nodded once in the pitch blackness of the room before pushing up from his knees and towering over the bed. I watched under my lids as he stalked out the door, his bare feet slapping against the wooden staircase as he made his way to the front of my tiny split-level condo.

A few minutes later, his footsteps came pounding back up those stairs, sounding both heavier and softer before a dark silhouette hovered on the threshold for a second longer than seemed natural. I didn't have time enough to question it because he rushed forward. Spreading my thighs wide and shoving them roughly back towards my head.

The first stroke of his tongue was hungry. Like this man I barely knew certainly *knew* me. The second teasing while the third had my legs shaking. My eyes rolled back and my chin pointed towards the ceiling. My spine wasn't even touching the mattress anymore as I tugged at the sheets for purchase. The sounds coming out of my mouth embarrassingly animalistic, if I cared enough to maintain my dignity right now.

I didn't.

Not when the first orgasm ran through me, and I shot up off the mattress like I'd been electrocuted. Not when he shoved me back down, his large palm sprawled across my face as he licked, nipped, and sucked me until I came twice more. My chest heaving and my muscles liquefied. And not when he circled his tongue, slow and methodical, up over my clit, then lower. His nose pressed against my pubic bone as he literally fucked me with his mouth. Moving in and out. Back and forth. And side to side.

I was overstimulated but too exhausted to do anything about it, as this man played my body like a well-practiced instrument. Moving to a rhythm shared between him and my nerve endings while I remained the not-so-silent observer.

A satisfied smirk curled my lips, just barely. Even those muscles were tired. Before my thighs dropped to my sides and my lashes fluttered closed.

That was how you fucked a girl into a coma.

50
EMILY

"*We're sorry. The number you have dialed has been disconnected or is no longer in service. Please hang up and try again.*"

It had been weeks, and Grant still wasn't returning my calls. No, that was a lie. Grant wasn't even *getting* my calls. I think the bastard blocked me?

I hung up, glancing at my phone like it had personally offended me and pulled up the spreadsheet with all the financials I had to review for the month, while trying to figure out where things went wrong. And I didn't mean with the numbers—which didn't add up all that well either, mind you.

I wanted to know what I had done to deserve being ghosted. *Again.* I mean, I thought we had a decent enough end to our night. At least for me it was.

Unless that was his problem? That I didn't reciprocate?

"Prick," I muttered under my breath, tossing my phone aside and clicking away at my keyboard. Too lost to my irritation to realize someone had crept up behind me and was leaning over my desk chair to eye my screen. Someone with a distinctly masculine scent and baritone voice.

"What'd that poor PC ever do to offend you?"

"Hmm?" I pivoted in my seat and stared up into the greenest eyes I'd ever seen. Closer to an olive tone than emerald, a dimple appearing on one side of his mouth—a mouth that was presently kicked up into a panty-melting smirk.

He brushed a strand of his shaggy black hair behind one ear before dipping his head towards my desktop. "Excel giving you trouble?"

"What?" I flicked my gaze from the guy standing in front of me, to my screen, then back again. "Oh no. Excel is fine. Men are the real troublemakers."

Shit!

"I mean, um, sorry... I shouldn't have said that. It's not very professional."

"No need to apologize, Emily. You're not wrong." He chuckled before adding, "And as far as professional goes, you wouldn't believe the shit I see in my line of work." I quirked a curious brow and he quickly extended a palm while clarifying, "Elliot Walker, IT department."

"Right. Bet you do." I shook my head until another thought came to mind. "Wait... How do you know my name?"

This time a full grin spread across his face, his pouty lips revealing some of the whitest teeth I'd ever seen. "Elliot Walker, IT department," he repeated. His way of saying *how do you think?*

"Of course." I smiled back at him before spinning my chair around and tugging myself closer to my desk. As nice as it was to eye my hot but slightly creepy coworker, I really did have a shitstorm of receipts to sort through and my libido had been enough of a distraction for one day.

Guess old cat lady was the life for me.

Elliot obviously didn't take the hint and continued to lean one of his arms over my headrest, his breath so close I could feel it on the side of my face. "There's an easier way to do that, you know." He tapped a finger against my screen. "Add a formula to the bottom cell and it will auto-calculate the sum."

"No?" I gasped while slapping a sarcastic hand to my chest. "You don't say. And here I was, using my teeny-tiny girl brain to manually add all those giant man numbers." I rolled my eyes before pinning Mr. IT-Hotshot with a seething glare. It wasn't his fault I hated his gender right now, but he was about to take the brunt of my annoyance. "I know what I'm doing, thank you very much. I add the formulas *after* I double-check the values. Relying on a computer to do all the work for you leaves room for error."

"Kinda like human error?" he countered without missing a beat.

"Oh, there's human error all right." I scanned Elliot from head to toe. "Pretty sure I'm staring at one right now." It was a low blow. An inaccurate one too, at least on the outside. And we both knew it. But I wasn't about to admit that out loud.

Instead of replying, Elliot rose to his full height and barked out a laugh. "Now I see why he likes you," he muttered under his breath as he turned on his heel and walked down the hall towards the boardroom and *not* the IT department.

It took me a moment to process his words and by the time I yelled out, "Who?" after him, I could barely make out his faint response.

"No one important."

THAT POST-LUNCH IRRITATION was in full effect as I entered the breakroom later that day. Cursing Grant, Elliot, and basically all of *man*kind under my breath as I swiped out an arm and grabbed my mug from the Keurig machine. I took a deep breath and sucked the scent of freshly brewed coffee into my lungs.

I'd landed this job in the financial department of Prescott Research and Development almost straight out of college, after graduating a year early. It was funny how productive I could be when my focus was shifting away from dumbass frat boys and onto my studies. Still, I realized how rare an opportunity this was. It was almost impossible to get your foot in the door, unless you were related to or sucking off the CEO.

Tate Prescott was as slimy as they came. And the office was a lot easier to tolerate without him slinking around the halls, trying to lure the newest youngest intern into the back room with the promise of some cushy secretary job. Which was code for: his personal fuck doll. And just like any spoiled brat with too many shiny toys at his disposal, good ol' Tate would toss the girl aside as soon as something better caught his eye. By better, I meant blonder or sluttier or with a larger set of tits.

Point was... none of us were questioning his absence. It'd be like looking a gift horse in the mouth. And I preferred this particular horse as far away from me and my mouth as he could get.

If I were being completely honest, Tate Prescott could drop dead in the middle of the office and I wouldn't give the fucker a second glance when I stepped over his corpse to get to the copier.

"Oh my god! He's dead!" Sarah came running into the breakroom, her eyes wide and her breathing frantic.

"Who?"

"Tate Prescott!" she gasped before covering her mouth with her hands to stifle her sobs. She was our boss's latest fling, and if I had to hazard a guess, I'd say the waterworks were more for his little black credit card than the man whose name was on it.

51
EMILY

He wasn't dead. It seemed none of us were that lucky. Tate Prescott was just missing... and *presumed* dead. Which was something else entirely, if you asked me.

There were cops everywhere, a sea of uniformed and plain-clothed officers taking over the various rooms of Prescott R&D. Warrant in hand, ransacking the labs and digging through private documents. As if our CEO would just pop up from one of the filing cabinets like a whack-a-mole waiting to be clubbed.

Bet if it were any of the rest of us, shit wouldn't be as accessible. The board of rich white men as obliging.

This was what happened when the wealthy went missing. Suddenly, overtime wasn't an issue and resources were unlimited. Time seemed to stand still for me while everyone else rushed by, everyone but the figure I saw leaning against the far wall staring directly at me. Mr. IT himself.

Good looking or not, I didn't like the way Elliot was seemingly watching my every move. His arms crossed over his shoulders and his head tilted to one side. That wasn't the way someone focused on a stranger. A coworker. It was the way you honed in on a target. His stare sent a shiver down my spine and had me dropping my head.

When I chanced another look, Elliot was gone.

Then everything seemed to stop entirely, the crowds parting when Mrs. Prescott walked in. The clicking of her heels on the tile flooring echoing in the silence of the bustling office space. And her long, tone legs and high, red-soled shoes adding an air of femineity to her perfectly pressed power suit while her jet-black hair was pulled high on her head in a cascading ponytail that landed midway down her back. Where Tate was like a gnat buzzing in your ear, Marisela was a wasp, her deadly glare nearly as venomous as the sting of her harsh tongue. Which was quick to tell you what she thought about you. The good, the bad, and the deeply insulting.

That said, I respected the woman. When it came to anything other than her choice in men, Mrs. Prescott was brilliant and unapologetic about that very same brilliance. She was the brains while her husband was the wallet—the wealthy name behind a brand that relied on the expertise of those who weren't born with silver spoons in their mouths. People who made the Prescott legacy look good to the rest of the rich fuckers at the country club. People who were invisible to the world around them. *People like me.*

"Ms. Shaw, I'd like to see you in my office now."

I'd been so lost to my thoughts, I hadn't noticed that the object of my fascination was standing in front of me, impatiently tapping one of her pointed heels.

"That wasn't a request," Marisela stated before pivoting in the opposite direction. Then her shoes were clicking again. This time down the long hall that led to the executive suites. No-man's-land as far as the rest of us pencil pushers were concerned.

I STARED at the perfectly white paint and opaque glass. The name Marisela Cruz Prescott, COO staring back at me from the gold-plated plaque mounted to the door in front of me. For far longer than seemed appropriate, given the fact I'd been summoned by the she-devil herself.

I didn't personally give her the office nickname, but it didn't make it any less fitting.

I took a deep breath and counted to three before finally pushing my way inside. Marisela was standing at the wall of floor-length mirrors, her back turned to me and the noise of the rest of the office chaos muffled as soon as I clicked the door shut.

I shuffled forward a few steps, stopping when I broached the perimeter of her sleek, modernized, white and gold, marble-topped desk. And waited for her to address me as I choked on the perfumed air of her inner sanctuary.

"Do you know what it is we do here, Ms. Shaw?" Marisela's voice had this way of wrapping around you whenever she spoke, and I didn't mean in a motherly manner. But more like a boa constrictor slowly strangling the breath from your lungs until you were left stumbling over your words, gasping for oxygen while your brain functioned on its remaining surplus.

"I, um, well..."

"It's a simple enough question. Did you or did you not do your research before accepting the very generous employment offer I drafted for you, Emily?" Her use of my first name had me snapping out of my stupor.

"Prescott R&D is the leading medical device developer and manufacturer in the United States, with a strong focus on innovating the way future generations will balance hands-on patient care and progressive scientific breakthroughs," I rushed out in one long breath.

"Cruz," she corrected in a sharp tone. "Cruz R&D. My husband already stripped me of my dignity. I will not allow him to strip me of my family's lineage." She finally spun around to face me, her shoulders pulled back and her posture pencil straight. "But that's not what we do, Ms. Shaw. That's a mission statement, a bunch of fluff words thrown onto our billboards, storefronts, and websites by the company's PR department."

I blinked back at her a few times, my lashes feeling heavier than the thick air filling up the room. "I'm sorry... I don't understand..."

"No, you wouldn't, would you?" Marisela sighed. Though something told me she wasn't talking to me anymore. "But you will in time..."

"Yeah, okay." I nodded. Because I honestly didn't know what else to do at this point. It was like I was stuck in a riddle I had no hope of solving.

"In the meantime, go see Josie in HR. She has some paperwork for you to fill out."

And once again, this woman's tone had a sobering effect. "Am I being fired, Mrs. Pres—*Cruz*?" I quickly corrected.

"Don't be silly," she hummed. "You're being promoted. To my new personal assistant."

52

EMILY

"I want the new logos up no later than Monday afternoon, the website live by Tuesday, the old ID badges shredded and replaced by midweek, and every current contract drafted, reviewed, and finalized by the end of the month. No exceptions."

It was Friday evening, several weeks after Tate Prescott had been first reported missing. Though, with the way things were moving, it was almost as if the man never existed. His creepy-ass remarks nothing but phantom whispers that haunted the halls *and* psyches of most of the female employees. Except for Sarah, who could be found wailing in the bathroom whenever anyone was close enough for her to put on a show—like the veritable Ghost of Mistresses Past.

It was also late, much later than normal business hours, the opulence surrounding us overshadowed by the fluttering crime scene tape that still clung to most surfaces of the Prescott family home. An ongoing, open investigation, the men in the brown suits and cliché trench coats had claimed. Nothing about the lack of police presence screamed "open" to me though. Truth was, it was one of the few times having shit swept under the rug actually benefited the greater good.

I didn't care enough to wonder what had happened to the man, and from the looks of things here, neither did anyone else. Especially his widow.

"And reach out to IT. The Wi-Fi's been lagging. That's unacceptable. Tell them to fix it or I will find someone who can." Marisela's heels click-clacked against the white tile flooring, which was a stark contrast to the bright red of her tight-fitted dress paired with a matching tailored blazer and fiery lipstick. Her voice echoing off the grandeur of her living room while my pen dashed across my notepad in quick shorthand, my sloppy scrawl trying to keep up with her rapid dictation.

It was no easy feat. The woman spoke almost as quickly as she moved across the room, her voice fluctuating each time she added and removed distance between us. I'd learned it was better to stay put instead of attempting to follow her. She never stood in one spot for long, especially when her brain was firing on all circuits. She also wouldn't repeat herself, something her last PA had learned the hard way. Or so the rumors went. Poor guy was supposedly locked up in some nuthouse somewhere.

I hadn't even realized she'd crept up behind me, my focus on the task at hand, until I felt her breath by my ear. Heard the soft hum that told me she was assessing my work.

"Did you catch all that, Emily?"

I quirked an incredulous eyebrow. Because she was doubting me and not because she was right.

Marisela responded with the makings of a smirk but never any words of praise. That slight twitch of her lips was the closest thing to a *good job* I'd ever get. And I was fine with that. I didn't need her approval. Or anyone else's, for that matter. It wasn't my preferred kink anymore. I wasn't sure it ever had been.

Whether or not I wanted to admit it, degradation had this way of sending my libido into overdrive. Which was probably some repressed trauma bullshit. But that was a problem for another day. When I could afford a therapist and wasn't afraid of scaring 'em off or ending up in a straitjacket myself.

"Right, well, you can go now. I expect to see you first thing in the morning. Don't be late." Marisela waved a dismissive hand before her polished nails clanked against the stem of the wineglass she swiped off the butler's tray. It wasn't until she took her first sip of what I could only assume was a bubbly champagne that the woman's mouth finally twisted into a real smile. Something that had nothing to do with me and everything to do with the alcohol currently breaking through her blood-brain barrier.

I might have been a numbers girl all my life, but I'd picked up more than my fair share of medical jargon during my time at Prescott R&D—though no one dare to call it that after the rebranding.

I didn't bother responding as I pivoted on my flats and made my way to the grand entryway of Ms. Cruz's *Downtown Abbey* style mansion. Dipping my chin to the man standing by the door as he swung it open while offering me a polite "good evening, Miss Shaw."

Then I descended the stairs, mindful to watch my step now that the sun was down and the estate was surrounded by eerie darkness. Each shadow bending and flexing with the breeze, waiting for the perfect chance to reach out and grab me. The manicured hedges resembling the sort of boogeymen that had us hiding under the covers as kids and the expansive landscaping and creaking gates like the opening credits in a horror movie just before the first jump scare. All that was missing was some creep in a mask hiding under my car or crouched in the back seat.

I shook off the sudden chill, my fingers curling around the handle of my off-white Chevy when the sound of my phone blaring through the night had me nearly jumping out of my shoes. I lifted one hand to my pounding chest while the other rummaged through my bag in search of my cell. Clicked answer and raised it to my ear without checking the screen.

I opened my mouth, my usual greeting forming on the tip of my tongue. But the person on the other end was already speaking. "Get home and get in bed. I don't like waiting."

"Excuse me? Who is this?" I didn't recognize the caller. But then again, I was pretty certain that was the point. It sounded like one of those text-to-talk devices rather than someone's actual voice.

"Oh, and, Emily, wear the blue one."

"The blue what?" *Click.* "Hello?" My eyes flicked from side to side, my heart rate picking up with both anticipation and fear. It wasn't a normal response. Normal girls would be running away. Calling the police and clutching their cans of mace. Not rushing towards the danger behind the robotic voice on the other end of the line.

Then again, I had never been all that good at being normal.

53
EMILY

The moment I stepped over the threshold that separated the hallway from my bedroom, I dropped my bag on the floor and stared at the different piles of lingerie meticulously laid out across my comforter, my off-brand sheets replaced by layers of red silk. Before glancing around the rest of the space. Nothing else appeared to be touched or taken and the front door to my tiny condo was exactly how I'd left it this morning. *Locked.*

I waited for that surge of fear to flood my system and send my fight-or-flight instincts into overdrive. Instead, my feet were sliding across the plush carpet, my curiosity propelling me closer and closer to the piles of lace and satin. I trailed a finger over the white almost see-through bodysuit, the black babydoll-looking nightgown, and the light-pink one-piece teddy before landing on the blue camisole and matching booty shorts. None of it was made for comfort and it certainly wasn't the type of underwear I would have chosen for myself. But it all appeared to be in my size—a fact that should have been alarming.

It wasn't. I was no final girl. I was the chick who got murdered five seconds into the opening scene. And some dark part of me was okay with that.

I glanced over my shoulder, towards the empty doorway, then back to the bed again. Snatching up the blue set, even though everything in me screamed to do the opposite. To lean into my natural defiance that urged me to throw on a pair of gray sweats and my favorite band t-shirt—the one I had since high school with all the holes in it.

A quick shower and a swipe of pink lip gloss later, I was on my hands and knees, climbing onto my double bed like a sacrificial lamb waiting for the slaughter. No idea whether or not I was about to be fucked into oblivion or chopped up into tiny pieces. My face spread across tomorrow's paper with some bullshit heading about me being a ray of sunshine and deeply missed by friends and family.

Truth was, I was closer to a storm cloud than a ray of anything. And no one would miss me. Except maybe Marisela. She'd also be the one most likely to show up to my funeral. If only to berate me for my tardiness.

I left the lights dimmed, all my focus directed at the open bedroom door as my chest rose and fell faster with each minute that stretched on. My lids were growing heavy, my muscles relaxing against the feel of the expensive sheets until I could sense myself slowly fading away as the first stages of sleep were taking over.

By the time I realized I wasn't alone anymore, it was too late. My eyes snapped open to a pitch-black room, my arms reaching out and trying to find purchase when a palm wrapped around my ankle and tugged me down the mattress. I slid with ease, the silk having a lot less traction than the cotton while leaving me nothing to grip. I blinked once, twice, then twice more. Trying to focus on the shadowy figure towering over me as slight recognition finally sank in.

"Grant?"

The question clung to the air, the figure neither confirming nor denying the accuracy as he ran a gloved hand along my collarbone. Over the peak of my right nipple, stiffened beneath the thin fabric of the camisole. Down my stomach, pausing when my breaths quickened, only to continue until the leather fingertips skimmed the waistband of the sleep shorts he demanded I wear. Then clearly decided I shouldn't as he yanked the material down my legs and tossed it across the room, the hood of his jacket making it impossible for me to see his face even as he lowered it between my thighs and buried his nose against my slick pussy. But I didn't have to see him to identify who it was. The way my body reacted to that first swipe of his tongue told me everything I needed to know.

I wasn't being stalked by some psycho killer looking to prop my head up on his living room mantel. I was being haunted by the ghost of the man who gave me the first orgasm I had in months. The guy who was too much of a pussy to break things off with me the next day. To face me and even tell me why. Another glorified dine and dasher.

I should have been annoyed. I wanted to be infuriated. But my brain was barely tethered to the rest of me as nerve endings I didn't even know I had thrummed to life. My head tipped back and digging into the mattress. My toes curling and my hips grinding against his jaw while he worked my pussy as though he knew it better than I did. Which didn't seem too far from the truth right now. Because I sure as fuck never made myself feel like this. And neither did my vibrator.

He was a mix of rough and gentle. Fast and slow. Calculated and sloppy. As he devoured me like I was both his first and last meal. Silently. But his actions no less ferocious than a starved man lapping up the sticky remnants of an empty soup bowl. He refused to waste a drop, his large hands spreading me wide and his frenzied breaths adding to the stimulation each time he exhaled through his nose.

I was rising higher and higher by the second, my muscles pulling tight like an overextended rubber band begging for release. At the same time, I didn't want it to end. I was both racing to the finish line and dragging my feet the closer it got. I knew it was hopeless though. I couldn't hold back, no matter how much I resisted. No matter how hard I tried to prolong the feel of his tongue flicking my clit at just the right rhythm. His gloved palms pressing into my thighs and his mouth adding the perfect mixture of suction and pressure. Until I had no choice but to give in to wave after wave of pleasure that had my body convulsing and the strangled sounds vibrating my vocal cords as I gasped and groaned in equal measure.

And then I was putty in his hands, my new sheets soaked through to the mattress with a combination of saliva and the aftermath of my orgasm, while the air was tinged with the familiar scent of one-sided sex.

An outcome that was his doing, not mine, by the way.

I had no problem returning the favor. In fact, I enjoyed giving head. Especially when the dick was pretty and clean enough to suck. He smelled freshly showered and my tongue was dying to know what he tasted like. Every part of him. But when I managed enough strength to lift my head off the bed, Grant was gone. The bedroom door pressed tight against the frame even though I'd never heard it click closed.

Well, fuck you too. Or I guess not.

54
EMILY

It was just another day in administrative hell. It was also a Monday, which only seemed to make matters worse. And I was two large coffees deep, a pile of documents clutched in one arm and a fresh mug in the other as I stopped a few feet short of my desk. I cleared my throat loud enough for most of the office to hear and watched as my chair spun back around to face me.

"Morning, sunshine." Elliot grinned like he hadn't just been caught with his hand in the *cookies* jar. His expression so smug it made my teeth grind in my jaw as I fought my need to slap him.

I waited, lifting a questioning brow. Urging him to explain without bothering to say more. We both knew what I was asking. *What the fuck are you doing going through my password-protected files?*

"Just updating your security software, Emmy. Shit's older than that dollar-store mug you're clutching." He gestured to my coffee, which I considered throwing in his face if it wouldn't be an insult to good caffeine, while attempting to disarm me with another smirk.

It didn't work.

"Emily, not Emmy," I was quick to correct before setting my mug down beside my keyboard and plopping my pile of paperwork with way more gusto than was necessary. "Sounds like IT isn't doing their job then, doesn't it?"

Elliot never dropped his grin as he pushed to his feet, making sure I took notice of the height difference as he *tsked* his tongue. "That's exactly what I'm doing, Emmy. *My job*."

I crossed my arms over my chest while tipping my head back to meet his glare. I didn't know what it was about this guy but he got under my skin. "Is that so? 'Cause to me, it looks like you waited until I left my desk to start snooping through my files."

"Looks can be deceiving, sweetheart. You should know that better than most."

"What's that supposed to mean?"

"Nothing. Nothing at all." He lifted one shoulder into a half-shrug, his hands tucked into his pockets and a cocky sway to his step as he turned to walk down the hallway, back towards the hole in the wall where all those zeros and ones went to die.

I watched until Elliot disappeared around the corner, then reclaimed my seat, tucking my legs under my desk and eyeing my screen. Not an icon, tab, or window out of place. Which didn't mean much of anything if the guy was as good as he thought he was. His attitude screamed *I think I'm the smartest person* in the room while his conventional good looks didn't do much to help matters. It was clear he was used to women fawning all over him. I just wasn't one of them.

Maybe that was his problem with me. The fact I wasn't throwing my panties in front of his keyboard. Because it was definitely something. He took every opportunity to try to unnerve me. If I were younger and a tad more naïve, I'd think the fucker was flirting. But this was the office, not the playground, and tugging a girl's pigtail didn't mean you liked her. It meant you were an asshole who needed to learn to keep your hands to yourself.

IT WAS NEARLY five before I peered up from my computer again, cracking my neck from side to side as I glanced around the almost empty office space. Marisela had back-to-back meetings with the board all day. Very need-to-know. And apparently I didn't need to know the shit that was going on behind those soundproof double-doors.

I was pretty sure I didn't want to know either.

I rested my palms on my desk, ready to slide back and stretch my legs, when a chat box popped up on my screen. I flicked a glare over one shoulder, that feeling of someone watching me sending a chill down my spine, before returning my attention to the little message tab.

UNKNOWN USER: It's late.

I rolled my eyes and typed out a quick response, some fucked-up part of my brain wondering if he was planning to ask me about my favorite scary movie. I was assuming it was a he anyway, seeing as the whole guy in a mask thing was popular nowadays. I mean, it wasn't my kink but I could certainly understand the appeal.

EMILY SHAW: Thank you, Captain Obvious.

UNKNOWN USER: Why aren't you home. Alone. In that empty bed of yours.

EMILY SHAW: That kinda talk isn't appropriate for the office. You do know these chats are monitored by HR. Don't you, Elliot?

It was a guess so I threw it out there. Worst case, I was wrong. Best case, I knocked the cocky bastard down a peg or two.

UNKNOWN USER: Keep calling me another man's name and you won't like the consequences, Emily.

EMILY SHAW: Oh, look at that. Now we can add threats to my sexual harassment suit. At this rate, my name's gonna be on this building by end of week.

UNKNOWN USER: Not before my name's on the tip of that tongue of yours. Begging me to stop… or maybe to keep going. We all know what a dirty little slut you are.

EMILY SHAW: We?

So this was a group effort? Likely one of the dozen applicants pissed off at me for landing a job I never wanted to begin with. That was before I'd seen the salary that came with my new title—there really was no arguing with all those zeros. Not with the amount of debt I'd accumulated over the years.

> UNKNOWN USER: I think the black is more appropriate for you tonight. Black like that shriveled-up little organ in your chest.

> EMILY SHAW: Grant?

I watched the little bubbles appear and disappear in the text box before they were replaced by one of those automated messages that informed me the user was *no longer available.*

55

EMILY

There were two kinds of assholes in the world. The ones who threw their *assholeness* in your face and the ones who were good at hiding it. Right now, sitting on my bed with my arms crossed over my chest nearly four hours after receiving those cryptic messages back at the office, I was trying to decide which category Grant belonged in.

Then again, maybe I was the real asshole. Or, at the very least, the dumb*ass*.

It was the only logical explanation for having a long-standing death wish that seemed to go hand in hand with my clear lack of self-preservation. That or all this pent-up sexual frustration had tossed my brain cells into a blender and pressed the puree button a few times.

When I glanced at my antiquated analog clock that reminded me of my college days and realized it was teetering dangerously close to midnight, I turned off the lamp on the bedside table and curled up in my sheets with a huff. I had to be at work in a few hours and I refused to look like a zombie in the morning meeting. Another couple of minutes and I was drifting off into a painfully unsatisfied sleep.

You know that moment between consciousness and unconsciousness where you're still not quite sure if you're awake or dreaming? Where that hand reaching out to grab you might belong to the burglar who climbed into your window or a complete figment of your imagination?

As my lashes fluttered but refused to open, my limbs immobilized by sleep and my brain refusing to reboot, I could only hope it was the latter. It felt like a weight was sitting on my chest, pinning me between the mattress and a faint warmth. And then something was brushing along my throat, over my collarbone, circling around my nipple before trailing across the underside of my breast to my abdomen and lower.

I didn't know where the nightgown had gone but the slight breeze from the ceiling fan told me I was naked, as that same something was dipping inside me. Testing the waters and coming out drenched. I wanted to arch my back. Grind my hips and give into the sensation but nothing above the waist seemed to communicate with the rest of my body.

Sleep paralysis. I'd heard about it before and could only hope that was what I was experiencing. Then again, if this was all a dream, I wasn't sure I'd ever wanna wake up.

The mattress dipped and then I was being straddled, two thick trunks pinning each of my thighs from the outside. My arms grabbed and stretched high above my head. Not that I could will them to move anyway. A warm breath bristled next to my ear before the meat of my hips was gripped up, my knees forced down against the bedsheets and my legs butterflied open. And then I felt it. That familiar burn at the apex of my thighs, my body being split in two as the weight drove forward over and over again to a rhythm my nerve endings knew all too well.

It hit deep in my gut, pulling out and plunging in. Harder and faster. A rumbling sound vibrating against my cheek in time with heavy breaths. I could hear the headboard knocking against the wall and feel the chill in the air from the open window. Smell the distinct odor of mint tainted by cigarette smoke and taste a hint of cologne whenever it bristled against my lips. But still my eyelids wouldn't pry open, my limbs as deadened as the rest of me.

I told myself this was a fantasy. My brain's way of doing what the men in my life couldn't. Sucked in a lungful of air through my nose and relaxed my muscles. Enjoying the push and pull of flesh against flesh, the friction and sloshing of bodily fluid. Until my lower abdomen was tightening. My toes tingling and my pussy pulsing.

I was so close to getting what I needed. Climbing higher and higher. My breath hitching in my chest and that slight moan trapped in the back of my throat. And then...

I woke with a start, shooting up in bed while my eyes flicked around the empty room. My temples were throbbing and the sunlight streaming in from my closed window and open curtains had me reaching up and yanking at the blinds.

It took me a few minutes to orient myself to my surroundings. I knew it was a little after five in the morning —the blaring of my alarm told me as much. And I knew I was in my condo but everything else felt hazy. Like my head was in a fishbowl and I was seeing the world through a thick layer of glass.

I dipped a hand between my thighs. Pushed past the hem of my nightgown and hissed. Everything burned, and when I pulled my hand up again, my fingertips were tinged red, a viscous substance clinging to my skin when I pried the digits apart. Blood.

I wasn't usually so reckless when it came to forgetting my least favorite time of the month, but then again, work had been hectic. Maybe I was more of a mess than I thought I was. Which was saying something.

I forced my feet on the floor and my ass out of bed, tugging the stained sheets off the mattress and shoving them into the washer. I set it to the quick cycle and prayed that I'd remember to switch everything to the dryer before I rushed out the door for work. Then I made my way into the bathroom, each step more painful than the last, the cramping in my lower stomach unlike I ever felt it before. I turned the water as hot as it would go and stripped out of my nightgown, allowing the material to pool around my ankles. Kicked it aside and jumped into the shower stall.

All I needed was a gallon of coffee and a fistful of pain pills and I'd be good to go.

56
EMILY

The halls were eerily quiet when I stepped off the elevator, the lights dimmer than I remembered them being, while the scent of freshly brewed coffee traveled all the way from the staff kitchen to my nostrils before I breathed the scent deep into my chest. It had this calming effect even though I was well aware caffeine's job was to aggravate your central nervous system, not settle it.

I decided to top off my travel mug, failing to question who powered on the machine until I was staring at an empty kitchenette. I was used to being the first one here. What I wasn't used to was having a full pot of coffee waiting for me when I arrived.

I glanced down each side of the corridor, finding them just as vacant, before making my way towards the machine. There was a cup already set out on the counter, not just any cup but my usual office mug, filled to the brim with my preferred blend of French roast—if the aroma was anything to go by.

I dropped my travel mug next to the sink and lifted the

cup to my lips, taking a tentative sip. One cream, one sugar. Just how I liked it. While the coffee helped warm the ache in my gut, unease chilled my spine. No one around here paid enough attention to me to know how I took my coffee. No one cared enough to ask either. I was just another face. Another name. Another person to dislike for their simple existence in the competitive field of research and development.

Truth was, I didn't need friends. Not in the office anyway. It was much better to separate business and pleasure.

I rinsed out my travel mug and tucked it under my arm, turning out of the staff kitchen and making a beeline for my desk. Only to stop in my tracks as soon as my computer came into view. The overhead lights flashed on, momentarily blinding me as I set my cups aside and reached a hand out towards the gift box sitting atop my keyboard. Its shiny black paper nearly iridescent at this angle and the matching velvet bow soft to the touch.

Pushing up on the tips of my dress shoes, I peered over the dividers, the silence that usually eased me into a productive morning suddenly eating away at my sanity. When it was clear that no one was jumping down from the drop ceiling or crawling out from under the conference room table to scream *surprise*, I tugged on the end of the bow and watched the paper slowly fall away. Then I placed the plain black box next to my computer screen and gradually raise the lid while a million different possibilities flitted through my mind. None of them good.

Black was a pretty ominous color. And tossing a gift box on someone's desk was a convenient way to trigger the whole building to blow. Also a good method of biological warfare, if history were anything to go by.

Still, my curiosity got the better of me as I leaned forward to peer at the contents. Lifting a questioning eyebrow when my fingers dipped inside and plucked out what appeared to be a man's dress shirt. A used dress shirt, off-white, with a thin peppering of cologne clinging to the fabric.

It wasn't exactly a bomb but it wasn't a gift either.

I deposited the shirt back into the box, shoving the crumbled paper and rolled-up bow on top of it before slamming the lid shut and pushing it all aside. Deeming it tomorrow's problem. Today I had work to do. Work that didn't include bullshit chat messages or creepy black boxes. Though whoever it was, they could keep the coffee coming.

I raised my cup in mock cheers at the thought before setting it next to my mouse pad again.

I slept like shit and that hyper-realistic sex dream left me on edge. In more ways than one. I had all the aches and exhaustion of being thoroughly fucked all night long with none of the benefits of an orgasm. It seemed the men in my fantasies were just as useless as the men in my real life.

It really was a shame I didn't bat for the other team. Would have made things so much easier if I could avoid the opposite sex altogether.

The repetitive rapping of knuckles against my divider wall had me simultaneously looking up from my screen and groaning in my seat. It wasn't even seven in the morning yet and the office nonsense was already in full swing, or so it seemed.

"Morning, Emmy," Elliot hummed while I pivoted in my chair to glare at him from over one shoulder. He was standing uncomfortably close, his hands tucked into his pockets and his posture too relaxed for a man well on his way to getting slapped. He leaned forward, not bothering to hide the fact he was snooping. "Whatcha got there? Is it your birthday or something?" He tugged a palm free from his pants and gestured at the box.

"Something," I muttered under my breath, quickly deciding to grab my discarded gift and shove it against Elliot's chest. "You know what? Why don't you take it? I think it would look much better on you anyway." I spun my chair all the way around and crossed my arms. My legs following suit as my lips curled into a smirk.

Elliot stared at me for a moment, clearly not knowing what to do with the items stuffed in his hands, before breaking out of his daze and dropping everything into the bin beside my desk. "No thanks. I don't do sloppy seconds," he grunted, his mouth twisted into an almost snarl.

Good. I didn't know what exactly put a damper on his mood or took the skip out of his step. But I was fucking grateful for it.

Without another word, Elliot raked an aggravated hand through his hair and stalked off. Grumbling to himself instead of *at* me for once.

The following week, another box appeared. This time with a pair of men's slacks neatly folded inside it. Not long after that, a man's watch. But it wasn't until the last package arrived on my doorstep with a wallet wrapped up in black tissue paper that everything finally sank in. And sent a fresh wave of panic surging through my veins.

The television was playing in the living room, white noise to help mitigate the suffocating silence that seemed to always surround me. The news anchor's voice carried into the kitchen as I set the small iridescent box on the table and started shifting through the contents of the wallet. Nothing out of the ordinary, besides the unconventional packaging. A few credit cards, a gym membership, and an ID that belonged to...

"A man's naked body was discovered by hikers last week, the remains mutilated and burned before they were dumped in a remote location just outside the city. After extensive testing conducted by the county's medical examiner's office, the victim has been identified as a Mr. Grant Nielson from..."

My head snapped up to the screen, while the rest of the woman's words landed on deaf ears the moment she repeated the name that was staring back at me from the little plastic card still clutched in my now trembling hands.

I knew what I should do. The right thing to do. What any emotionally stable individual would have done under similar circumstances. Left everything where it was and immediately reached out to the proper authorities. And definitely not do whatever they could to contaminate a potential crime scene.

Instead, I tugged on a pair of rubber gloves I used to scrub the dishes. Wiped my prints off the cards in the wallet and tossed any piece of evidence that could have possibly linked me to Grant into an industrial-size trash bag. Including the freshly laundered lingerie and bedsheets. I wasn't a criminal, but for some reason, I had no problem thinking like one.

Then I dropped the bag into the trunk of my car, glancing over my shoulder before slamming it closed. I didn't know where I was going but I would figure it out when I got there. I was on autopilot, acting without much thinking as I jumped into the driver's seat. Backed out of the spot and turned on to the main road. Every stop light and street sign a blur as I stared through the windscreen without seeing much of anything at all. Just streaks of color and flashes of movement.

A short ride later, I was pulling up to the large iron gates that welcomed you to Prescott Manor—it was the one thing Marisela couldn't tack her name on. The estate was owned by Tate's family, passed down from generation to generation with no wiggle room in the language of the deed. Something I learned after extensive legal research I was forced to sift through when one of the man's many mistresses tried to claim she was pregnant with his rightful heir.

Marisela and Tate didn't have any children together, which was more of a blessing than anything if you asked me. Even if it made her stake in his holdings weak at best.

For as long as my former boss's body was missing, his wife was permitted to reside on the property. But once a trace of him was found, she'd be out on her ass and everything would be turned over to the only remaining Prescott. Tate's half-brother, born out of wedlock and never given the privileges that came with the paternal blood that ran through the bastard's veins.

I couldn't tell you what led me to Marisela's doorstep. I was her employee, not her friend. But something in my gut told me she would understand. Maybe even help me. At the very least, provide some guidance. She knew better than anyone else that it didn't matter if you were guilty or not. It only mattered what it looked like. And right now, it looked like I had a dead man's belongings shoved inside the trash bag currently clutched in my hands.

Before I could knock, the large ornate door was swinging inward and I was being escorted into the parlor room by Marisela's butler. I offered the man a tight smile and he dismissed himself, after assuring me Ms. Cruz would be with me shortly.

There was a tray of sweets already set out on the sideboard, a few fancy cups, and a carafe of fresh coffee from the smell of it. But I didn't have the stomach to eat, while caffeine would only serve to heighten the pounding in my chest.

If the electric chair didn't kill me, a heart attack just might.

I was too stunted—perhaps still in shock—to realize

how much time had passed before I heard the familiar clicking of heels travel down the grand staircase. Clack against the tile flooring of the foyer and pause at the threshold to the parlor. I pushed up from the plush sofa as soon as I felt Marisela's glare boring through the side of my head. And took a tentative step forward.

She lifted a palm to stop me. "First thing's first, *nena*. Did you do it?"

58
EMILY

"Did I do what?" Even as I asked the question, I knew there was no point tiptoeing around the truth.

Marisela could smell a lie a mile away. Hell, the woman could practically taste it in the air. Like a cobra waiting to strike. All that was missing was the forked tongue. It was what made her so ruthless in the boardroom. What made it nearly impossible to pull away before she was already sinking her teeth into you.

It was also why I was standing in the middle of this fancy-ass version of some rich lady's living room, clinging on to the thinnest thread of hope that someone with more money than God wouldn't have the cops on speed dial. That I could find something to say that wouldn't have her throwing my ass out on her gilded doorstep before I had the chance to plead my pitiful case for mercy.

I mean, surely someone with a dead husband (allegedly) would understand the plight of someone with a very dead *kinda* boyfriend. At least that's the logic I was going with.

She quirked a manicured brow and gestured to the trash bag I was twisting around in my hands. "Whatever brought you here. Whatever you're hiding in there. Did you do it?"

"I... well, no," I fumbled over my words. "I didn't do anything. I swear."

She eyed me for a moment, the green rings around her pupils disappearing at the same time she scrutinized my every feature. Her nostrils flaring and her expression blank. I watched soundlessly as Marisela took a deep breath and threw an arm out towards the sofa. Then she pivoted on her heels, drawing the antique pocket doors closed and latching them in place. Before pinning me with another laser-sharp glare.

"Good. That makes things much easier. Now have a seat and start at the beginning. And, Emily?"

I peered up at the sound of my name.

"Do not leave anything out. The devil's always in the details, *nena*."

I went as far back as college, way too sober to discuss everything that came before it. Truth was, no amount of liquor could dull my brain enough to bring up the topic of my mother and all the underlying trauma that came with being the daughter of an abusive drunk, whose boyfriends all seemed to prefer little girls warming their laps over the grown-ass woman they were supposed to be crawling into bed with at night.

Instead, I touched on my unhealthy relationship with a certain med student, dug deep into how it felt to suffer through the loss of a child on my own with no one to hold my hand or help me navigate the emotions that came with the fluctuating hormones, and admitted how humiliating it was to never hear from the son of a bitch again. I rattled off the name of every guy who never called back. Summarized every message that went unanswered and acknowledged every part I played in choosing walking-talking red flags with chiseled jawlines and the mommy issues to match.

I described that first night with Grant and the several strange interactions that followed it. Explained how I discovered that someone had not only killed him but chopped him up into tiny pieces, and then sent me his belongings—all wrapped up in grotesque gift boxes with perfectly creased corners and even edges. Like a psychopath's fucked-up version of arts and crafts.

How that same psychopath knew where I worked. Where I lived. How I wasn't safe. And how I had no one to turn to. So here I was, curled in on myself in my boss's parlor room, asking her what I should do. While we both knew what I was really asking her was how to cover up a crime I didn't commit but sure as hell looked good for.

Marisela's face remained a mask of indifference. No word too dark or depraved when it filtered through her ears. No unspoken implication perverse enough to draw a hint of emotion from her stoney demeanor. I could only imagine what this woman experienced in her life to remain so unaffected. But some deranged part of me was thankful she *had* experienced it.

I wasn't ready to deal with anyone's judgement right now. Instead, I needed someone to think logically. Take charge. And that was Marisela's exact area of expertise.

Her long perfectly painted nails tapped against the fabric of her white slacks, her bright-red lips even brighter when she pinched her mouth and hummed thoughtfully to herself. "Honestly, *nena,* the timing couldn't be better."

"I..." I forced down a barrage of questions before finally

landing on one I could articulate. "For me to be a person of interest in an ongoing murder investigation?"

"Did you tell anyone else about this..." She twirled her wrist in the air as if trying to decide on the word. "...boy?"

"Well, no—"

"Then, I fail to see how you're an interest to anyone."

It was a statement, a hidden meaning, that landed like a one-two punch to my gut. Because she was right. I was just another name in Grant Nielson's little black book. That's really all I was to anyone anymore. I'd made myself disposable. A realization that had a rather sobering effect on my rattled nerves.

I dipped my chin with a curt nod, bending forward to grab the trash bag off her Persian rug when Marisela grabbed hold of my wrist to stop me. "How do you feel about Spain, Emily?"

"The country?"

One side of her mouth curled into a near smirk as she appeared to hold back whatever snarky response was on the tip of her tongue. "Yes, *nena*, the country."

"I'm not sure I feel any particular way. If I'm being honest, I've never stepped foot outside the midwest."

Marisela nodded once, something she did whenever she was certain she was on the winning side of an argument. "Then I think it's time you did."

I CURLED up in the back of the town car Marisela had hired to drop us off at the airport—I didn't care where we were going, just that we were getting away—and closed my eyes.

The exhaustion taking over as the adrenaline seeped its way out of my system. Which left me trapped somewhere between the nightmares in my mind and the nightmares that had become my reality.

I also didn't know where the voices were coming from. Just that they were there. Making their way into my ear every now and then without carrying much significance. Almost like the language wasn't my own. Even though it was. It was a coping mechanism I'd learned as a kid. To tune out all the yelling and pretend like it didn't exist.

Sometimes, if I tried hard enough, it really didn't.

"Fuck me over and I'll fuck you harder. Or don't you remember?"

Marisela was hissing into the phone, her tone harsher than I'd ever heard it before. I was used to the eerily calm woman whose glare did the talking for her. So maybe I really was just imagining it. And the only voices I was hearing were the ones in my head. There was a reply. A distant shouting I couldn't quite make out before she spoke over it.

"Good luck keeping your dog on a leash when you have nothing to offer him anymore."

With that, my world went silent. And then I was drifting away from all the white noise. While inching closer to the demons that always seemed to be chasing after me. In some form or another.

59
EMILY

The truth was I never wanted to be rich. Money gave you a false sense of security. Weakened your survival instincts and softened you against a world that had no problem eating you alive.

So, no, I couldn't say being rich was my end goal. Being able to afford my next meal certainly was. But I also had to admit that being *rich-adjacent* sure was nice. Seeing it all from the outside—just close enough to not have to look in—was a comfortable way to live without ever getting *too* comfortable. Because I was well aware it all could be yanked away from me again without a moment's notice.

That's what the last five years had been like while traveling with Marisela. Late nights, lots of champagne, more money than I'd ever seen in my life. Her sights set on extending the company's global influence while she dipped her sharp talons into every eligible tailored pocket within arm's reach.

She may have been a widow, according to the courts

that had recently deemed Tate Prescott legally dead, but that didn't mean Marisela was in mourning.

Me, on the other hand? I'd given up on dating altogether. Not that there hadn't been offers. Plenty of men were ready to jump into bed with me just to get close to my boss. But I'd learned my lesson the hard way. I couldn't trust my judgement—just one reason of many I was in a dedicated relationship with my brand-new vibrator and a Kindle full of smut.

Book boyfriends did it better anyway. Speaking of...

I tugged my e-reader from the adapter still plugged into the outlet. Wrapped the cord into a small bundle and tucked it all into my backpack.

The usual click-clack of Marisela's heels echoed off the terracotta flooring in the little Spanish villa as she made her way down the hall towards my bedroom. I didn't bother looking up as I packed the last of my belongings in my carry-on suitcase while she glared at me from where she was perched against the doorjamb.

"Ready, *nena*?" she hummed in that too-sweet voice she used whenever being sweet was the last thing she wanted to do.

I nodded once before dropping my suitcase onto the floor, popping the handle and swinging my backpack over one shoulder.

We were catching a red-eye to the States in a couple of hours, something Marisela seemed to decide we were doing on a whim. Then again, this woman never really did anything on a whim. She just didn't always let on to what she had planned.

Good on her, I guess. You were better off when the only one you trusted was yourself.

A few minutes later, we were navigating the circle

driveway, the colorful gardens bouncing by us on the dirt road. I never did bother to learn the names but the bell-shaped ones were always my favorite. There was something about those little orange flowers that was hauntingly beautiful. The way they seemed to hang their petals rather than flaunt them.

It was like they knew showing off just meant you were more likely to get plucked.

I'D BARELY RECOVERED from the ten-hour flight, and I was already standing inside Marisela's office at Cruz R&D. The cityscape lit up by the bright sunlight that was streaming in from the floor-to-ceiling windows behind her.

I glanced around the room, taking in the fresh paint and additional gold frames. Staff had come and gone but other than a few modest updates, not much had changed.

Marisela took two steps forward, closing the distance as she reached out a hand and snatched a small brown box with thin white ribbon from the top of her desk. She glanced at it for a moment, then peered back up at me. The top of her head illuminated like a halo while shadows darkened her newly sun-kissed features.

"I've dropped you a pin with the address." She dipped her chin towards the phone clutched in my palm before tossing the box in my direction. Far more confident than I was that I'd actually catch it.

I could hear something bouncing around the sides as the package settled against my palms, before I tucked it into my bag and hiked the strap higher on my shoulder. I didn't have enough caffeine in my system yet, which meant dumb questions that deserved *dumber* answers came tumbling out of my mouth with little to no warning. Questions like...

"What's in it?"

Marisela grinned, her version of a grin—if I were being honest it was more like a strained grimace—and waved a dismissive hand. "Open it and find out."

I shook my head before she'd barely finished speaking. "I'd rather not."

Curiosity killed the cat after all, and I only had so many lives left before I was tail up beside Mr. Whiskers.

"That's your choice, *nena*. But once that box leaves this office, it is not to be tampered with. Straight to the drop-off location. Understand?"

I dipped my head into a curt nod, and Marisela clicked her tongue.

"Words, Emily. The entire future of my company hinges on that box making it to its intended recipient."

"Then why don't you take it there yourself?" I was already reaching a hand inside my bag when something had me pausing to look up at her again.

Marisela arched a challenging brow, and my arm pulled back and snapped down to my side.

"What I meant was... are you sure you don't want to ask someone else? Since so much is at stake." I could feel the heat creeping up my neck as I quickly added, "I'm not sure I'm the one who should be doing this..."

She watched my face for a moment, almost as though she were considering my offer, before landing me with a glare that replaced the heat with a fresh chill. A coldness that seeped into my bones. "That's where you're wrong, *Emily*. You are the *only one* who can do this."

60

EMILY

I stared up at the towering brick building, my glare catching on the endless barred windows that left me to wonder if they were meant to keep people in or prevent them from getting out. It sounded like the same thing but I promise you there was a difference.

If you'd ever felt trapped somewhere, you knew what I meant.

Then I lifted a tentative finger and pressed the button, waiting for the buzzer that would grant me access to this Amityville horror house with a hint of that *just lobotomized* charm.

When the metal doors started moving inward on their own, I jumped back a step and caught a glimpse of the little red blinking light that told me I was being watched. The rundown loony bin didn't seem the sort to have automated anything, so it took me by surprise when I crept forward and was surrounded by bright-white paint and a high-tech security system—all welcoming me to Briarwood Sanitorium.

I glanced at a few outdated photos framed and propped

up on a table near the main door and had to admit it was a little jarring. Imagining what it would be liked to be trapped within these walls, dropped off on the doorstep because your family didn't want to deal with your version of crazy anymore. A thought that sent a shiver down my spine and accompanied a chill that landed at the base of my tailbone.

The place was soundless, other than the squeak of my shoes against the matching white tiles. I could only imagine how much the janitor had to invest in bleach to keep everything so... shiny. While the maze of hallways and doors left me feeling like Alice, ready to jump down the rabbit hole at the same time my inner voice mumbled something about not drinking any potions I happened to stumble across along the way.

"Hello...?" I called out and listened as the word echoed back at me. A little fainter and a lot more breathy. But it didn't change the fact I was alone. Or at least that was the way someone wanted it to seem.

I took another tentative step to my left, my hand creeping into my pocket and grabbing my phone. And glanced down at the screen, only to realize I didn't have any bars. I wasn't so far out of the city that I should be losing service, which meant something or someone was blocking the signal from the inside.

Just one more reason I should have been spinning around and looking for the closest exit. Instead of moving farther down the abandoned halls as the lights seemed to sense my presence and flick on over my path so that I could make out the next few feet of tile. Then the next. And the next. And the next. Until I was standing at another junction, walls and doors climbing as far as the eye could see.

This was getting me nowhere but lost. And quick.

Though I didn't know what choice I had, considering I wasn't sure I could find my way back to the entrance if I tried.

Drop the box off, Emily.

It was meant to be simple. Deliver a package and be on my way. But there was no mention of what to do if there was no one here to accept it. I highly doubted Marisela would appreciate me tucking the thing under the mat and calling it a job well done. While something in my gut told me letting her down came with more than a spot in the unemployment line. It didn't matter how long I'd known her, the woman didn't make friends. She made connections and then she severed them.

Just ask Tate... if you could find him. The cops couldn't.

I took a deep breath, deciding I was better off trying to navigate a hall of funhouse mirrors than figuring out which direction to turn in this literal nuthouse. Pivoted around and headed back the way I came. Except I wasn't headed that way at all.

I peered to the left and then over to the right. Nothing looked familiar—in reality it all looked familiar because it all looked the same—and the lights weren't following me anymore. And before I realized what I was doing, I was running. Turning corners. Stopping short and changing direction. The package the last thing on my mind by this point.

My heart was pounding against my chest, thudding and fluttering in a rhythm that felt completely unnatural as I attempted to find a way out, succeeding in finding a way further *in*. Running around in the dark was a lot like staying in one spot while everything seemed to run around you instead.

None of my other senses did the thing where they were

supposed to compensate for my lack of sight. It was the opposite really. I couldn't hear anything but the thumping behind my ears, couldn't feel anything but the prickling of my own skin, and all I smelled was the fear radiating off my body in waves. Until I came face-first with a wall.

A wall that was somehow able to reach out and clamp down around my shoulders, my arms pinned to my sides as I was lifted in the air and tossed into a metal cart. *A wheelbarrow,* I realized as my ass slid deeper into the slanted bottom, my hands fumbling for the sides as I tried to pull myself up. Only to be shoved back down before a bag was thrown over my head and yanked tight.

Everything was muffled after that. All I could hear were the squeaking and occasional clanking of metal wheels along the sleek tiles, the interior of the bag puffing out and quickly clinging to my mouth as I tested the breathability of the fabric each time my chest failed to completely rise. The lack of oxygen rendered me immobile, my limbs growing heavy and slipping to my sides. My head dipping forward and my neck twisted at an odd angle—which should have been painful but wasn't.

And then the world was quiet. Warm. Dark. *It wasn't so bad actually...*

PART FOUR

THE PRESENT

You see what's holed up in the basement?

I see everything, dumbass. Including what you're doing right now.

Always looking and never touching ain't no way to live, bro.

61

EMILY

"... If I'm careful enough, you'll sure make for one pretty corpse."

The tip of the knife gleamed beneath the fluorescent lighting at the same time recognition slipped past the fogginess of my brain and settled on the tip of my tongue. I couldn't tell you what clicked the final piece of the puzzle into place. Maybe it was my very real demise I saw staring back at me from the corner of the room. Or maybe some part of me had known all along. Knew and refused to accept it.

It didn't matter. Because all that knowledge did was make things much, much worse. For me.

"Cohen! Wait! I... I lost the baby..."

His pupils dilated and his nostrils flared as he sucked in a harsh breath. His glare flicking from my reflection in the knife to my face and back again. I could feel the moisture pooling beneath my lashes, dripping down my cheeks and onto my chin. I didn't bother to wipe it away as I waited for my words to land and stick just long enough to give him pause.

Then I grabbed for his wrist and pivoted myself under-neath his arm, putting as much distance as the space would allow between him and the blade still clutched in his palm. I knew there was nothing stopping him from rushing forward and driving the tip of that same blade into my gut over and over again.

My heart was pumping too fast, my body buzzing with a sudden surge of electricity and I knew in that moment that the bunny on the tv didn't just lie there and wait to die. She squealed and thrashed and clawed. She'd gnaw a limb off if she had to. Because that need to survive was innate. It kept her struggling for air even as she slowly suffocated. Kept her scrambling across the room long after logic told her she was trapped. Had her fighting for her life even when she knew there wasn't a chance in hell she could win.

And right now I was that little bunny, while Cohen was the predator looking to tear me apart.

He forced out a laugh through his tight-set jaw. A sound I didn't recognize coming from a man who was briefly a lover and ten years a stranger. "You didn't lose shit, Emily. Our kid wasn't a packet of gum you accidentally ran through the rinse cycle. No, you allowed some quack to shove a tube up your cunt, blissfully doped up as he tossed the little chunks of shredded meat in a container with the rest of the medical waste. Like it was nothing. Like *I* was nothing." Cohen gestured around the room that had become my prison. "Now who's nothing."

"I didn't—"

The first blow to my face echoed off the stone walls and left me dazed. While the second had me tasting copper as I instinctively tried to swallow it down. And before I realized what I was doing, I'd already returned the favor. My palm swollen and throbbing. His cheek marked with the raised imprint of each of my fingers and his mouth bleeding at one corner.

I watched his tongue peek out and swipe along his bottom lip, a deranged smirk tugging at one side of his face as he stalked forward while I continued to stumble back. Until I was pinned against the closest wall, my chest heaving and my glare defiant.

Cohen grabbed my jaw between his damaged fingers and squeezed until my lips were pinched tight and puckered. "Don't fucking lie to me, pet. I saw the records. I know the date, the time—and good luck finding the fucker who signed off on that shit. He's been rotting in a shallow grave for nearly a decade now. A life for a life. Seemed fair."

Now I was the one laughing, the strangled noise vibrating low in my throat as he continued to squeeze my mouth closed.

"What the fuck is so funny?" he hissed, shoving my head back so hard against the wall I was surprised my skull didn't crack open like an egg fresh out of the carton.

"You. You and that goddamn ego of yours. Seems not much has changed, has it?"

"Make your point, Emily, or I'll make one for you. A nice sharp, shiny point. Jabbed through that smart-ass tongue of yours."

I pushed at his chest, watching as Cohen shuffled back a step, and brushed my wild hair behind my ear as I got my first good look at the man behind the name. Tilting my head to one side as I eyed him from head to toe. Feature to feature. Scar to eye socket.

His jaw was more defined with age, as if he didn't know what it was to smile. Not that he'd smiled much in college either. He carried a different kind of arrogance on his shoulders, though. Almost as though his posturing was a shield instead of the blatant egotism that used to straighten his spine.

But his eye, his one piercing blue eye...

Other than the fact its counterpart was missing, that piece of him was the same. Nothing changed when it came to the way he looked at me, no matter what hatred he was spewing from his lips. His glare was hitched on my every move like it hypnotized him. Like he didn't know what it was to be in this world without me. Like I was the one reason he woke up in the morning. What kept his heart pumping in his chest and the air filtering through his lungs.

"I don't know what it is you think you know, what you think you saw in the medical records I'm sure you obtained illegally, but you might want to read them again. Maybe get a second fucking opinion from someone who isn't so caught up in themselves they fill in the blanks instead of seeing what's right in front of their fucked-up face." I crossed my arms over my chest, my attention laser-focused even as I felt the little droplets of blood trickling down from my forehead before sliding down my chin. "Go on, Dr. Michaels. Phone a friend. I'll be waiting right fucking here with bells on."

62

COHEN

I should have just left her bare ass to rot in that room, stopped feeding her and waited until she slowly withered away to a pile of fucking bones. Borrowed Donnie's wheelbarrow, the same one he used to drop her at my bedroom door, and tossed her in the incinerator. Watched as that pile turned to ash. Along with the poison she injected into my veins every time she looked at me like I was the villain in this story. When she was the one with a perfect face, flawless fucking skin, not a visible scar to indicate all the ugliness beneath her surface.

Instead, I slammed the door and stomped into the freight elevator, pushing the button that would take me out of the basement and land me two floors up. Right outside Adrian's office with Emily's records tucked under my arm and a fifteen blade concealed by my sleeve. First lie flung my way would have me popping out his eye and using as a stress ball.

I didn't have patience for anymore bullshit today. Least of all from the fucker currently smirking at me from behind his desk.

Adrian didn't spare me another glance as he tossed a small cardboard box in the air, catching it twice more before shoving it into his desk. "Finally coming up for air, Dr. Michaels?"

I dropped the brown folder in front of him, the pages worn by both time and obsession. Truth was the file itself didn't have much purpose anymore. Not when every word was archived in the deep recesses of my brain, imbedded there like a core memory I couldn't forget even if I wanted to.

I didn't want to. I wanted to remember what she did. And I wanted her to remember it too.

Adrian flicked his eyes downward. Blinked once and then pinned me with a glare. His expression as cold as the organs we had packed in ice a couple of rooms down.

"Something you wanna tell me?" I ground my teeth, feeling the ache radiate up my jaw and make itself at home at the base of my skull.

There was that pounding again.

Tension thickened the air until Adrian slammed his palms down on the piles of paperwork spread across his desk before pushing up from his chair. "No, Dr. Michaels, is there something you wanna tell me? *Thank you* would be a good start."

"For what?"

"For bringing your little chick home to roost..." He walked his fingers across Emily's folder, a single brow arched with the same arrogance that curled the top of his lip. One of these days, I'd cut that smirk right off his fucking face. I just wasn't sure if that day was today. "You didn't think you'd find her without me, did you?"

"You don't know that."

We both knew it was a lie. But only one of us cared to

admit it. And it sure as hell wasn't me. Adrian had given me the occasional picture over the years. Always blurry. Always at a distance. Always promising me more. If I rolled over and showed the fucker my belly. Didn't really have any choice but to play nice. At the time. He had the resources, the funds, and I had an addiction to feed. One that had been building up and was close to exploding.

So I did what I had to do to get here, jerking off to those same images and the memories I'd had so engrained in my brain I could still smell her cunt, all while the fucker shoved more empty promises down my throat and cash in my hand. The latter I squirreled away, slowly adding to the room that had become her cell. Maybe even her tomb, depending on how things went.

I liked to plan but I wasn't afraid to improvise if it came to that either.

"Five years, Cohen. Might as well have been an eternity of watching you obsess over that girl. And now that you have her, you come bursting into my office with that sour expression on... half your face. Why?"

I uncrossed my arms and gestured to Emily's folder, my fingers itching to tug my blade free and see the gray steel turn red. "I want the original."

"Why?"

"I wanna know what you're hiding, what parts you took out."

Adrian lifted a shoulder into a half-shrug. "It's all there, Dr. Michaels. Just because you don't see something doesn't mean it's missing."

"What the fuck is that supposed to mean?"

"It *means* take another look with a fresh set of..." He trailed off while twirling a dismissive finger in the air.

"Well, you know how the saying goes. No need to open old wounds."

He extended an arm, and I snatched the folder out of his hands before throwing my ass into the closest chair.

Female patient, age nineteen, seen at Mercy General on the 28th of October for a scheduled D&C. Four-hundred micrograms of misoprostol administered orally three hours prior to scheduled procedure. Evacuation completed by attending without incident. Patient alert and oriented...

I could recite this shit word for word. Nothing was different. No annotation missed. I threw the chart back across the room, watching the pages flutter towards the ceiling before scattering along the floor.

This was a waste of my fucking time, a way for Lambert to get his rocks off by watching me squirm in my seat. No matter how much she may have wanted to, Emily couldn't argue facts. Everything was right there in black and white.

Adrian didn't spare me a glance as he yanked the bottom drawer of his desk open and withdrew a duplicate file. Though something told me it wasn't the original either. Fucker probably had a stock room of those things just waiting for the right moment to shove them in my face again.

He cleared his throat before repeating the same words I'd already read for myself. "Female patient, age nineteen, seen at Mercy General on the 28th of October for a sched-uled D&C—"

"I already—"

He slapped another heavy palm down on his desk. *So*

much for the cool façade. "Stop using your mouth for one goddamn second and maybe your brain will finally catch up." Then he cracked his neck from side to side, quietly tucking away his hair-trigger temper like it was never there. "I'd hoped you'd come to the conclusion on your own, but seeing as a decade has done nothing but thicken that skull of yours, I'll explain it in terms even you can understand."

It didn't matter how many years you spent under Adrian's thumb, how many more you saw in your future, the guy always had this way of reminding you that you were lower than the shit under his polished shoes. And that he had no problem scraping you off as soon as he was done with you.

I took solace in the fact that one day someone was gonna bend him over and shove that same shoe up his ass. The left side of my mouth tugging into a smirk at the thought while he continued to enjoy the sound of his own voice.

"A dilation and curettage procedure has more than one use, Dr. Michaels. Something you should be more than aware of if you attended even one day of your gynecological rotation." He shot me a glare from across his desk. "To force a surgical evacuation and—"

"Assist in the shedding of the uterine wall after a spontaneous abortion..."

"Among other therapeutic and diagnostic uses, yes." He nodded, white noise filtering through the air, but I wasn't listening anymore.

My feet were already taking me towards the door, muscle memory guiding me down the hall, my brain in search of the closest vice to quiet all the static in my head. Didn't care if it was liquor or pills as long as it did the trick.

A few minutes later, I found myself at the bottom of an

empty vodka bottle. Never liked the taste of that shit but Casper always had a stash somewhere in his bunk and I wasn't above raiding it. I tossed it against the wall, watching the glass shatter before reaching an arm under his bed and grabbing another. Rinse and repeat until the rest of me was as numb as my hand.

63
CASPER

It took Frankie's little fuck toy several long moments to realize we were watching her. But fuck if the look on her face wasn't worth it when she did. Her eyes flicked to the hospital blanket just out of reach and back to the open door behind us.

I could see all the wheels turning in her head. Chick was trying to decide what was more important. Her freedom or her dignity when the answer was simple.

Neither. Not here at Briarwood. Little Miss Golden Pussy—*how else do ya explain Frank's addiction*—was in Renegade territory now. Which meant the only way out was after a visit to the chop shop. A couple of pounds and a few garbage bags at a time.

I saw it. The second she decided her bare ass was the lesser of two evils, her toothpick legs rushing forward as fast as they could take her before Bugs stepped out to block her path.

I could picture the smirk tipping up the fucker's mouth even from behind his mask. It was the way he tilted his head to one side, something he always did whenever he enjoyed fucking with someone. Guy had to get out more—it was only a matter of time before all those screens rotted his brain and shit started oozing out his ears.

Couldn't imagine it was all that easy to be a tech genius without the whole *genius* part. But not my fucking circus. I liked my monkeys with a lot more coke and a lot fewer sticks up their asses.

I dropped my arm from where I was resting it on the metal frame, silently urging the walking-talking set of tits to make a run for it. What I wouldn't give to see those fucking balloons bounce a few times before I snatched an ankle out from under her.

But our little blow-up doll seemed to think better of it, crossing her arms over her pebbled nipples and eyeing me like I kicked her goddamn puppy. Thing was I was always more interested in pussy cats. Speaking of...

My gaze shot to the fuzz peeking out from between her thighs, enough to tell me old Frankie boy didn't trust his girl with a razor.

Smart. Considering she looked ready to slit my throat. Correction: bitch looked ready to slit *both* our throats.

"Who the fuck are you?" She spat the words between the two of us. Me and Bugs. But they landed on me.

"A friend," I mumbled through the rubber of my favorite mask, tasting my own sweat pooling on the underside. Frankie kept shit hot down here. I grinned at the realization. Sly son of a bitch was doing it for her. He didn't want his princess catching a cold.

Real considerate, that one. Shame about his fucking face.

"Whose friend?" Princess Peach tipped her head back to level her jaw with my chest. "The clerk from the Spirit of Halloween store?"

"Yours, of course." I shrugged before ripping the fabric

hood off my head and tossing it aside—I had a dozen more where those came from. When a Ghostface was too bulky for a job, a little black and white paint did the trick. Nothing made a chick scream like seeing a glow-in-the-dark skull climbing in through her window. Nothing 'cept the cock swinging between my legs of course. "We could be very good friends, Emily. Hell, I could even be your knight in shining armor, if ya let me?"

I reached out a hand to brush her hair out of her face, and the ungrateful Ice Queen slapped my arm aside. "No thanks. And don't fucking touch me."

"Okay, not friends. Got it. Acquaintances, then?" I pivoted on a boot before spinning back around again so that there was barely an inch between my chest and her chin. "Or maybe I'm just the guy who was fucking you in your sleep." I watched her eyes widen as recognition turned our Elsa into an Olaf, and my lips curled into a full-on fucking grin. "Oh, I'm sorry, babe? Did ya really think that shit was a dream?"

"It was... that was you..." Our Sleeping Beauty fumbled over her words as she slowly backed herself into a corner.

I quirked a brow. "Maybe."

"What the fuck do you mean *maybe*?" She stepped closer until she realized what she was doing. And quickly stepped back again.

"I mean, most of the time it was him." I gestured a thumb behind me and her eyes bounced from me to Bugs. "Nah, not him, sweetheart. Unless...?" I glanced over one shoulder. Bugs shook his head from side to side and I turned back around. "Most of the time it was Franks. Some of the time, *maybe* it was me. Can't fault a guy for wanting to know what all the fuss was about."

I pushed off the wall and barely made it a half a step

before the Bride of Frankenstein was lunging for my face. "You fucking asshole!"

I shifted to the side, in time to watch her tumble forward and crack a knee against the cement. I'd help her up but chivalry didn't seem to get me very far with this one. "Maybe. Maybe not. Maybe I never touched you at all. Maybe I just liked to watch through the window. And maybe, just maybe, you're better off not knowing." I rushed forward, jumping up and twisting into a backflip. A hand reaching out and snatching Bugs's mask clean off his head as I landed silently on the heels of my boots. Then I rose to my full height. Grinning wider when our wilting flower choked on a name the moment her eyes swept across his profile.

"Elliot...?"

I slammed the door shut on her face while she pounded those cute little fists of hers against a metal panel that had no chance of opening. "Ya know, a lady shouldn't curse so much," I yelled out, and listened as the cursing got louder.

A for effort. B for creativity. I'd been called worse names by the time I reached my ma's knee.

I pivoted down the hall of doors, only to be tugged back by the collar of my shirt a few seconds later. "Did you really fuck Frankie's girl?" Bugs whispered like the walls had ears, and I guess they did. He should know. 'Cause he was the one who put 'em there.

"I'm gonna tell ya the same thing I told her..." I whispered in reply, my left shoulder jumping up without me even feeling it. "Maybe I did."

"Yeah, well, maybe you have a fucking death wish."

"Ya know what? Maybe I do. Maybe I fucking do," I sang out, shoving my hands into my pockets while the sound of my whistling followed me farther into the shadows, dying off the moment I stepped into the freight elevator and turned around to shoot our one-man IT department another grin.

It seemed Elliot Walker had just as much explaining to do as I did. Difference was I was much better at keeping secrets. Especially when they benefited me.

64
COHEN

A day could have passed, maybe two, before a kick to my ribs had my eyes shooting open and staring into the face of a kid stuck in a man-sized body. At least that was the only theory I could come up with to explain Casper's obsession with Halloween masks. I mean, I had a reason to wear ʼem. Fucker chose to. And something told me it had to do with a lot more than anonymity.

"What the fuck do you want?" I grunted, closing my eyes and dropping my head back down on the cold tile.

"Did ya know Lambo only has nine toes?"

I could feel the fucker staring at me. I didn't care. He could stare all he wanted. I wasn't moving. "Cool, thanks for the intel, Snapple Facts."

"Also, this is my room and you drank all my liquor so get the fuck out."

He had me there.

So I pulled my ass off the floor, using the bedframe to prop myself up before meeting his scowl with a shoulder-check. Everything I could feel was aching. Everything I *couldn't* creaking and cracking with each step I took towards the supply closet. Then I holed myself in a corner and shot my veins up with enough fluids to have me pissing like a racehorse every five seconds.

But at least the headache was gone. Though I couldn't be sure how long that would last as I disengaged the lock on Emily's door and shoved my way inside.

As soon as she caught sight of the movement, she pushed up from the floor and came rushing forward, the hospital blanket draped around her looking like the aftermath of a drunk sorority girl at her first frat party.

If she was hungry, she didn't show it. Crossing her arms over her chest as I lunged an apple in her direction. Her stuck-up ass not even bothering to try to catch it as she watched the fruit hit the ground with a splat.

"What the fuck was that?" she hissed.

"You know what they say? An apple a day keeps the doctor away... Unless you don't want me to stay away. Have you missed me, pet? Your legs trembling with need for me? All wet without any relief for days?"

"Fuck you."

I leaned against the closest wall and eyed her for a few seconds, her face flushed with a hint of anger and a whole lot of lust. And grinned. "You were gonna keep the baby, weren't you?"

"I don't see how that matters now, Cohen. It was ten fucking years ago, and my body seemed to make that choice for us so I didn't have to. Get over it."

I rushed forward and grabbed her by the throat, squeezing just enough to get her attention. "Never. You loved me and wanted to have my kid. Admit it."

"*Never*," she spat, her tone mocking and her confidence far more elevated than it should be.

"You don't have to say it for me to know the truth.

Pretend all you want, pet. Do whatever it is you have to do to convince yourself you weren't obsessed with me. That you didn't seek me out in every room, touch yourself when you were alone in that little twin bed of yours. That you weren't begging me to fuck you with those long stares aimed my way, hoping I'd offer you the slightest hint of attention."

Her mouth twisted to one side, her nostrils flaring with the long breath of air she sucked into her lungs before forcing it out on a huff of annoyance. "I don't even know what to say to that." Emily shook her head. "It's goddamn laughable."

"You don't have to say anything. Your body told me everything I needed to know about you." I lifted a challenging brow. "It still does." I kept guiding her backwards until an uneven divot in the floor had her stumbling, her legs giving out from under her as she landed on her ass.

She peered up at me, her glare just as piercing as when she was standing. "You're so fucking full of yourself."

"So were you. So very full of me. Not all that long ago either. Is that your problem right now? You need to be full of me again." I crouched forward, my knees hovering above the floor, my feet spread wide and balancing the brunt of my weight as I reached out a hand to brush a stray lock of hair from her face.

"Don't you dare touch me." Her teeth were clenched, her jaw set tight as she slapped my palm aside.

"Close your eyes. I smell the same, feel the same. Just imagine I look the same. And I promise you won't be saying that for long." I grabbed her wrists and pinned her arms against her sides before pressing my lips to her cheek. "No, you'll be begging me to touch you, princess."

"The way you look? You honestly think that's the issue I

have with you? With the fact you have me chained up like some dog you found on the street?" She tugged an arm free, fumbling for the scalpel I was concealing in the palm of my hand. I knocked her back down on her ass and sat cross-legged in front of her.

"Sure, let's say that's the only reason." I shrugged a single shoulder.

"I take that back. You're not full of yourself. You are straight-up delusional."

"Or maybe you just can't admit how shallow you are. So narrow-fucking-minded you can't accept the fact you loved a monster. Because he was a pretty monster. And really, what does that say about you, Emily Shaw?"

"I did not love you, Cohen."

I slapped her hard enough to draw blood, and she returned the blow with one of her own.

"I let you fuck me for a brief period of time. I enjoyed the release of endorphins. More than anyone, you should know that is not love. Truth is, I barely knew you. *We barely knew each other*." She laughed, the sound dry and humorless before dying off into a choked noise that bubbled in the back of her throat. Or maybe it was all the blood she was swallowing down.

I shuffled my boots on the cement flooring until my back was pressed against the closest wall, my chest rising and falling in quick succession as I allowed my grip on the blade to loosen. My other hand reached up to swipe at the blood trickling from my lip, the metallic taste resting on the tip of my tongue.

"Oh, I knew you, pet. Inside and out. There's no more intimate a way to know someone than when they're carrying a piece of you inside them." I grinned, watching her face for any hint of emotion. Any sign that she felt something towards me. Even if it settled on hatred. I could work with that.

"You've been here... all this time. All these years. And instead of manning the fuck up and knocking on my door," she hissed, little droplets of red saliva peppering the air before silently dotting the blanket as it slid lower on her chest. "Hell, how about just making a phone call or sending a goddamn letter, you've been here. Doing what? Seething? Plotting? Throwing an adult-sized tantrum because life didn't turn out the way you thought it would? For ten fucking years."

"What was I supposed to do? Show up on your doorstep looking like this?" I circled a finger around my face, observing the way her pupils dilated when her glare hitched on the thick layers of scarring. A stress response. "Take you out to all those fancy dinners *like this*?"

"Who wanted the fancy dinners, Cohen? Because it sure as hell wasn't me."

This time I was the one throwing my head back as I barked out a harsh laugh. "You're telling me you don't like nice things, Emily? You didn't want to be wined and dined before I got my hands on that tight little skirt of yours?"

"So much energy focused on hunting me down and it's like you don't even know me. Maybe you lost some brain cells along with that eye."

I jumped up, my movements silent as I closed the distance so quickly she didn't have the time or ability to react before she was forced to stare me right in the eye. Barely a breath between us as I grunted against the soft skin just under her ear. "Watch your mouth, pet. Or I'll be forced to watch it for you."

"It is your specialty, isn't it? Watching but never really learning a goddamn thing."

"Emily..." I warned. Truth was I liked how close she was to tipping me over that edge. To forcing my hand.

"Shut up for once in your life and listen, Cohen." She shoved at my chest.

I didn't resist, baring my weight on my left palm while my right had my blade at the ready. In case my pet had some more fight left in her.

"Pay the fuck attention. I'm not the one who wanted nice things, who was obsessed with fancy things, who was so hyperfocused on *things* in general. I may not have loved you, Cohen. But given the chance, I could have. I probably would have if it all worked out differently and we had a kid together. And *things* had nothing to do with that."

"I'm not a good man, Emily." Another fact neither one of us could change.

"You don't think I know that? You didn't think I knew that back then? Long before any of... this?" She waved a hand around the room, her eyes bouncing over the various medical equipment I had at my disposal.

And I grinned as an idea started to take shape in my mind.

65
EMILY

Cohen canted his head to the side, his glare penetrating as he twirled the knife in one hand while watching me from the corner of his eye. Almost like the gears inside that cracked skull of his had stopped turning the second his brain settled on its next twisted little thought. My gaze bounced from the look on his face to the way his fingers wrapped tightly around the blade. The tips brushing along the metal. Working it far more gently than those same fingers ever worked me.

I could only imagine what the man was thinking. Actually, I couldn't. And I didn't want to. Some thoughts were far too dark. Even for me.

"I think it's time we dated," he said a bit too calmly.

There was a damn good chance I was hallucinating. Hearing things. Maybe even hysterical. Or I could have been dead and this was my version of hell. Who knew anymore?

Whatever was wrong with me, or him, or both of us... it had me cackling until my chest hurt, my breaths coming out on a wheeze as I choked on a mixture of saliva and blood before forcing both down my throat. A poor man's liquid diet. It did nothing to stave off the hunger pangs but it did ease some of the burning of the acid as a whole lotta nothing churned around in my stomach.

Funny enough, I knew starvation. It was an old childhood friend of mine. And it sure as shit wouldn't break me. Cohen Michaels would have to try a little harder for that.

"Pretty certain we gave that a go in college. And look how well that worked out." I snorted, quickly covering the sound with a hand as I continued to giggle behind the shelter of a cupped palm.

Yeah, probably hysterical. Definitely mad.

Cohen lifted his shoulder into a half shrug. "I don't know. Ten years is a long time to be in a relationship. Can't just throw that all away, now can we, pet?"

"What relationship?" I laughed.

He threw out an arm while gesturing an index finger between the two of us. His expression blank as he replied with as few words as possible. "You and me."

"We are not in relationship, asshole. Hell, what we did back then probably shouldn't have been considered one either."

"I took you on dates before. I enjoyed myself. We should go on more." Cohen nodded once, and I had no doubt that in his head it was a done deal.

That hadn't changed either. It was always about what the *almost* but *not quite* a doctor wanted. Though his arrogance went far beyond the almost part. And landed on the far end of undeniable. Everyone else could get on board or they could get fucked. To him it was just that simple.

"Oh sure, just let me grab my purse and slip into something a little more comfortable and then off we go into the sunset—*you fucking kidnapped me, you psychopath!*" I scooted forward on the heels of my feet, my hand primed and ready to land another slap. Only to have Cohen swipe out and grab my wrist before I could make contact with that look on his too-fucking-smug face.

"You're starting to sound a little bitchy, babe. Are you on the rag or some shit? It's fine if you are." He paused. His glare flitting downward and snapping back up again as a smirk danced across his lips. Before it was gone entirely. His mouth now curled into a snarl that was clearly aimed my way. "I mean, what's a little blood on your dick, am I right?"

Cohen tugged me forward, dragging my top half over his lap as he lifted the thin material of the hospital blanket and exposed my bare ass to the stagnant air. I struggled to pull myself up but his grip was too tight as I shivered without meaning to, my body reacting to the sudden change in temperature as he landed a rough palm against my right cheek. The sharp sting traveled up and down my backside, nearly ringing in my ears before I realized where his hand was going. Then he pried my thighs apart as he dipped a finger as far as he could reach inside me, twisting it around then drawing it out as I glared back at him from over a shoulder.

"What the fuck are you doing?"

"Just lifting the hood to check the oil. Nope, not bleeding," he grunted. "Just being a cunt then." He issued another slap to my left cheek before shoving me aside. Then he was up on his black combat boots, his steps slapping against the concrete—much louder than they needed to be —as he stalked towards the door and slammed it shut again. Also louder than he needed to.

I sat rooted to my spot, the skin on my ass burning and probably two shades darker than it was a few minutes ago as a small part of me considered chasing after him. Seeing if I could escape somehow or at the very least not make it so goddamn easy for everyone. Because now I knew there was an *everyone*. A whole bunch of them. Working together with the shared goal of doing who the fuck knows.

I guess I didn't see the point in pretending anymore. The fantasy where this had been random was gone the moment Mr. IT's creepy-looking bunny mask was tossed aside and I realized just how *very not random* it had all been.

Nope, nothing was coincidental. Not when you're the fucking target.

66

COHEN

What I wanted was a stiff drink. What I needed was a good fuck. After I finished what I started back in college.

I knew she wasn't bleeding. She may have been hiding for the last five years but that didn't mean I stopped keeping track of her ovulation cycle. No, bending Emily over my knee was more about making a point. Reminding her I owned every part of her. And being bratty wouldn't earn her any favors.

That shit wasn't cute anymore.

I had no doubt she'd be knocked up with my next kid by month's end, if she wasn't well on her way already. She'd give me that little piece of herself I'd been missing and I'd figure out what to do with its mother later. That didn't mean shit was forgiven and forgotten. The details might have been a little obscure but none of it changed the fact she'd been whoring around on me for nearly a decade.

Didn't matter if she knew I was watching her or not. She should have felt it. Just like I felt her down to my fucking bones, so ingrained I couldn't take my first real breath until we were in the same room again.

I hiked my bugout bag on one shoulder, pushing through the door before slamming it in place again. I already knew I had a runner and I wasn't in the mood to be mowing anyone down.

Tomorrow might be a different story. There was something to be said about the chase, about that first whiff of fear permeating the air.

Emily didn't say a word as I stalked over to the metal table I had bolted to the floor and dropped my bag on top. The sound of me wrenching open the zipper broke the silence before I shoved a hand inside. Tugged out the blue dress I'd pulled out of storage and tossed it in her direction.

"Put it on." My tone should have been enough to warn her it wasn't an option, but Emily's smart fucking mouth had always been her biggest flaw.

"Why?"

"Can't have the mother of my child walking around bare-assed where any old creep could see."

"I'm locked in a room, Cohen. The only people seeing shit are the ones you're working with."

"Exactly my fucking point. A buncha creeps." I didn't bother looking up as I laid her dinner out on the table. She needed more protein. I'd let her snack on nuts when she wasn't too busy emptying mine.

She'd gotten too fucking skinny without me around to make sure she ate, her collarbone protruding out of her neckline and barely any meat left on that ass. Which was just something else we had to rectify. Had to plump her up a bit so that shit jiggled when I gave it a decent slap. Couldn't risk her having another miscarriage because she didn't know how to take care of her-fucking-self.

Then again, that's why she had me. To make sure she did what was expected of her for the next nine months or so.

I dragged the new chair I brought her across the room —metal, in case she got anymore bright ideas about stabbing me in the remaining eye this time—and dropped it in front of the table before gesturing for Emily to sit.

She mumbled under her breath while yanking the blue fabric of the dress over her head and smoothing it around her body. Taking slow, begrudging steps forward until her ass was firmly planted on the seat.

"Eat."

Another command she was remiss to follow until the contracting of her abdominal muscles, the body's way of ensuring its survival, had her reaching out a hand and plucking up one half of the sandwich I'd made for her. Prosciutto and provolone. She needed the sodium.

I also knew it was her favorite. Because I paid attention.

"See how much better things can be if you just do as you're told, pet." I slid over to perch myself on the edge of the desk. My legs spread out in front of me and my arms crossed over my chest. I still had a blade tucked into the pocket of my tac pants but I'd wait to see if she needed to find out the hard way again.

"I'm just hoping that if I eat quick enough, I'll choke. Or maybe today's my lucky day and the shit's actually poisoned." Emily's lips curled into a sneer as she bit down on the bread and tugged roughly with her teeth. Likely pretending she was tearing into some part of me instead.

That was fine. Like I said, she could hate me as much as she wanted. Shit was so close to love I might as well be dropping down on a knee.

"Don't speak with your mouth full, Emily. It's not

polite." My grin grew as her scowl deepened. And I had to admit it was a nice change of pace.

I finally understood why Casper liked getting under my skin so fucking much. Shit was entertaining. *Damn fucking cathartic.*

I reached into the bag, pulling out a bottle of water and popping the cap. I took a long swig before passing it to Emily. "Unfortunately, this isn't poisoned either."

She swiped the bottle out of my hand, nearly draining the whole thing in one long gulp.

I swiped it back and slammed it on the table. "Slow or you're gonna make yourself puke."

"Thanks, Doc. Where would I be without you?"

I lifted a shoulder. "Probably married to some small-dicked prick in a cheap suit. Who'd throw your legs in the air, forcing you to stare up at a dusty old ceiling fan while faking your way through orgasms. Night after night, year after year, until one of you died."

"Guess I'm lucky you decided to kidnap me, then, huh?" she countered, her voice dripping in the kind of sarcasm I ate for breakfast with a glass of whiskey to wash it all down. Emily shot me another glare, and before she could look away again, I grabbed her chin with my thumb and index finger, wrenching her face in my direction.

"You have no fucking idea how right you are, pet. But you're about to find out."

67
EMILY

"..."You're about to find out."

Cohen's voice took on that eerily calm tone again. The one that told me he was anything but *calm*, his expression absolutely feral when he reached forward and ripped the chair out from under me before tossing it aside.

I didn't know what I'd said or did to trigger him this time. But my reflexes had me jumping to my feet so that I wouldn't land my ass on the solid floor and then he was behind me. His thick thighs pinning my hips in place and a heavy palm shoving my head down on the table in front of us. My cheek pressed to the solid surface while he tugged the hem of the dress he forced me to wear up until it was covering the exposed side of my face.

Light streamed past the porous fabric enough that I could see movement but not much else. My hearing though? It was never fucking better. I could hear everything.

The sound of his zipper as it lowered and the wrenching down of his pants. The freeing of his cock and the shuffling of his boots as they scuffed the floor behind me. How heavy his breaths seemed each time he sucked in a lungful of air and hissed it back out again. Then there was the slapping of skin and the sloshing of bodily fluid. The pounding of my waist against the table's ledge and the creaking of its legs. The way the lights buzzed in the background, baring witness to my humiliation while doing nothing to stop it.

It was okay though, because I didn't do anything to stop it either. Finally understanding what it meant to be a deer caught in the headlights. Watching the oncoming traffic barreling towards you but finding yourself unable to get out of the way.

Not long after that the grunts started, followed by the knocking of the table against the concrete behind it. I could hear it all while feeling absolutely nothing. Even as his lips pressed next to my ear, whispering their ownership at the same time the rest of his body proved it.

Deep down, I thought knowing who he was would somehow make it better. Easier to accept. But I think all it did was shut me down. Strip some of the fight I'd always thought was innate.

It was a weird way to prove that it wasn't.

By the time his rhythm was quickening, jerking, his breaths more stuttered and the friction between my thighs more intense, I was already miles away. Aware that my body was responding to him even when my brain was detached.

It wasn't until I felt my dress being smoothed back into place, my vision no longer obscured by a light-blue haze, that I noticed the stream of warm liquid trailing down one leg before dripping onto the top of my foot. Then the sandwich was rising up in my stomach, and the next thing I knew, what was left of it was spewing from my mouth and splattering on the floor.

And suddenly I couldn't hear anything but the thumping of my temples and the condescending tone of Cohen's voice.

"Another thing you'd do well to remember, Emily. We do not waste food in this house."

I WAS STILL IN A DAZE, no recollection of moving or being moved, while my current surroundings told me that was exactly what had happened. The black-and-white tiles a stark contrast to the all-gray room I was used to seeing. But it was the shock of the scalding water hitting my back that sent me crashing into reality.

I didn't remember the last time I took a shower, let alone a bath. But I had to admit that once the initial surprise wore off, the feel of the bubbles popping up around me was nice. Much nicer than anything I'd experienced in days.

I sank deeper into the water. Leaned farther back against what I now realized was a chest tucked up behind me. I lifted my chin and found myself staring into a single blue eye. Then his rough hands, much rougher on one side, were rubbing up and down my arms. Swiping the bubbles aside and working the kinks out of my neck.

This was exactly why Cohen Michaels was so bad for me. Far more deadly than any poison I feared he might slip into my food. It was his intoxicating yo-yo effect, giving you just enough string at the end to hang yourself before tugging you back towards him again.

The worst part was the fact that I knew it. Recognized it. Leaned into it. Then tried to fight against it.

I hummed to myself when he combed his fingers through my hair and worked out the knots, unusually gentle on the same scalp he had no problem yanking in every direction whenever he was grinding up behind me.

I could feel my muscles relaxing under his touch, my head resting on his chest and my eyes starting to close even as he shifted me onto his lap, his cock dangerously close to the spot that landed me here in the first place.

My lashes didn't flutter open again until long after the tub water had turned cold and I was already wrapped up in a sheet, my body curled up on the softest thing I'd slept on since I stepped through the front doors of Briarwood—*that lost memory was now haunting me too.*

I dug my elbow into the mattress, attempting to roll onto my side, only to have a large arm tug me back against the bed. Cohen's bed. This room far different from any of the others I'd been lucky enough to peek inside during the entirety of my confinement. But no less terrifying.

68

COHEN

I didn't have any plans of taking Emily out of that room *or* bringing her to my bed, but I slept much better when she was within arm's reach. It was why I often found myself knocked out in my chair in the observation room, my feet kicked up on the desk after hours of watching her both through the two-way glass and on the camera feed. I liked knowing that when I opened my eye, she'd be there.

Which also meant I wasn't letting her get away again. I didn't care what it took to keep her under lock and key, how much money I had to drain into upgrading my equipment and security procedures. Hell, I'd turn the damn basement into a fucking nursery if I had to. A mausoleum after that. Whatever it took to ensure my pet was never out of my sight.

I glanced down, my gaze tracing over all the soft curves of her profile, and had to admit she was beautiful when she slept. More than fuckable when her mouth parted on a sigh. And downright perfect when she wasn't able to talk back.

I watched her for another moment, then reached out a

hand and ratcheted her restraints in place. One on each wrist and ankle. Then I shot her thigh with a hefty dose of adrenaline to counteract the sedative I slipped into her water bottle. My pet should have paid better attention. Then maybe she would have noticed I didn't swallow.

That was her job. When she wasn't too busy puking everything back up again. Lucky for us enough made it into her system or else I would have had a lot more work ahead of me and she would have had a lot more pain in her future.

Once again, I was only looking out for both our best interests.

Emily's eyes shot open, her mouth popping wide on a sharp gasp as she sucked more oxygen into her lungs. Her airways dilating and her skin blanching as blood flow was diverted to her heart and brain. When she started thrashing against her restraints, I knew it'd made its way to her musculoskeletal system.

"Morning, sunshine. I assume you slept well?" I arched a questioning eyebrow as she slung a few very unladylike words in my direction. "Now, now, is that anyway to treat the father of your child?"

"I'm not pregnant, asshole."

"Not yet, you're not," I hummed, snapping my gloves on before laying out each of my sterile instruments across the tray. Don't get me wrong, I thoroughly enjoyed doing this shit the old-fashioned way. But patience wasn't a virtue I had time to indulge anymore.

I could feel her eyes on me, watching my every step as I prepared the syringe. Flicking the side with my thumb and index finger until the fluid settled at the bottom. Then ripped off the light-blue surgical mask and tossed it in the medical waste bin. Most of this was unnecessary. For aesthetics. It had been a while since I had an audience and I had to admit I missed all the attention. It was a goddamn aphrodisiac if the grinding of my zipper were anything to go by.

There'd be time for that later. Right now I had a patient to attend to.

I stepped around the metal surgical table until I was positioned between Emily's legs, grabbing each ankle and drawing them apart before forcing her knees to bend with the makeshift stirrups I'd fashioned for just such an occasion. She responded with another sharp gasp and a lot more expletives.

I ignored the filth coming out of her mouth as I reached for the syringe I'd left to settle on the tray. Time was of the essence after all. The sample needed to be fresh, less than thirty minutes from preparation to insertion if we wanted the best results. Which we did, of course. Emily just didn't know it yet. Motherhood would grow on her. I was sure of it.

I lifted the hem of her new hospital gown, seeing as my little pet didn't appreciate the dress I'd gifted her, and peered up at Emily from between her spread thighs.

"What the fuck are you doing, Cohen?" she hissed between her teeth, but I could see the terror in her eyes.

It did things to me. Sent a shiver down my spine to the base of my balls. The kind that would have me popping a button if I weren't careful.

I remained statue still, refusing to show her the effect she had on me, before I allowed one side of my face to tug back into a smirk. "What does it look like we're doing, Emily? We're making another baby."

Before she could respond, I jammed the syringe into her tight cunt, rolling back a bit on my stool to watch the way her pussy ate it up. Inch after inch disappearing between a pair of pretty pink lips. Like her body couldn't wait to get another taste of me.

The thing was... Emily could call me delusional till she turned blue in the face. Claim I was out of my mind and only seeing what I wanted to see. But none if it changed the way she responded to me. How pliant she became in my hands or how easily she caved beneath the pressure of my touch.

She was just as obsessed as I was. I just wasn't in denial about it. And after a little more coaxing, my pet wouldn't be either.

I tugged off my gloves, one at a time, before tossing them across the room. Not bothering to see where they landed before yanking down my zipper and pulling my cock free. A few quick strokes from base to tip and I was ready to make sure the first dose stuck. Then offer her another, drenching her womb with so much of my cum my spermatozoa would be seeping through her uterine walls and finding their own damn eggs.

69
EMILY

My heart was beating much faster than it should. Almost like the damn thing was trying to pump its way out of my chest. My stomach fluttering in waves and sweat beading on my forehead. Those very same little droplets of moisture then dripping down my temples and pooling in my hair. I was gulping in breath after breath, my lungs expanding and contracting at double the speed and my skin hot all over.

I felt like I was both dying and being resurrected at the same time.

I needed to get out of here. This room. This building. But no matter how hard I tried to yank myself free, the straps on my arms and legs wouldn't budge. A realization that seemed to send my anxiety into overdrive. Almost as much as the idea of being forced to have a kid with the madman playing the part of a mad scientist.

I'd take a coat hanger to myself before I'd let that happen. He'd figure that out soon enough.

I felt like I was fucking dying as Cohen dropped a knee onto the table, leaning forward before quickly shoving himself inside me. The first thrust left me gasping. The second and third had me squeezing my eyes shut while everything after that didn't really register as my lashes fluttered open again and I stared past the top of his skull into the blinding whiteness of the overhead lights.

His voice was close to my ear again, his rough facial hair scraping across my cheek as he whispered a mixture of promises and threats. None of them meaning much of anything. They were just words. And this was just a moment in time. Like everything else, it would all pass.

At least that's what I kept telling myself until his hand migrated to the space between where our bodies were joined. His fingers circling. Making slow, sensual movements over my clit. While he continued to grind on top of me, matching the speed and rhythm. Each soft flick sent goose bumps rising across my skin, the hair on the back of my neck standing on end and my toes curling.

I didn't want to enjoy it. The things he was doing to my body. I didn't want to acknowledge the tightening in my lower stomach or the pressure building between my legs. But it'd be so much easier if I did. If I pretended I liked it as much as my nerve endings seemed to.

It wasn't giving up. It was giving in. It was getting by until I could get out.

So I did. I closed my eyes, tipped my head back, and surrendered to the sensations. The push and pull. The delicious friction. The smell of soap and cologne. It may have been ten years since I allowed myself to bend to his will, but something about it was so familiar. And strangely nostalgic. Like my body recognized him even when I couldn't.

I knew I was fucked. In every possible way a person could be fucked. But I couldn't be bothered to care when my thighs began shaking. My nipples tenting the thin fabric that barely separated us and my walls contracting and sucking him deeper. Keeping him close. Trapped. Until we both got what we wanted from each other. Then I hit that point of no return, allowing wave after wave of ecstasy to wash over my body as I twitched and trembled beneath him. One, two, three more pumps and Cohen was right there with me. A single eyebrow raised and a stupid fucking grin on his face.

"Do you know what happens to a woman's body when she experiences an orgasm?" It was one of those questions that wasn't really a question, seeing as he kept talking anyway. "Besides a natural rise in blood pressure and release of oxytocin—the hormone that bonds you with your partner and makes you much more receptive to inter-mingling your DNA—the pelvis muscles contract, raising the cervix while pooling the sperm at the point of entry, which is believed to increase the likelihood of conception by nearly fifty percent."

He didn't have to explain what he was telling me without telling me anything—and I didn't mean all the self-inflated doctor talk. No, he was saying this entire exchange had been about him and what he wanted. My pleasure just a byproduct of his manipulation.

Then he was pushing off the metal table, the smell of sex and shame permeating the air as Cohen tugged his pants back in place and adjusted his zipper. I watched him walk into a storage closet, reappearing a second later with a pillow tucked under his arm and a bottle of water in his hand. Two more steps forward had him standing between my legs again as he shoved the pillow under my ass before using the restraints on my ankles to raise my knees. He bent down, locking something in place and then his head was popping back up again.

"There's no scientific evidence to suggest lying flat does much of anything. But it sure as shit doesn't hurt to try, now does it, pet?" Cohen said with a wink, which wasn't much different from blinking when you only had one eye, as he maneuvered around the table to position himself by my head. His crotch at eye level now.

He twisted off the bottle top with his teeth before taking a long swig of water, his cheeks puffing out as he held it there. Using his fingers to pry my mouth open and pinch my nose closed as he lowered his face and allowed the water to slowly drip through his lips onto mine.

I had two choices. Swallow or choke. Which wasn't much of a choice at all.

70
COHEN

I continued our little sessions for the next three days. Sedating and securing Emily to my surgical table. Inseminating her with my carefully collected... *supply* and fucking it deep into her cunt. Refusing to waste a drop. Even going as far as scooping up whatever was left over and shoving it back inside her. Drawing my fingers in and out until she was squirming against my hand, cursing my name as much as she was begging me not to stop. Which was just more proof I knew what she wanted far better than she did.

The girl was fucking stubborn. So I did my best to fuck that stubbornness out of her.

Truth was I didn't need to keep her strapped to my table for more than a day. The ovulation window thirty-two hours max. But even the most skilled physician knew it was only practical to give yourself a little buffer room. Biology was one of those areas that had a lot of shades of gray while the human body was as much a guessing game as it was an exact science.

But Emily's body? There was no mystery there. It was the kind of puzzle I had all the pieces to. Especially now as I stared down at layer after layer of her unmarked skin. Just waiting for me to claim it as mine as I pulled up a stool and positioned myself between her splayed legs. Her angled knees opening her wide for my viewing pleasure. Every part of her screaming at me to claim it as mine. Until there was no doubting it ever again.

I mean, the things she'd forced me to do for her. The lives I took, the frozen cadavers I'd cut up and the viable organs I'd wasted. The evidence I'd burned and the time I'd lost. No matter what I did, it never seemed like it was enough.

The thought had me reaching for an alcohol swab, my fingers making quick work of prepping the area to reduce the chances of infection. Wiping down the incision point with some clean gauze before swapping that out for my scalpel.

This time my pet would come to with a different surge of adrenaline, brought on by her central nervous system's natural pain receptors rather than forced on by a hypodermic needle, as I took the first slice into her pliant flesh. The elasticity telling me it was healthy as I cut past the epidermis and headed for the spongier subcutaneous tissue before her eyes were snapping open and she was flailing against her restraints.

There she was, the hellion behind the halo.

"Careful, pet, or I might slip," I hummed through my surgical mask, my eye focused on the task at hand rather than my disgruntled patient as my steadied blade hovered just above her femoral artery. The slightest nick could turn a little knife play into straight-up exsanguination.

And no one wanted that, now did they?

She couldn't see what I was doing but I was certain she could feel it as each fresh stream of blood added to the one next to it, collectively pooling on the surgical pad I'd placed under her leg. Almost as if my subconscious knew what I was planning before I did.

When the string of expletives turned to a softened plea, my lips curled into a grin. I fucking loved how weak her voice sounded. Knowing that I'd broken her even momentarily.

"Cohen, please..." Her breath hitched on a silent sob as my blade made the final curve of the C. Then shifted over two centimeters and started on the first line of the M.

Why, look at that...

Now there was no second-guessing when it came to who she belonged to. Me. Mind and *body*. As for her soul, that was mine a long time ago. When I spent all those nights corrupting her. Ensuring the only place she was going was down. On me.

You see, I didn't believe in an afterlife. 'Cause if I did, we were all fucked.

"Stay perfectly still or you'll ruin your clothes."

"What did you do, Cohen?" she hissed, gnashing her teeth as she attempted to chew through her restraints. She wouldn't get very far. It was medical-grade, used to keep a noncompliant patient strapped to their hospital bed. And my little hellcat was the epitome of noncompliant, teetering dangerously close to downright disrespectful.

"What I should have done a long time ago." Ask a vague question, get a vague answer. My pet should have known better by now. She tried to play that game with me already and we saw how far that got her.

I glanced down at the sundress I'd presented her with today, canting my head to one side as I watched the red seep into the white fabric. It was fitting really. This woman was as much a stain on my sanity as I was a mark on her flesh. Then pushed up from my stool before slipping inside the med supply closet. Grabbing a bottle of iodine and some liquid skin adhesive. Both of which I'd use to ensure proper scarification of the wound.

Healing would be an extensive process, an art form that required a proper balance between staving off infection and ensuring the flesh remained as damaged as possible.

I'd hate to have to start over on the other thigh.

I'd lost count of the days, the hours both rushing by and dragging on. Something that seemed to go hand in hand with having nothing to look at but four walls, a concrete floor, and one watchful eye.

I passed the time searching for patterns in the cracks in the ceiling, staring at the overhead lighting until one of us was forced to look away—*no surprise it was always me.* When it came to Cohen, it was usually me too. His glare even more penetrating than the searing light.

Like how he was using it on me right now, somehow stripping away every layer and seeing through me. As he took a step forward. Then two. Until he was standing in front of me. Not even a breath between us when he grunted the first words he'd spoken to me all morning.

"Blood or piss. Dealer's choice, pet." He slammed the tiny plastic cup on the table to my left, before presenting me with the needle and test tube he had wrapped up in one gloved palm.

When I peered back up at him, he was grinning. A light-blue surgical mask cupped over his ears and one eyebrow lifted in challenge. I noticed he was doing that more frequently now. Covering his face. I glanced around the room, my gaze sweeping across the cobwebs and insect corpses piled up in the corners before landing back on Cohen again. I also knew the mask had nothing to do with the sick fucker wanting to keep a sterile environment.

No, it was his little insecurity peeking out. The fact he honestly thought I'd rejected him because of the way he looked. Instead of the horrendous things he'd been doing. Truth was, the scars didn't bother me. Neither did the eye socket he refused to hide. Which was just another contradiction that made him the level of crazy that he was.

Must have been hard for an egotist to lose the thing that made him so egotistical in the first place. Or so I could only assume. It wasn't like he'd ever tell me.

I snatched the plastic cup off the table without another word and stalked over to the little metal bucket in the corner. The one I was forced to use when Cohen wasn't around or willing to escort me to an actual bathroom. I'd gotten over the whole invasion of privacy thing real quick. I didn't see the point in stressing over the fucker's literal take on an open-door policy.

If watching me... do *everything* disgusted the man, he sure as hell didn't make mention of it. No matter how much that might have worked in my favor.

I hovered over my makeshift toilet, my thigh muscles used to the strain this position put on my lower back, and tried to think about waterfalls and sprinklers as I coaxed my bladder to empty. I wasn't a shy pisser or anything. I was just dehydrated. Seeing as the man in front of me controlled everything that went into and came out of my body. Though some part of me had to admit he was much better at it than I was when I was living on my own.

The thought gave me pause. *Was this living?*

There was oxygen in my lungs. Blood coursing through my veins and a heart pumping in my chest. But it still felt more like existing than anything else. Which honestly wasn't all that different from what I was doing before, I guess.

When the cup was finally full enough to call it a sample, the color a few shades darker than I knew it should be, I pushed up off the wall. Finding my balance before closing the distance between myself and the good doctor.

Cohen eyed my every movement as he reached out a hand from his crossed arms. His posture stiff as I shuffled forward a step to meet him halfway. Until some deranged voice in my ear had me falling short. I tilted my head to the side and watched the dark-yellow contents flip over and splash across his boots.

I couldn't tell you why I did it. Maybe that little devil resting on my shoulder got the best of me. Maybe I was bored. Or maybe defiance was just my second nature. Either way, the look on his face as he tugged off his surgical mask and tossed it aside and the quickness of his steps as he backed me into the closest wall told me I'd fucked up big time.

His hand speared out and pressed against my jugular, his knee digging into a pressure point in my thigh as his other fist white-knuckled the small knife he always kept on his person. He touched the tip under my left eye, just enough to sting as he brushed his lips over the shell of my ear.

"I should cut it out, you know. Give us a matching set. What a pretty pair we'd make, don't you think, Emily?"

I tried to swallow past his grip on my throat, tried to form words, and quickly realized he had no intention of letting me speak. All I could do was suck in whatever air I could force through my nostrils, squeezing my eyes shut as Cohen pressed an open-mouthed kiss on my lips before dragging his tongue over my face. From chin to temple. Then temple to chin again.

"Blood it is," he whispered against my cheek, seconds before he replaced his breath with the blade as he sliced into my skin with a quick flick of his wrist.

7²
COHEN

The negative result stared back at me from the test window of the rapid serum HCG test I'd set on the counter five minutes ago. I swiped a hand out and sent the cassette flying across the room. Not bothering to see where it landed.

I didn't like losing. More than that, I didn't like when shit didn't go my fucking way. And this was both. Now I had to wait another four weeks before doubling my efforts.

Don't get me wrong, I didn't mind the act itself. Fucking Emily was up there on the list of my favorite pastimes. Right next to fucking *with* her, of course. And I had a full five years of both to make up for. But I also had to get back to work before the cash dried up. I had a feeling Adrian didn't believe in IOUs. Unless he was the one asking for 'em.

I pivoted on the heel of my boot, keeping my expression neutral as I approached the metal table. Where I had Emily strapped down and waiting for me. I'd shoved a gag into her mouth and was a hair trigger away from sewing the damn thing shut as I pulled up my stool and rolled it closer to her head. Three quick sutures should do the trick.

On her cheek, not her lips. I hadn't made a decision on the last part yet.

She was watching me with wide eyes as I adjusted my headlamp and lifted the needle to her face. If I were nicer, I'd numb her up a bit first. But my pet needed to understand there were consequences for her actions. Especially actions that resulted in me being covered in human waste.

Truth was, she was fucking lucky all she got was a superficial kiss from my fifteen blade. Shit wouldn't even scar unless I wanted it to. I could make a damn paper cut scar *if I wanted it to.* She was also lucky I didn't make good on my threat to take her eye.

It'd be hard for her to look at me with disgust when she saw the same goddamn thing in the mirror, now wouldn't it? But that was an idea for another day.

Today, I needed to work on fattening her up a bit. Clearly her body was unfit to carry my child or she'd already be well on her way.

I released her legs before moving on to her ankles, then offered her a palm to help lower her back down to her feet. She scowled at me the entire time but didn't dare say a word.

Someone was learning.

It took two steps down the hall for me to realize I was giving my pet far more credit than she was due. She dug her feet into the ground, forcing me to look over a shoulder to glare at her.

I take that back. Emily hadn't learned shit.

"Where are you taking me now, Cohen?" She liked to use my name a lot. I think she thought it humanized me. It didn't. It just turned me the fuck on. Something she claimed she didn't want. Yet she kept doing it anyway.

"To my bedroom, Emily."

"For what?"

"For whatever I damn well please," I grunted before tugging her behind me again. She had to know I only paused in my steps because I chose to. Otherwise we'd still have been moving.

I didn't have to look back again to know she was trying to take in her surroundings. Count doors. Memorize landmarks. There was no point. The tunnels beneath Briarwood were a maze of connecting rooms and dead ends. It took me years to figure them all out for myself. Longer than that to add the additions. Like my bedroom and her little cell. But I'd let her think she had a chance of finding a way out. Because it would be so much more amusing when I finally got to see the expression on her face when she realized she couldn't.

A few minutes later, we were pushing through the metal door of my underground bunker. The room where I spent most of my time when I wasn't out there looking for Emily. It wasn't much to write home about, especially compared to my former life, but it sure as shit beat pissing in a bucket and sleeping on a concrete floor.

I dragged Emily inside and pressed the button on the panel that had everything locking from both sides. One of the little bonuses that came with making nice with Bugs. I helped him with medical shit and he helped me with the techy shit. Everything with the Renegades was about a fair trade—or at least it needed to appear that way. No one really sat down and made sure.

And, yeah, I still thought the name was fucking stupid. But I'd given up on trying to change Casper's mind while

Adrian liked to appease the fucker wherever he could. His way of keeping the kid out of trouble. A feat that was almost as fruitless as whatever plan my pet was concocting in her head as she shot me what I could only assume was supposed to be a scathing glare.

I pulled the chair away from the little dining set I'd positioned in one corner of the room and motioned for Emily to sit down. She complied begrudgingly as I took my seat opposite her, lifting the dome of the plate I'd had Donnie deliver about thirty minutes ago.

It seemed my pet decided to sacrifice a hot meal for acting bratty, so now we both had to suffer and eat our food cold.

I handed her a dulled-edge fork—I wasn't stupid—and began cutting up her steak into bite-sized pieces. Placing the utensil out of her reach but well within mine as soon as I was done. Then I stabbed a soggy piece of broccoli with my own fork, setting it into my mouth and forcing it down before landing my reluctant dinner guest with a smirk.

"Eat up, Emily. We have so much to discuss."

73
EMILY

I eyed the plate in front of me. Portions far larger than anything I'd seen since my last meal on the outside. And could feel the saliva pooling in my mouth.

I knew it would be stupid not to eat. First of all, I was starving. Second, refusing Cohen wasn't an option. He'd get what he wanted. He always got what he wanted. Eventually. Me being here proof enough of that for everyone while the matter of how remained the only question in the equation. That said, I also knew the shit could be laced with any number of things. And the more of myself I gave to him, the more he would take.

It was a lose-lose situation. So I decided I'd rather lose with a much fuller belly and a bit clearer head.

The first bite of cold mashed potatoes had me holding back a moan and quickly scooping up another until I could feel his eye on me. Watching me. Following my every movement. Like I was the most interesting thing in the room. And considering where we were, maybe I was. This place was a far cry from the Cohen Michaels I knew. Or rather knew of. The one who always needed the fastest bike between his legs and the most popular girl... well, also between his legs. It was another reason his interest in me in college never made sense.

Besides the occasional insecurity, I didn't question it all that much at the time. Mostly because I didn't want to know the answer. But now I had to wonder...

Was there something about me that called to him? Something about the darkest parts of him that were drawn to the darkest parts of me? The parts that had me creeping closer to the sound of footsteps in my house instead of running away? Had me waiting for some shadowy figure in my bedroom instead of locking my door? Had me rushing to stash evidence in the trunk of my car instead of bringing it to the police?

Deep down, I had to admit the last five years felt almost empty without that hint of danger that seemed to follow me everywhere. Almost like if adrenaline didn't have my heart rate spiking, I wasn't sure if the damn thing was beating at all.

Maybe some of the demons in this room were my own... Or maybe Stockholm Syndrome was a very real thing and I was starting to sympathize with the devil a little too much. Fuck if I knew anymore. Fuck if I cared about anything other than some more butter melting on my tongue.

By the time my plate was practically licked clean, I was actually grateful for the airiness of the green dress he'd forced me to wear today, which gave my extended belly room to breathe. I set my little shaved-down fork on the table—smart move on his part—and glanced at the man in front of me.

"So what is it that you wanted to discuss, Cohen?" I quirked a questioning brow while settling my hands on my lap. No matter how much I was itching to grab for the knife at his side.

He shrugged a single shoulder. "Our future of course."

"Do we have a future?" I flicked my eyes down, staring at the bruises on my wrists before peering back up at him from beneath my lashes. My expression a mixture of feigned innocence and flat-out sarcasm. "And here I thought killing me was always the end game? Or were all those threats of yours as empty as that socket of yours?"

"The only thing empty in this room, pet, are going to be my balls. When they're through with you." He grinned, clearly proud of himself and his not-all-that-clever retort. "But as far as our future goes, I think you already know the answer to that question."

Cohen leaned forward, and I instinctively leaned back.

"Tell me, Emily. What was your life like without me? When you couldn't feel me in every room with you—never mind. Let me tell you what life was like for me first and see if it sounds familiar, hm?"

He took my silence as a prompt to continue speaking. And I guess it kinda was. It would kill me to admit aloud. But I was a little curious as to what the psycho had to say.

Cohen tipped his chair against the wall behind him and kicked his legs up on the table, not bothering to look down when the plates were jostled aside before shattering on the floor. "The first thing on my mind when I woke up in that hospital bed was you. Then our kid. Followed by how both of you would react to seeing the same shit I saw in the mirror every morning. But ya see, I also didn't care. Because you were mine in every way possible. I'd made sure of that when I knocked you up—"

"On purpose?" The words caught in my throat but I

forced them out anyway. "You fucking got me pregnant on purpose? Why? How?"

He landed the chair on all fours with a loud smack, his palm slamming down in front of me. "*Shh*, you're ruining the best part of the story." Then he cleared his throat. "I thought that would be enough to keep my sweet Emily from going astray—we both know how that ended. However, at the time, I was missing some of the…" He paused to wave a hand in the air. Almost like if he fished long enough he might catch whatever he was searching for. "…*particulars*. Still, I remained faithful while you, my pet, did not."

"You lef—" Another slap on the tabletop had me biting my tongue.

"I never fucking left, Emily. Not once. Ever. In ten fucking years. But you…" Cohen lifted an accusatory finger while venom practically dripped from every word he directed my way. "I had to watch as you whored yourself out to every prick in the city. But that fucker you lured into your bedroom… that was the last fucking straw. You forced my hand. Forced me to show you all the things I did for you behind the scenes. And then you were the one who fucking left. Not me."

74
COHEN

The rage was simmering beneath the surface, reaching its tipping point and quickly boiling over as my arm shot out and closed around Emily's throat. I didn't remember putting it there. I barely registered my fingers as they clamped down on her pressure points, and I watched her struggle for her next breath of air. Her hands flailing out and her nails clawing at my knuckles. If she broke skin, I didn't feel it. I couldn't feel anything beyond the compulsion to destroy. Her and everything that came with her.

Including the things she made me do at every turn. Things like lose my cool. Things like almost kill her without meaning to. Things like this.

When I noticed the color start to drain from her face, her fight waning along with it, I tossed her motionless body over one shoulder. Scanned my thumb over the keypad to the door and took a sharp left. Stalking down the darkened hallway without bothering to flick on the lights. Truth was I didn't need them. Everything was mapped out in my brain like an extension of myself.

I didn't know where I was headed. But I had no doubt I'd figure it out when I got there.

I stopped short when I caught sight of the large metal tub pressed up against the far wall in one of my various surgical rooms. I liked to use it to keep body parts on ice before shipping them off for disposal or prepping them for a secondary buyer. But right now, I had a better idea.

I leaned forward and flipped Emily onto the metal surgical table. Her ass wasn't moving anytime soon so I didn't bother tying her down as I tugged open the freezer door and grabbed a few fresh bags of ice before tipping them into the tub. Repeating the process until it was filled to the brim. Then I dumped in a few buckets of water, giving the whole thing a quick stir with my arm. The chill penetrating through several layers of skin down to the bone. Exactly how I wanted it.

If she were already pregnant, I couldn't risk the safety of the fetus. But seeing as that wasn't an issue right now, I had free rein. Could do with her what I wanted and then patch her up again. Like my own fucked-up little rag doll. A fact that had me scooping her into my arms and tossing her into the ice bath without much thought as to the consequences.

The moment her head went under, I reached in and tugged Emily back to the surface by her hair, watching as she sputtered out a mouthful of water and gulped in a lungful of air. Frozen droplets splashing out and dripping onto the tiled flooring. I leaned over the edge of the tub, grinning wider as her lips turned that familiar shade of blue that told me she was well on her way to hypothermia.

Blue always did suit her best.

"Ya ever heard of hydrotherapy, pet?" I didn't wait for her to answer before continuing with today's history lesson. "The thought behind it was that the cold water constricted blood vessels, reducing inflammation and congestion while redirecting the blood from the brain towards the internal organs."

I lifted a hand to brush the damp hair out of her eyes and Emily snapped her teeth at me. Her expression screaming rabid dog while mine was more the cat who ate the canary.

"It's why you look so pale right now. They also thought it'd reduce agitation caused by increased brain activity— clearly that theory has been proven incorrect. Then again, some people believe it was all a bunch of snake oil, more about control rather than offering any real therapeutic value. What d'you think, babe?"

Her teeth chattered in her jaw, her muscles expanding and contracting and her body trembling in an attempt to produce energy and warm itself up. "F-f-f-f-fuck y-y-y-y-you," she hissed, and I counted to ten in my head before finally reaching back into the tub and tugging her out.

Any longer than that and I would be fucking a corpse tonight. Which, believe it or not, wasn't my thing.

Emily didn't fight me as I threw her over a shoulder again and made my way back to the bedroom. Though something told me it had more to do with a lack of ability than a lack of will.

I threw a hand up and smacked her across one ass cheek, listening as she cursed me under her breath. "Next I'll tell you all about what they thought an orgasm could do for female hysteria."

75
EMILY

The stiff black fabric pressed close to my face and tied in a knot behind my head meant I couldn't see the first rays of sunlight that streamed across my cheeks. But I could feel it. The warmth that kissed my skin and added a hint of color I was certain was missing after weeks spent underground. While the air I sucked into my lungs tasted like freedom instead of death and dust mites. Somehow lighter each time I funneled a new breath through my nostrils and forced it back out my mouth again. My hands were bound and my hearing was dampened yet I felt more free than I had since waking up in that fucking hospital bed.

It was funny how much you missed the little things like fresh air and sunlight when they weren't an option anymore. And what I wouldn't do for a cup of stale coffee from the office breakroom. They could keep the cream and sugar. I'd drink that muddy water straight black right now. Coffee grounds floating around the bottom and all.

I didn't make it a few steps onto the damp, newly cut grass before I was scooped up and tossed into the back of some sort of vehicle. A van? The rumble of the engine followed by the jostling of metal told me we were already moving. Away from wherever Cohen was keeping me, towards who the fuck knows? It wasn't like the asshole gave me an itinerary. For all I knew, he was about to knock me over the head with one of those giant landscaping shovels and drop me in a shallow grave in the middle of the woods. Though I didn't think that was really his style.

Cohen liked shit with a little more flair. And much more theatrics. Fucker really missed his calling. Could have been the next lead in the Phantom of the Opera. He already had the whole messed-up face thing going for him.

A sharp right turn had me gripping on to one of the paneled walls, trying to steady myself before I felt my arm being tugged upwards and then the clank of metal was the only warning I got that I'd just been handcuffed to the ceiling.

"Didn't know it was bring your bitch to work day," a muffled voice called out from the front passenger seat. That creep who got off on watching. I recognized his pattern of speech. Guy sounded like his words were always two steps ahead of the rest of him. But ten steps behind whatever he was thinking. Almost as if his brain and his mouth didn't know what it meant to work in tandem.

"Shut the fuck up unless you want that stupid-ass smirk embedded in your stomach lining," Cohen grunted. Then his mouth was pressed up against my ear, the smell of his cologne an odd sense of comfort all of a sudden. I could only assume it was the familiarity in an unfamiliar setting that had me relaxing against my restraints instead of tugging harder to get free. "Don't give me another reason to kill you today."

"Today?" I muttered under my breath without meaning to.

"Yeah, today. Who knows what I'll decide tomorrow?" Cohen whispered, while pulling a piece of my hair away from my face. Tucking it beneath the blindfold far more gently than his tone suggested he was capable of being.

Then his hand was creeping up the hem of my dress, his fingers dancing across my freshly shaved pussy—something Cohen had insisted on doing himself before we left. And really, what choice did I have when I was strapped down and at the mercy of a madman with a straight razor?

I bit down on my bottom lip, forgetting to keep track of the number of turns the van took the moment the first finger slipped inside me. Moving back and forth in a slow rotation while his thumb circled my clit.

A moan parted my lips before I could swallow it down and then Cohen's breath was by my ear again. His hand continuing to work me as he hissed, "Don't you dare make a fucking sound or I'll be forced to cut out your larynx."

I nodded once because what else could I do? Getting lost to the pleasure was far better than whatever was waiting for me wherever it was we were headed.

Cohen's free hand shot out and clamped around my throat as he shoved me against the closest paneled wall, his hips pinning me in place as he ground his cock into my stomach in time with the curling of his fingers. The flicking of his thumb. The panting of his breath next to my cheek.

I didn't know if it was intended to be a distraction so that I couldn't keep track of how long we'd been driving, or if the crazy son of a bitch really just got off on almost fucking me in front of his friends. It was a moot point either way, because I honestly didn't care about anything else right now. Nothing but the feel of his hand, the building pressure in my lower belly, the wetness pooling between my thighs and dripping down my leg. Everything combined had my head reaching forward, my mouth seeking his even as he pressed harder on my neck. Then his tongue was choking me too. Darting past my lips and thrusting down my throat.

He tasted like mint and nicotine. Flavors that shouldn't go together but for whatever reason worked for him. And did something *to me*.

I could tell he was two seconds away from yanking down his zipper and fucking me for real when the van came to a stop, a few strokes too short for my libido, and then I was left panting as Cohen dropped his hands and stepped back. Leaving me in a pool of my own arousal when he jumped out and slammed the door shut behind him. Not a word shared between us while the lingering silence in the seemingly empty space was more than a little deafening, especially when the only other sound was the whoosh of my own breaths.

I combed an aggravated hand through my hair, slamming the van door shut and padlocking the back before following Casper and Donnie across the manicured driveway of Prescott Estates. Truth was I didn't know what the fuck we were doing here a handful of years later. Though returning to the scene of a crime didn't seem like the smartest move on our parts.

What I did know was that Adrian had another job for us and leaving Emily behind didn't feel like much of an option. Not when one of us was always conveniently absent whenever there was heavy-lifting to be done. It was the same one of us who had eyes on all the live security feed both on and offsite.

It fucking irked me. The way Bugs leered at something he knew damn well didn't fucking belong to him. And that fucker had access to every camera in my possession. Probably a shit-ton of them that weren't too. Which meant my pet was better off locked up in the back of our travel van than at the mercy of a Peeping Tom with too much time and lotion on his hands. She had enough air to last her an hour or so before the heat got to her. Wasn't about to leave that shit idling and chance her running off with the keys.

I also wasn't about to analyze why I suddenly gave a damn about Emily's welfare. *I didn't.* The fact she was mine was more than enough reason for me to justify bringing her along. Besides, I was gonna have to start giving her a bit of a longer leash. Couldn't have our future kid being born in some mold-infested basement. That shit seeped into the air sacs and caused all sorts of respiratory issues. But I had a good few months before I had to worry about any of that. Thanks to another fucking negative HCG test. Until then, I needed to train my pet to come to a quick heel.

By the time we were approaching the front doors, I was reaching out an arm. Tugging Casper behind me by the collar of his toddler-sized t-shirt. Cocky bastard loved showing off his... well, everything.

He tilted his head to grin at me in that way he did whenever he was about to say something stupid. "Ya gonna let me join in next time? Or just keep playing the cock tease?"

"Depends..." I kept my tone low and calm, despite the way my skin was prickling beneath the surface.

"On?"

"On whether or not you want your balls delivered to ya in a glass jar or a pine box."

He barked out a laugh, slapping the backside of my shoulder as he teetered dangerously close to earning himself that male soprano spot.

"What's this shit about? Didn't think we did house calls," I grunted, watching as the crazy fucker practically bounced on the soles of his boots.

"All we do is fucking house calls, Franks."

I dropped my glare, eyeing the fucker's hand until he

was smart enough to remove it. "Not during the day, we don't."

Before I could get a straight answer from the ass clown with more coke in his system than brain cells in his skull, we were being guided inside by some old guy in a penguin suit. His bald head gleaming beneath the light of the chandelier that looked far more gaudy now that it was all lit up.

The fact Bugs wasn't currently chirping in our ears told me this would be an in-and-out sort of thing. While the fact we weren't climbing in through a cracked window suggested it was no ordinary job. Shit seemed off the books. Like Adrian was sending us out as his personal errand boys. Wouldn't surprise me if that were true. Though it would piss me the fuck off. I didn't work for free. Not for anyone.

The clearing of a throat had us pivoting around on the heels of our boots before the clicking of heels told me this chick didn't know the meaning of a quiet entrance. She was decent enough looking. Long, thick, black hair pulled into a tight ponytail that cascaded down her back in waves and the kind of curves that were meant to be gripped up at the waist. But the tight pursing of her lips warned me the woman was a problem I didn't have the patience to entertain. The kind of bitch who didn't know when to keep her mouth shut. Especially when it was in her best interests.

Casper popped a piece of chewing gum between his teeth, one side of his face pinched back into an unnatural grin as he lifted his arms and folded them over his chest. "What can we do for ya, *mami*?" He laid on a thick accent that had me groaning and the woman's nostrils flaring in disgust.

Couldn't blame her for that one. Shit was cringy as fuck but that was Casper's style.

She eyed him for a second or two, the iciness of her

glare brisk enough to send a chill down your spine before landing it on me. "I'm told you're good with a bone saw." She lifted a curious brow. "But I don't believe anything I'm told until I see it for myself."

The chick didn't bother saying more before pivoting on her too-high heels, clearly expecting us to follow her without needing to be asked.

77
EMILY

I could feel the sweat dripping down my forehead, the air growing thicker and staler as the oxygen was slowly replaced by carbon dioxide. The sun beating down on the metal van and the blindfold creeping lower on my face before the fabric covered my nose. I tried to flare and scrunch my nostrils, wiggle my top lip and tug at the material with my teeth, but all that seemed to do was make matters worse.

My arm ached, the raised position forcing me to switch between bearing my weight on my thighs and stretching out my upper limbs. While dehydration didn't seem to alleviate the growing pressure in my bladder.

I had to pee so goddamn bad my thighs were shaking. The sweat accompanied by a weird chill that lingered on my spine and urged me to just let it all go.

What I wouldn't give for that fucking bucket right now...

I was doing my best not to panic or piss myself, whereas my brain was doing *its best* to send my central nervous system in to a frenzy. Which was why it took me a moment too long to feel the sudden breeze bristling against my skin. I hadn't even heard the door open but I was grateful for the rush of fresh air that streamed in from the seam. Even more so when the metal around my wrist was loosened and my hand slipped free.

I sucked in a sharp breath, rubbing at my arm while my head shifted from side to side, even though I still couldn't see past the blindfold. Until it finally occurred to me...

I reached up a hand. Tugged the fabric off my face and glanced around the back of the van. Finding it just as empty as it was before the cuff was removed. As much as my brain was cautioning me that this shit was a trap, it didn't stop my feet from shuffling closer. My arm from reaching out and pushing the door wider and my body from propelling forward.

I didn't register the crunch of the gravel beneath my feet. The way my ankle rolled or how my knees stung when I tripped and scraped them across the concrete. What I did notice was the swatting of wind on either side of my face. The buzzing of insects by my ear and the bright-orange of a familiar bell-shaped flower...

I stumbled in my steps and took a deep breath as realization hit me at the same time the scent of Marisela's perfume made its way into my nostrils and embedded itself in my lungs. She was here. Or she had been. There was no mistaking her presence. It had this way of lingering long after she was gone.

I tugged the hem of my tattered dress in one hand while peering back at Prescott Estates, the large manor silhouetted by the towering trees that surrounded its perimeter. I didn't know how deeply involved my former boss was in all this. Just that she was. There was no other explanation for why it was so important for me to be the one to land on Cohen's doorstep that day.

I remembered everything now. Including how she had been the one to send me to that creepy-ass asylum in the middle of nowhere.

You are the only one *who can do this,* she'd said.

And why exactly was that? What did she have to gain from what I was certain was a deal with the devil? Because if I knew anything for sure, it was the fact she had *something* to gain from it. Marisela didn't do anything if it didn't benefit her in some way.

Which also left me to wonder how much of my life had been planned out for me. Down to what I'd assumed was an accidental teenage pregnancy but hadn't been accidental at all. How many coworkers and acquaintances were used to shuffle me one direction on the board and then the next? How many friends were really just players in a game I wasn't invited to join in on?

But I didn't have time to think about any of that now. Not when I should be running. Why wasn't I running?

And then I felt it. His eye on me. I couldn't tell you how I knew or where it was coming from. Just that he was coming.

I forced my aching feet to pick up their pace as I navigated around prickly bushes and downed trees. Jumped over a few puddles and pushed past some overgrown vegetation that told me I was getting farther and farther away from civilization and closer towards the density of the woods.

My heart was past the point of pounding. It was fluttering in my chest, barely able to finish the cycle of its first beat before it was starting the next. I didn't know what it really felt like to be hunted until now. Because that's what this was. I was the prey doing whatever I could not to fall into a trap. While everything in me said Cohen had his sights set on taking me down.

78
COHEN

The moment I stepped foot on the circular driveway, I knew something was off. And it had nothing to do with the bag of body parts currently slung over my shoulder. Or the bloodied bone saw Casper was holding up like he'd just hit the jackpot with one of those light-up claw machines and that rusty power tool was his prize.

This shit was the norm for us.

No, this was something else. Something that hit me like a punch to the gut when my glare landed on the back bumper before skidding across to the door. Which I now noticed was swaying when a gust of wind swiped past us. I didn't bother saying a word to either of ' em as I shoved the industrial-sized trash bag against Donnie's chest and took off at a full run. My boots sending up a cloud of dirt and sand at the same time my clenched fists swished back and forth at my sides.

I could hear the guys trudging towards the van behind me. Probably doing what I didn't and peering inside.

Thing was I didn't have to check shit to know that

Emily was gone. I could feel it. I also didn't have to guess where she was headed. Her footprints in the mud did that for me.

I was equal parts pissed the fuck off and turned the fuck on as I pushed saplings aside and stomped across carefully manicured flower beds. Pounded grass into the dirt and maneuvered around trees. In search of my little runaway bride. Couldn't say for sure when I'd come to that conclusion. But I had. She was gonna marry me. As soon as I caught up with her.

Maybe it was the very real possibility of her getting away. Or maybe nothing had changed since I decided she was mine back in college. Whatever it was, I knew I wasn't letting her go. Even if it drove us both mad.

I was certain it would.

It didn't take me long to spot her. My little pet was anything but quiet as she tripped over dried brush and stumbled across fallen branches. And fuck if she didn't look edible with her chest heaving. Her damp hair clinging to her face and the hint of red smeared across her cheek.

I could smell it. Her blood. I could taste it too. It didn't matter how unlikely it was at a distance. It didn't make it any less true. Sensory memory. The spark of something familiar that had your brain tricking you into believing it was actually there. The neuroreceptors in my parietal lobe were stimulated to the point saliva was pooling in my mouth. My jaw clenched and my zipper chaffing with each step I took closer to my prize.

One side of my face curled into the lopsided grin that had become my regular as I slipped out from behind the tree and gave chase.

Emily froze. Peering up like one of those antelopes in a nature documentary seconds before the lion was set to appear and snap its jaw around the creature's throat. It wasn't all that far from the truth either. Not when I closed the distance and pounced. The force of my body slamming into hers sent Emily toppling sideways and crashing onto her back. Then had my little pet staring up at me again. Her eyes wide and panicked. Just the way I liked them when I was propped up on top of her.

"Tag. You're it," I grunted against her ear, lowering my face to that spot where her neck curved into her shoulder before suckling on the salt that collected and dried there.

She shoved at my chest, pounding her tiny fists against my arms and torso as I yanked the hem of her dress up around her stomach. Using one hand to release my zipper. Pull my cock free and sink into her tight cunt. Which was weeping for me to claim it.

Two quick thrusts and she'd stopped fighting me altogether. Her head tipping back and her fingers closing around my shirt and tugging me forward. Clumps of dirt and gravel scuffed against my knees with each drive of my hips, the overgrown grass pricking the undersides of my hands as I braced myself on the ground and fucked my little pet into submission.

I could feel that too. The moment she gave in and accepted her fate. The moment she realized it was so much more satisfying to fuck me than fight me. And then her leg was wrapping around my ass, holding me in place while I held her down.

This was what she needed. What would make sure she wouldn't try running again. This and the ring I was gonna nail to her finger if I had to.

79
EMILY

When I blinked my eyes open again, it wasn't to the image of the cloudless blue sky that stretched on above me or to the feel of the damp grass tickling my back. Instead, I was left staring at a dark ceiling, beam after beam that made up the underside of a basement. Cohen's bedroom. The drugs starting to flush out of my system while the ropes on my wrists and ankles ensured I didn't need another dose of whatever concoction had been rushing through my veins.

It didn't matter. I wasn't gonna try to run again. Not that there was anywhere to go. I'd had my chance at freedom and watched it slip through my fingertips at the same time something else slipped between my thighs. And then it clicked. The realization that I didn't want to get away. That being trapped was so much more exhilarating than the long leash that would have me yanking so hard I'd end up strangling myself. That I enjoyed the thrill of being chased. Because Cohen Michaels wasn't the only one with an ego problem. I was shamelessly addicted to being the center of his world.

With him, I wasn't just another face in the crowd. I was the only one he saw. And I enjoyed being seen. So much more than I liked being invisible. Which made me almost as narcissistic as the man glaring at me from across the room. And twice as self-destructive.

I barely had the chance to blink before Cohen closed the distance. His large frame towering over me at the foot of the bed. He clicked his tongue, his arms crossed over his wide chest as he eyed me like I'd just been caught sneaking in after curfew.

"It's not a good look, ya know?" he grunted while lifting a challenging brow.

I shimmied higher up on the mattress, so that my shoulders were resting on the headboard, my arms still overextended at my sides. "What's that?"

"You running off. Gives the rest of the guys the impression I don't know how to handle what's mine." Cohen climbed over the bed, using his knee to spread my thighs wider apart. "And if I can't fucking handle you, ona them would be more than happy to step in and do it for me." He brushed the loose strands off my face, his stare penetrating as he gawked at me for a moment too long to be comfortable. "Is that what you want, Emily? To have someone take my fucking place? You think someone else can take better care of you than I can, is that it?" Cohen's jaw was practically clicking in his mouth, his tone much calmer than the tension in his face.

I shook my head from side to side, my wide eyes answering for me. Truth was I much preferred the monster I knew than the ones I didn't.

One side of Cohen's lips tugged up into a smirk as he brushed a hand across my cheek, the same one he'd stitched back up not all that long ago. "I didn't think so." He shrugged a single shoulder while bearing his weight on the other arm. "I knew it had to be a... misunderstanding. That you wouldn't make the mistake of running from me again."

I wanted to tell him I didn't run the first time. That the years I spent traveling with Marisela had nothing to do with him. But that would have been a lie. I was looking for any excuse to get away from the things I'd found in those black boxes. The same things I'd stuffed into a trash bag and dropped over the bridge on our way to the airport. Which I now knew had everything to do with Cohen and what I was certain he'd done to what was left of the man they found in that car. I couldn't say his name. And I didn't dare think it without the images I saw on that television screen flashing in my head.

I could only guess Cohen could read the indecision on my face, the lies warring with the truths on the tip of my tongue. Because the next thing I knew, he was grabbing my face between the meat of his palm and squeezing. So I had no choice but to look him in the eye.

"No one will ever do the things I've done for you. No one will ever care for you the way I've cared for you. And no one will ever fucking love you the way I've loved you. From the first moment I knew you were meant to be mine, Emily."

"You don't love me. You love the way I make you feel," I mumbled between pinched cheeks, watching as Cohen barked out a loud, humorless laugh that had his teeth gnashing and his lips curling into a snarl.

"Isn't that the same thing?"

I shook my head, as much as I could while my jaw was being pressed against my neck. "No, it's not."

Cohen smirked, dropping his mouth so that it was just a

breath above mine before he whispered against my lips. "But it could be. It could be whatever I want it to be, pet. And I think it's time we've both accepted there ain't shit either of us can do about it."

80

COHEN

Emily had a healthy glow to her. Her skin more rosy than pale. Her cheeks fuller than I ever remember them being and her thighs thick enough for me to grab whenever I felt the need to pry them apart and take the plunge. With my cock balls-deep inside her. She was listening better too. Just enough sass to keep things interesting and compliance to keep me from having to cut out her tongue.

She also seemed more at ease, now that she realized running wasn't an option. Like a house cat that had finally accepted the fact she was much safer indoors. So, by the time the nondescript box had arrived several weeks after her failed escape attempt, I was all too eager to show my little pet what I had in store for her next.

I eyed her on the screen for a minute longer. Enjoying the bounce of her larger breasts, the parting of her plumper lips each time she took a deep breath. I had no idea why I got off on watching her almost as much as I got off on the real fucking thing. But I did. There was just something about seeing a side of Emily no one else got to see. Being a part of her most private moments that had my dick harder than steel. I didn't think I'd ever get enough of it. Or her, if I were being honest with myself.

Then I closed out of the surveillance app and shoved my phone back into my pocket. Swiping the box off the van's dashboard before making my way inside. Adrian had sent me out on another job. Which had me flying solo for the night while everyone else got to kick up their feet with their cocks in their hands.

If I had to take a guess, I'd say the fucker did it on purpose. His way of ensuring I didn't get too complacent. A little reminder that he fucking owned me, and if I didn't play nice, he'd take my favorite toy away. *Again.* Seeing as a tiny voice in the back of my head told me Dr. Adrian Lambert, Briarwood's own certified sociopath, had something to do with Emily's disappearance from the jump. It was the only thing that made sense after you put all the pieces together.

How else did ya explain the part he had in getting her dropped off at our doorstep?

You didn't. That was how.

The elevator creaked and moaned as it made its way down to the basement, jostling when it finally landed at the lowest level and opened up onto the maze of hallways. If I took a left, it would bring me to Emily's former cell while a quick right would land me in my personal bedroom. Where my pet was waiting for me. There was no need to keep her locked up anymore, not when she looked much better tied up on my bed. Her hair sprawled out across my sheets and her pussy wet enough to take my full fist if I felt the urge to punish her.

I tucked the box under my arm, punching in the code to the door and pushing my way inside the room. Emily was seated at the dining table in the corner. Her blue dress perfectly pressed. Her hands secured to the hook I'd screwed into the wall and her hair combed back into a high ponytail—just begging me to wrap it around my hand and tug her up and down on my cock.

But first thing was first.

I dropped the box in front of her, carefully peeling back the flaps to reveal the smaller velvet case inside. Emily watched as I cracked it open, the knitting of her brows a clear sign she wasn't understanding what she was seeing or what it meant as I removed the metal collar from its padding to set it down on the table between us. Then I freed her wrists and took a step back. Observing her reaction as she reached out a hand to run her fingertip along the cool, sleek edges.

I waited until she dropped her hand to peer up at me through a fan of dark lashes—those were thicker too now —before closing the distance again. Brushing her hair over her shoulders to give myself better access to her throat.

"What is it?" she asked with a hint of hesitation to her voice.

"A present. For you, pet."

My girl had learned not to question me. It was much better when she accepted the things I gave her. For her, not for me. I didn't mind putting her in her place whenever a quick reminder was needed. Especially when that reminder ended with tears in her eyes and my cum down her throat. I didn't give a fuck if she choked on it as long as it got my fucking point across.

Emily nodded her head. Once. The questions running through her mind not daring to make it to her tongue as I pulled the collar apart at the hinge before placing it around her neck. Where it would stay. If the scar on her thigh didn't tell everyone who she belonged to, the little charm dangling from the center that said "Property of CM" sure as fuck would.

I flicked a finger over the permanent locking mechanism, listening to it click into place as a smirk kicked up one side of my face. "Every good pet deserves a pretty collar," I hummed while trailing a hand along the metal. Down the soft skin beneath it and over the swell of her breasts before rubbing my thumb back over her new jewelry. Tapping it once when I told her, "This will stay right here. Until it falls off your bones. You're mine forever, pet."

EPILOGUE
THE CLIENT

ONE YEAR LATER

There was too much testosterone in the room. It thickened the air and made it difficult to choke down the cheap coffee staring back at me from the bottom of my mug. Too many supposed alpha males holed up in one space all thinking the same thing. That the fact they were born with an outie instead of an innie made them superior.

It didn't. It made them easier to manipulate. Which was exactly what brought me to their doorstep. Claiming to be interested in their services. I wasn't. I was interested in them. In what made them tick and if they were worth the hefty bounty on their heads, should my team decide to bring them down. It wasn't a question of whether or not we could. It was a question of whether or not I thought it was a challenge.

I clicked my nails across the conference room table as I waited for the children to quit scratching their balls and start settling down. I was the client after all. I expected a little more professionalism in my presence. But boys would be boys and all that nonsense that allowed men to act like neanderthals without consequences.

Dr. Adrian Lambert sat at the head of the table. The Surgeon. I respected his work far more than I respected him, which was saying something. His hands steepled and his head tilted to one side as he eyed me like a weed he wanted to pluck from the garden and squash in his hand. On his left were the brothers. Not much was known about them other than the fact one was a computer whiz and the other couldn't find his way out of a paper bag. The Russian sat to the right, his stare nearly as crazy as the reputation that preceded him. Leaving two empty spots between us.

I could only assume they belonged to the one-eyed freak they'd taken on a few years back and the newcomer we'd yet to pull a file on. They called him "The Negotiator." The guy was in charge of the details, laid out the rules for every hand-off and had the last word when it came to the final take-home rate. Odd, considering no one could tell me a thing about him, other than he was a fucking ball-buster. But then again, so was I. And everyone was always so eager to drop their pants and allow me to do it too.

I spun in my chair at the sound of the door opening, telling us the last members of the Renegades had finally arrived. But it wasn't the first guy's face—as horrifying as it was to look at—that had my coffee nearly coming back up the way it went down. No, it was the petite figure behind him, her swollen belly entering the room several seconds before she did that had one side of my mouth tipping up into a sickeningly sweet grin.

"This is my wife," the man grunted in my direction before guiding the woman over to the seat beside me. "Emily Michaels."

I scooted my chair another inch closer and offered Emily a hand, while my glare dipped to the metal collar around her neck and back to her face again. "Pleasure to meet you, Mrs. Michaels."

She cocked a challenging brow, taking a moment to eye me up and down. "Is it?"

"It is. Makes things interesting," I hummed. Far more pleased with this sudden turn of events than I should have been.

"Oh, yeah? How's that?"

I lifted a shoulder before pinning the woman with my most-disarming grin. "Well, from what I hear, Mrs. Michaels, you're one hell of a negotiator."

THE END

BONUS CHAPTER
CASPER

ELEVEN YEARS PRIOR

What did crazy feel like?

Good fucking question. Best way to describe it was a million different conflicting thoughts zapping through my brain. Buzzing and bouncing around until one of them finally stuck the landing. Then veered off again. Kinda like me.

Come to think of it, guess you could say my ass was the epitome of crazy. Unpredictable. A little unhinged. But a lotta fucking fun. Especially in the bedroom.

The things I could do to a chick's body. Hell, the shit I could do with my own body. Mind-fucking-altering. Back-breaking.

I reached down and gave my cock a good squeeze through the thick fabric of my jeans. I'd take care of him later. I had a job to do first. And Big Daddy AKA Surge AKA Lamb Chop AKA Lambo AKA the man who paid for all the blow I liked to shoot up my nose and liquor I liked to pour down my throat would be more than a little peeved if I made a pit stop to get my nuts off. Guy had a stick up his ass the size of the Mother Land. But I owed 'em life and limb. In the very literal sense.

The moment the neon-yellow bike whizzed by like a big fat bumblebee calling my name, the engine cranking and whining down the street, I jumped in through the driver's side window of the little beater car and followed the fucker with a big ego and a small dick—I assumed, couldn't tell you for sure until I got an eyeful. You'd be surprised how many guys in this city had thimbles hanging between their legs.

Okay, maybe not hanging. Shit just kinda poked out like a turtle head. No idea why micropenises were such an epidemic all of a sudden. Maybe there was something in the tap water. One of the reasons I stuck to straight vodka.

No teeny weenies in these jeanies, ladies.

I kept just enough distance between me and Buzz Lightyear to maintain my tail, my palms drumming across the steering wheel to the rhythm of the loud bass I was playing in my head. Couldn't turn on the radio as much as the stereo button was begging me to touch it.

Press it. Come on, you know you want to. FUCKING PRESS IT ALREADY.

I shook my head. I had to resist the impulse because the fucking noise would give me away. And just when I got to the best part. Really leaned into my silent solo, my palms tap-tap-tapping in rapid succession, the bike came to a stop at the light.

I grinned, slammed the car into fourth and gunned for the Buick sandwiched between me and Mr. Quick-Nut Cheerios. The poor driver didn't know what hit him and neither did the prick on the bike. Fucker skid across the pavement like the smoothest skipping stone, leaving a wide streak of blood and gore from the middle of the street over to where he stopped, dropped, and rolled up next to the barrier.

Chicago's finest hose jockeys would have been proud.

The Buick took off and I cruised on by, pausing when I heard a groan coming from the mass of mangled limbs that shouldn't have enough brain matter left in his skull to be making noise. I flashed my busted headlights in the fucker's direction and watched the steady rise and fall of his chest. The twitching of his foot. The stretching of his right arm. And then he pulled himself onto his side.

Might not have had a big dick, but the prick sure as hell had steel balls. Didn't know if I'd have it in me to be feeling around the grass for my missing fingers. The best thing to do would be to back over the guy's skull and put him out of his misery.

But that shit wasn't up to me. Surge would have to make that call. Whole thing had to look like an accident according to the client. Rat… or was it Rath? Or maybe Weasel. Guy sure looked like a couple of weasels piled up and wearing a lab coat. And while I loved pushing my boss's buttons, I'd also learned my lesson. A week of forced bedrest—and I mean physically forced 'cause your legs don't work no more—will do that to you. Especially when your version of hell is being confined to a chair.

Just the thought sent a chill down my spine, which was a feat all its own, considering I couldn't feel shit from the base of my neck to that spot right where my dick started.

Thank God for small favors, am I right?

I shoved a hand into my pocket. Tugged my burner phone free and pressed dial on the only number in my contacts. He answered on the first ring but didn't speak. It was the way we did shit. If I was calling from this line, it was because I had something to say and not because I was asking him what we were having for dinner tonight. Though the slight chill in the air had my stomach rumbling and my mouth watering at the thought of my mother's solyanka.

"Minor hiccup." I could hear him breathing but the boss man wouldn't respond until I gave him a reason to do so. "Fucker just doesn't want to stay down. Should I take care of it?"

"No." One word. Cold and definitive as always.

"You sure?"

"Yes." *Click.* That was it. Honestly, I didn't expect more.

With one last glance in the rearview mirror, I shifted gears and sped off in the opposite direction. The night was young. Plenty of time left for me to crash this car in some ditch and still find a pussy or two to warm my cock. My reward to myself for a job "almost" well done.

I mean, even the best hitman this city had ever seen couldn't win 'em all.

FROM THE AUTHOR

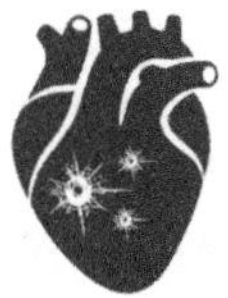

If you enjoyed SKIN, or even if you didn't because that is okay too, I would be so grateful if you took a moment to leave a review. Nothing is too short and no amount of effort goes unnoticed.

Thank you so much for reading my book. I couldn't do this without readers like you.

Click here to leave a review!

COMING SOON

CURIOUS AS TO WHICH ONE OF THE RENEGADES WILL BE THE NEXT TO FALL?

PREORDER **LAMB** NOW AND DISCOVER WHO HAS MORE THAN A PIECE OF THE SURGEON'S HEART.

THERE WERE THREE THINGS AND ONLY THREE THINGS I KNEW FOR SURE ABOUT THE WOMAN SITTING ACROSS FROM ME AT THE FAMILY DINNER TABLE EVERY NIGHT FOR THE LAST WEEK. SHE WAS COMPLETELY OFF-LIMITS. MY BROTHER'S FIANCÉE. AND MY ABSOLUTE OBSESSION.

FACT OF THE MATTER WAS, I'D ALSO SEEN HER FIRST. WHICH MEANT IT WAS ONLY FAIR THAT I CREPT INTO HER BRIDAL SUITE THE NIGHT BEFORE THE CEREMONY AND TOOK HER VIRGINITY. SHE RETALIATED BY SLIPPING INTO MY HOTEL ROOM AND TAKING SOMETHING OF MINE. AN APPENDAGE. THE FIFTH TOE ON MY LEFT FOOT. TUCKING IT AWAY IN A BOX AS A SICK LITTLE KEEPSAKE OF OUR SHORT TIME TOGETHER.

BLOOD FOR BLOOD, OR SO SHE CLAIMED.

AND THAT'S WHEN I KNEW THE GIRL WAS IT FOR ME. HER KIND OF CRAZY THE PERFECT ACCOMPANIMENT TO MY OWN... PECULIARITIES.

The newspapers liked to call me *a butcher*. I preferred the term *surgeon*. After all those years in medical school, I deserved it.

The truth was, I was a saint compared to *her*. Because Mari didn't just know how to crack open a rib cage. She knew how to fish around with a pair of perfectly manicured nails and dig out a guy's heart. Something my brother found out the hard way.

Now she was back, looking to make amends. Or at least pretending to. And I was more than ready to lead my little lamb to slaughter...

LAMB is a dark spin on the nursery rhyme "Mary Had a Little Lamb" and book two in <u>The Renegades Series</u>. Each title is a standalone in an interconnected world while each story is a retelling of a fairy tale, nursery rhyme, fable, etc. The focus is dark romance so please heed the trigger warnings at the beginning of every book.

The Renegades Series:
Book 1: SKIN (Frankie's story)
Book 2: LAMB (The Surgeon's story)
Book 3: BELLS (Casper's story)

ACKNOWLEDGMENTS

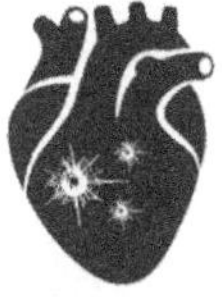

THANKS TO EVERYONE WHO HAS BEEN A PART OF THIS LONG-ASS PROCESS. TO EVERYONE WHO HAS SHARED, LIKED, COMMENTED, AND PREORDERED. TO THOSE OF YOU WHO TOOK A CHANCE ON ME AND MY FUCKED-UP BRAIN.

I COULD NOT HAVE DONE IT WITHOUT YOU, AND I AM SO VERY HUMBLED.

I ALSO WANTED TO SAY THANK YOU TO MY ARC READERS, WHO ARE TAKING TIME OUT OF THEIR BUSY SCHEDULES TO READ AND REVIEW MY BOOK. AND THANK YOU TO THOSE OF YOU WHO WENT AS FAR AS TO READ AND REVIEW MY PRIOR PUBLICATIONS TOO—I SEE YOU AND I AM SO GRATEFUL FOR YOU.

LASTLY, A SPECIAL THANKS TO LEAH POLUMBO, ZOEY DAY, COLBY BETTLEY, DEB DUNFIELD ROUNDTREE, ANGELA VOORHEES, AND ALICE FARMER FOR HELPING ME NAME BRIARWOOD. WELCOME TO THE CRAZY HOUSE...

ALSO BY SYBIL KNIGHT

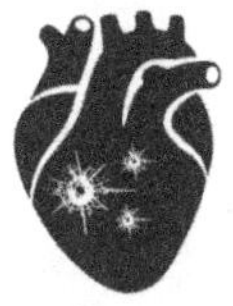

THE HARSHER THE TRUTH

THE SWEETER THE LIES

SINS OF OUR FATHERS

HALF COCKED

SKIN

LAMB

MORE TITLES TO COME...

ABOUT THE AUTHOR

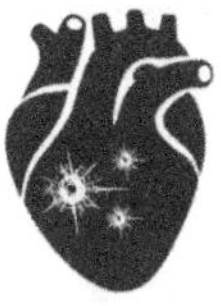

Sybil is a career-driven Philadelphian native. A crime show enthusiast by day, and a BDSM club hopper by night. When she isn't working or writing, she is talking about working or writing. She is a single mom to her beta fish (Fish) and way too many dead houseplants.

Her stories range from gray to black, with darker themes throughout. She prefers heroines with a kick-ass mentality and the heroes who know how to rein them in. The mental and medical aspects of her books are well-researched, though they are given a humanistic approach and diagnoses aren't the focal points. She believes her characters don't need to wear labels in order to get their messages across.

Her books are mostly standalones, though her characters may interact and intersect worlds. Additionally, she works closely with and writes alongside author Dahlia Reign and some characters will appear in cameos in each of their publications.